ANGEL

— OR —

DEVIL'S

ADVOCATE

Dear Gino,

Thank you for being such a great friend + surgeon. I hope you'll enjoy the read.

ONWARD

fondly,

CW

ANGEL

OR

DEVIL'S

ADVOCATE

Catherine DeAngelis

ARCHWAY
PUBLISHING

Archway Publishing books may be ordered through booksellers or by contacting:

Archway Publishing
1663 Liberty Drive
Bloomington, IN 47403
www.archwaypublishing.com
844-669-3957

Because of the dynamic nature of the Internet, any web addresses or links contained in this book may have changed since publication and may no longer be valid. The views expressed in this work are solely those of the author and do not necessarily reflect the views of the publisher, and the publisher hereby disclaims any responsibility for them.

Any people depicted in stock imagery provided by Getty Images are models, and such images are being used for illustrative purposes only. Certain stock imagery © Getty Images.

Scriptures taken from the Holy Bible, New International Version®, NIV®. Copyright © 1973, 1978, 1984, 2011 by Biblica, Inc.™ Used by permission of Zondervan. All rights reserved worldwide. www.zondervan.com The "NIV" and "New International Version" are trademarks registered in the United States Patent and Trademark Office by Biblica, Inc.®

ISBN: 978-1-6657-2581-1 (sc)
ISBN: 978-1-6657-2582-8 (e)

Library of Congress Control Number: 2022911585

Print information available on the last page.

Archway Publishing rev. date: 07/20/2022

To my husband and soul mate, Jim. He died
April 5, 2021, but has not left me.

CONTENTS

Part 2: Investigations

Part 3: Resolution

PREFACE

When I first decided to write this story, it was to be a straight-forward murder mystery taking place in a hospital. I had no specific plan beyond that simple idea. However, as I wrote each day, the story soon evolved into two parallel plots that wove in and out and came together nicely in the resolution at the end of the story.

I wrote almost the whole story while my husband, Jim, and I were in self-isolation from the COVID-19 virus at our family home in rural Lackawaxen, Pennsylvania, during the summer of 2020. My routine there has always been to walk slowly, listening to the silence and the sounds of the Delaware River and the woods. That summer, I walked about three miles on a road along the Delaware River every morning, contemplating what I might write that day. I was surprised that I never really knew what I'd write until I sat down and started writing. Somehow, the characters developed, thoughts came, and I wrote them. It was as simple as that.

After a while, the characters and places became so much a part of me it was frightening. At times, I felt as if I were in a parallel universe when I wrote. I believe that's why the second parallel plot came about. My personal thoughts and inner existential struggles with my spirituality became part of the main character and the plot. At times, it was almost impossible to differentiate which was the real me.

In 2020, when I wrote the first version of this novel, my

husband and I were professors at the Johns Hopkins School of Medicine, and thankfully, he was a psychiatrist. He assured me it was not rare for authors and actors to become as involved with the characters they were portraying as I was with mine. That was reassuring to me and allowed me to continue writing without thinking I was going crazy.

Then my husband died after a short illness in April 2021. Losing my soul mate stimulated me to revise the novel, allowing my spirituality and emotions to be incorporated into the story.

Clearly, the story is fiction, and any resemblance to actuality is accidental. The patient scenarios I use to develop the protagonist are based on my personal experiences as a physician. However, I have changed the names, places, and circumstances of the scenarios, so they also are fiction.

I am a Catholic Christian, which is probably obvious in the story, but a reader's faith or lack thereof should not matter in the read. Anyone facing truth and justice decisions of any sort, from parenting to legal decisions, should be interested in the decision process of the protagonist.

Some persons might find the story more engaging if they are interested in existentialism or spirituality, but that's also not necessary.

My wish is that anyone would enjoy the book and learn as much from reading this story as I did from writing it. In any case, onward.

Catherine DeAngelis

ACKNOWLEDGMENTS

Because in many ways this book is a culminating story of my life, there are so many persons to thank I cannot name them all. To my family, friends, and colleagues, I thank you all for helping to make me what I am.

But of those who played a direct role in my writing this book, I must first thank my husband and soul mate, Jim, who carried me through the ups and downs of authorship. My sister, Grace Herron, encouraged me to write a murder mystery when I was seeking a project to keep busy during COVID-19 isolation. My niece, Kathy Pasko; Monsignor Robert Vitillo; and Jack Hanley read the first draft of the manuscript and offered valuable suggestions. Drs. Howard Markel and Chris Zink and Gary Wilson provided suggestions regarding publishing. Amy Rutter-Hanzel provided invaluable assistance and suggestions in uploading my manuscript for publication. I thank you all.

A DASTARDLY DEED

▷ MAY 2017

Unaware of the horrendous deed about to be forced on him, the patient was asleep in his room at St. Joseph's Hospital. A laboratory technician walked silently into his room and gently woke him. She said, "I'm very sorry to wake you, sir, but I must start an IV—that's an intravenous—and draw some blood in preparation for the test you are scheduled to have later this morning."

The sleepy patient mumbled, "That's fine. I was expecting you."

The technician put on the dim wall light but not the bright overhead light, so the patient would be less likely to fully awaken. She proceeded to insert the IV, draw his blood, and hook up to his IV the solution she had hung on a bedside pole. She watched to make sure the solution was flowing properly, which was essential so that later in the morning, the necessary contrast material for the cardiac catheterization test could replace the solution. This early morning procedure saved time later for the cardiac catheterization team and reduced the time the patient needed to be in the catheterization room.

She smiled, turned off the light, and whispered, "Good night, sir." She then left the room.

The drowsy patient thought how nice the technician had been as he looked at the dimly lit clock on the wall near his bed. It was 4:45 a.m. He figured that because his procedure was not scheduled until 8:00 a.m., he could sleep for at least another two hours. He closed his eyes and thought about the wonderful steak dinner prepared by the hospital chef, complete with two glasses of red wine, or spiritus frumenti, which he had been told was the medical term for the alcoholic beverages he had consumed the night before.

Of course, he expected to be treated especially well at St. Joseph's Hospital, and all Catholic churches overseen by the bishop, because of his prestige and his having donated a lot of money, precious time, and effort to them.

A little while later, the patient was almost asleep, when someone in a white doctor's coat came quietly into his room. The room was dark, so except for the *MD* on the coat, the patient couldn't quite read the doctor's name or see the face, but he didn't care because he was very sleepy. So he closed his eyes.

The doctor whispered, "Sir, I won't put on any light, because I am only going to put some medicine in the well of your IV. You won't feel anything. Please go back to sleep."

After injecting a liquid into the IV well and tubing using a flashlight, the doctor whispered, "Goodbye," and then mumbled something else before leaving the room.

The patient thought, *Did he or she really say goodbye and mumble something? I must have fallen back to sleep and been dreaming.*

He then felt his heart skipping beats, and he couldn't breathe. He tried to call out, but it was too late. He was gone. Goodbye.

PART 1

PEOPLE AND PLACES

CHAPTER 1

DR. MARY ELIZABETH DAVINO DEFAZIO

▷ JANUARY 2018

As Mary gazed out the window into the gloom, she thought about the depressing morning she'd had. She essentially had pronounced a death sentence to a fifty-year-old man, who, with his wife, had sat dazed and shocked at the news. It had been her obligation, as the doctor, to tell the patient that he had metastatic pancreatic cancer.

The weather matched her mood. The cold winter wind on that dark, cloudy day was blowing hard, making the branches on the trees sway. Dr. Mary Elizabeth Davino—or Dr. D, as the staff fondly knew her—was one of the hospitalists at St. Joseph's Hospital. She was sitting at her favorite table, one by the window, in the hospital cafeteria.

On clear days, when the sun shone, a crystal someone had placed by the window would spin slowly and send rainbows across the room. She enjoyed watching the children in the cafeteria giggle and point as they watched the phenomenon. It always lifted her mood, no matter how tired or sad she might have been.

Unfortunately, the crystal was not shining that day. But she had taken her dinner tray to her favorite table anyway. On most Wednesdays, after her shift ended at 3:00 p.m., she would stay in the doctors' on-call room for five or so extra hours, working on the never-ending paperwork required by medical insurance companies. It was the only day when she ate dinner in the hospital's cafeteria. All other times, she ate with her mother, with whom she lived. Her mother was an excellent cook and enjoyed cooking for two or more rather than only for herself.

When in the hospital, Dr. D preferred to wear scrubs and a white coat, which were required by all staff who worked with patients. She wore little or no makeup, except for lipstick, and wore no perfume when working but used lavender soap. She was five foot six and carried her one-hundred-twenty-pound frame with great dignity. She was a beautiful woman who wore her thick dark hair just above shoulder length in the winter and shorter in the summer.

It was now 6:00 p.m., and Dr. D had taken a break from the administrative work. She was hungry after skipping lunch to care for a very sick patient. Dinner was baked chicken, mashed potatoes, broccoli, and a garden salad. She skipped getting dessert.

Once again, she marveled at the delicious food served in the cafeteria and to the patients. And the prices were reasonable, to ensure patients' families could eat there without concern for cost. It was one of the many reasons private-practice physicians admitted their patients to St. Joseph's.

She looked up as the hospital chaplain, Father Dan Murphy, known by all as Father Dan, asked if he might join her, with a tray in his hand. She smiled and said, "Of course, Father."

He thanked her; sat down; and, between bites, asked if she

might tell him a bit about herself. "I've known you since you were a nurse here many years ago. And I was delighted when you returned as a doctor. When was it—a lucky thirteen years or so ago? The whole time you've worked here, you've helped me as a eucharistic minister, for which I am very grateful. But I know so little about you."

After a smile and another "Of course, Father," she said, "I was the younger of two children and raised by very devout Roman Catholic parents. My father, Frank, died about thirteen years ago as the result of a freak accident. He worked as a Catholic school bus driver and general fix-it man for the nuns who ran the school and convent. And my mother is Elizabeth—or Beth, as her friends know her, and Mom to our family. She was a lunchtime waitress in a local restaurant when my brother and I were growing up.

"When my brother went off to college, my mother stopped working at the restaurant and instead did volunteer work at the Catholic soup kitchen. Years later, after my father's death, I moved back home so I would be able to take care of my mother when she was no longer able to take care of herself. But at this point, I think she mostly cares for me.

"My brother's name is Francis, or Frank now that my father, who shared that name, is gone. He lives close to the house occupied by my mother and me. He graduated from law school, much to the delight of our parents. They were ecstatic, to put it mildly, when I graduated from medical school. To have their two children become professionals was considered amazing by their friends who also had grandparents who were immigrants from Italy.

"Frank is now serving as a judge in the city courthouse. It's an easy five-mile drive from his home. He is married to a wonderful Irish American Catholic woman, Megan, whom I know you'd like very much. They have two children, who have been the delight of my mother's life and very much of mine: Mark is twenty-four years old and in law school, and Katie is twenty-two, working on a doctorate in psychology. Neither are married yet, much to the dismay of their parents."

Mary shook her head and smiled. She considered the many conversations and hints that occurred every time Mark or Katie was home from school. "When they were growing up, I spent a lot of time with them. At least once a month, I would babysit them on a Saturday night so Frank and Megan could have a night out. I'm afraid I spoiled them terribly, just like my grandparents spoiled Frank and me.

"Luckily, Frank and Megan had the sense to counteract that spoiling, just as my mom and dad did with Frank and me. At least I hope that is true for me. When my niece and nephew come home from school, we have a lot of fun together.

"We have a close-knit family. We spend most Sundays and holidays having dinner with Mom, who is a marvelous cook. In fact, years ago, when I was a novice straight out of high school and a nun, she and my father would drive to the convent almost every Sunday to deliver a delicious dinner of Italian food made specially by Mom. The nuns there looked forward to those dinners. And they could not understand why my family were not obese. I joked with them, saying, 'All my family in Italy are five feet tall and five feet wide and have small black mustaches. Of course, those are the women; the men are a little taller.'"

Dan laughed loudly, and people in the cafeteria looked at them.

Mary continued. "Frank was grateful that I decided to live with Mom. It relieved him and Megan of worry. Frank and I were educated in parochial schools. Immediately after graduation from high school, at age eighteen, I joined the Daughters of Charity in a local convent. The mother superior arranged for me to attend one of their affiliated colleges to become a nurse. The plan was, ultimately, for me to take care of the sisters, especially those who had retired. But during the end of my senior year, something happened on a clinical rotation that completely changed my life.

"One night, I was caring for Yuliana—or Julia, according to the medical chart—Morales, a twenty-two-year-old Mexican American woman. She was dying of a very serious infection caused by her inducing an abortion with a knitting needle. Julia's temperature was over a hundred and five degrees, and she was going in and out of a coma, despite strong antibiotics and antipyretics to keep her fever down. I was Sister Mary Elizabeth then and was very moved by watching this woman's suffering. We were the same age, but Julia told me she had been married at age eighteen, had three children under three years of age, and had again become pregnant.

"I could barely imagine what that must have done to her psychologically and physically. She and her husband were devout Catholics and followed the church's teaching about birth control. Her husband had two full-time jobs, and she tried to take on ironing, but that became impossible with three little ones. They lived in a two-bedroom apartment in a poor part of the city and could barely keep food on the table. She just couldn't bear having another baby to take care of.

"Because there were very few sick patients on my ward that night, I tried to spend as much time as possible with Julia. A little after two o'clock in the morning, she cried out and began sobbing. I was just finishing with another patient, so I rushed over to her and held her hand, trying to comfort her. Julia told me that she was very frightened.

"She knew she was going to die and was going to hell because of what she had done. I was very moved by my personal feelings for this poor woman. I held Julia in my arms and told her that the God I knew would never condemn her for dealing with such a horrible situation in that way.

"Julia said, 'Do you really believe that, Sister?' To which I said, with full conviction, I truly did believe what I said. She then smiled, relaxed, and died in my arms."

Mary stopped talking. She was dealing with deep emotion and had tears in her eyes. After swallowing and taking a sip of water, she continued, saying, "At that moment, just before she died, I felt a powerful, peaceful warmth throughout my body that I think was grace. Because for the first time in my life, I truly felt at one with God.

"I was shaken by that experience. I couldn't stop thinking about Julia's suffering because of her belief in the church's teaching about abortion. That and some of the other teachings and rules of Catholicism concerned me.

"After several weeks of deeply thinking about my feelings on the issue, just before graduation from nursing school, I told the mother superior what I was going through and said I had decided to leave the convent. I promised to pay back the tuition for my education. Mother Superior told me there was no need to pay back the tuition, and if I should change my mind about being a nun, I would always be welcomed back. She only wanted to be assured I was going to remain a Roman Catholic, which was never a question, so that was an easy promise. My faith was not in question, but I needed time away to contemplate my feelings about some of the church's rules and teachings.

"After graduation in 1992, as you know, I worked as a nurse at St. Joseph's Hospital while taking courses for an advanced degree in nursing. In one of those classes, I met a wonderful man, Thomas Defazio, whom I married. As a devout Catholic, Tom had spent one year in the seminary but decided that was not the life for him. Instead, he decided to study something in college that would lead to a different kind of life. He graduated with a degree in, of all things, business management and took a job working for a local real estate firm.

"I continued working as a nurse and taking night courses needed to apply to medical school, which was a dream for me and supported by Tom. We were very much in love and happy, sharing so many ideals and spirituality. To our profound joy, I became pregnant after we'd been married eight months, but I miscarried at nine weeks. Unfortunately, I never became pregnant again, because less than two years after our wedding, Tom was killed in a freak accident involving a runaway truck whose brakes had failed. The truck came out of a side street at high speed and crushed the driver's side of Tom's car, and he died at the scene."

Mary again was clearly moved and stopped speaking for a while. When she gained control of her emotions, she continued. "I was decimated and deeply grieved for several months but knew I still had an amazingly wonderful life and needed to get on with it. That was when I decided I would devote the rest of my life to caring for the sick as a doctor, as Tom would have wanted. I would use my grief at losing my soul mate and love of my life to better understand the grief and sadness of others, especially when those emotions were caused by illness.

"My friends were aghast at my decision to become a doctor, because I would be over thirty years old when I finished medical school. I told them I didn't understand their logic, because I would be the same age of thirty at that point in my life no matter what I did in the interim years, and I'd much rather be a doctor than anything else in the world.

"Much to my surprise, Tom had a substantial life insurance policy, which, together with the settlement from the truck's insurance company arranged by my brother, Frank, provided me with sufficient funds to pay the rest of what I owed to the Daughters of Charity convent, leaving enough to pay for medical school if I could obtain some scholarships. That was what happened, and I graduated from Georgetown School of Medicine and then completed an internal medicine residency at Johns Hopkins. In 2004, I returned to St. Joseph's Hospital as a doctor. And the rest you know, Father. After hearing all this, I hope you won't think less of me now."

As she was speaking, Father Dan was thinking that being an old man and a priest didn't mitigate his appreciation of her outer beauty. However, he knew it was her kind and compassionate inner beauty that was responsible for her being so beloved by all the staff and patients.

When she commented on his potentially thinking less of her, he looked at her and shook his head. "Doctor, how could I think less of you, when I share at least some of the feelings you've expressed about Catholicism? Incidentally, may I call you Mary and you call me Dan? I think we are going to have a wonderful friendship beyond sharing Mass. Would you like that?"

Mary gave him a mischievous look and said, "Of course, Dan. Being friends should be an interesting adventure for both of us. Now that I've told you about myself, how about sharing with me your background and some of those doubts and feelings?"

Dan readily agreed to share his background and feelings about Catholicism.

Little did either of them know the full extent of what their adventure together would involve.

CHAPTER 2

FATHER DANIEL PATRICK MURPHY

▷ JANUARY 2018

Father Dan thought about how he might best respond to Mary's fair request for him to share a bit of his background with her, as she had done with him. To stall for some time to think more about it, he said, "Let me finish this delicious cherry pie made by the masterful hospital chef, and then I will tell you about myself."

While he stalled for time, Mary watched how he took his time eating, all the while obviously deep in thought. He was seated close enough that she noted a pleasant fragrance of some masculine soap, which probably had been a gift from someone. She thought their dinner together might be the beginning of what would become a beautiful friendship. Dan had much to teach her, and she hoped she could reciprocate in whatever way might come along. In any case, she wanted to encourage a close relationship with him, sharing spirituality and a love of St. Joseph's Hospital.

As promised, after swallowing the last bite and taking a sip of his coffee, Dan told her his story.

"I am the third of four children born to a very religious Irish Catholic family here in the community. As I was the first of two sons, my parents were delighted that I decided to enter the seminary in the diocese after graduating from high school, and I think my mother believed she was in heaven when I, her oldest son, was ordained in 1963 at the age of twenty-five." He smiled and added, "Don't bother to calculate, Mary; I am now seventy-nine years young and still going strong. The only problem is that now my mind is like a steel trap. It keeps everything out."

She laughed and said, "I think you are a very sharp thinker, and you surely don't look that age."

He replied, feigning shock, "You mean I look older?"

Mary shook her head and laughed loudly because Dan was a handsome, physically fit, and well-preserved man. She estimated him to be at least six foot two and about 190 pounds. He still had a full head of thick gray hair, with a well-groomed gray beard. She knew him to be a compassionate, kind, high-energy priest who was loved by all the hospital staff. He also had a good sense of humor and a hearty laugh. The patients looked forward to his daily visits, when he took the Eucharist to the Catholics and blessings to all those of any or no faith.

He continued. "All of us went to parochial school. My two sisters are retired teachers who graduated from Notre Dame College in Baltimore, and my brother graduated from the city's police academy and is a retired captain of the police department in the city. My parents are deceased, and all three of my sibs are married and moved away years ago. However, we all try to meet at least once a year, usually at Christmastime, in a centrally located hotel. In the tradition of the Irish, I have five nieces, four nephews, and a slew of grandnieces and grandnephews."

Mary smiled broadly at his obvious pride in being an

American of Irish descent. Dan looked at her with feigned surprise and said, "Why are you smiling?"

Mary replied, "Because you sound like all my relatives and me. We are as proud of our Italian background as you obviously are of your Irish background. I guess we never lose the sense of our heritage when we grow up in a close-knit family."

Dan said, "You are so right. The customs were part of every day, even though at the time, we were not aware that they were different from the customs of others."

Mary then said, "I'm sorry. I didn't mean to interrupt you. Please continue."

Dan sat back and said, "OK, let's see. Right after being ordained, I enlisted in the army and was assigned to be the Catholic chaplain in an army hospital here in the States. There I experienced the horrible effects of war's violence on older and young soldiers, some of whom were still only teenagers. At that point in my life, I simply was not prepared for that experience, and it threw me for a loop.

"The first few weeks, I was shocked by the number of soldiers who had lost limbs or died from their wounds despite the excellent care of the army physicians and nurses in the hospital, not to mention those soldiers who had succumbed on the battlefield. Providing last rites, as the sacrament was then known, to those who were only a few years younger than me was just too much for me to bear.

"When I said Catholic Mass at funerals, I found my eyes tearing up while praying over the caskets. While that didn't seem to bother and, in fact, was respected by the families, I felt embarrassed. That shows just how young and inexperienced I was.

"You see, you and I are similar in that I questioned how the God I chose to spend my life serving could possibly be so cruel to these soldiers and their families. Nothing I learned in the seminary had prepared me to deal with this deeply negative feeling about God and his son, Jesus, whom I so loved, not to mention what I felt about the Holy Spirit. I had many times experienced anger and disappointment with people I loved, but this feeling was much deeper and difficult to deal with. I didn't know how I, as a priest, could possibly bring the solace of God to these soldiers, who had so much more reason to feel anger with or abandonment by the God in whom they believed.

"For weeks, I went through the motions of providing what was expected of a Catholic priest, saying Mass daily, ministering the Eucharist to the bedridden, hearing confessions, providing the sacrament of the sick, and so on. But my heart and soul were not really in it. I fervently prayed for guidance and forgiveness, hoping that both would come. The irony of praying to the God with whom I was having trouble was not lost on me. But it was the only way I could cope. So I guess I was not totally lost to my loving God.

"Then, one morning during my third week at the hospital, I was slowly walking in the beautiful garden outside the main building, praying silently for guidance, when I heard loud laughter. I looked up, and on one of the concrete paths ahead, I saw a soldier with bandages over both eyes pushing a wheelchair occupied by a soldier who had had both legs amputated below the knees. Clearly, the blinded soldier was being directed by the soldier with no legs, and the latter soldier was being transported by the former.

"What a beautiful sight that was. Both soldiers were obviously in very good spirits and continued talking and laughing. I wanted to understand how they found the strength to cope so wonderfully with their injuries caused by war. So I walked faster to catch up to them and, smiling broadly, as it was easy to catch their good cheer, I asked what was so funny.

"The soldier with the eye bandages stopped the wheelchair

and looked a bit sheepishly toward my voice. The soldier in the wheelchair whispered something to the blinded soldier, which was probably that a priest had spoken.

"The blinded soldier said, 'Good morning, Father. We were just telling jokes and having a good time.'

"I smiled and asked them if they'd share the joke with me because I needed a good laugh. The soldier in the wheelchair said, 'Uh, Father, the joke we were telling each other is too raunchy to share with a priest. It's one of those we heard while on the front lines, waiting for the enemy to strike. The jokes made us laugh and helped to take the tension out of the air.'

"I told them that I was a man and not a saint and that I doubted they could say anything or use any words I had not heard many times. So they shared a very funny, if somewhat raunchy, joke with me, and we all roared with laughter. It was one of the funniest jokes I had ever heard."

Mary, feigning innocence, asked if Dan might share the joke with her. He looked at her with surprise but then realized she was pulling his leg to see his response. In like response, he said, "Sure, and we can share it over a shot and a beer in a bar near St. Joseph's Hospital." She laughingly declined, saying she only drank wine and never in any bar.

Dan continued with his story. "I then asked the soldiers how they were feeling about what had happened to them and how they had come to be such good friends, taking care of each other. They explained that they had come to grips with their situations, knowing that one of them would soon have the bandages removed from his eyes and that while he might need another operation, there was a good chance he would see again. In any case, his family were very supportive and promised to read to and guide him if that became necessary. That gave him the courage to carry on with his life.

"The soldier with the double amputations said he was

already being fitted for prostheses and being trained to walk by the hospital's physical therapists. It was a grueling experience but would be well worth the pain and effort if the result was that he could walk again. He was engaged to a wonderful woman who, despite his double amputation, still loved him and wanted to set a date for their wedding. He told me he considered himself to be a very lucky man to have such a wonderful woman with whom he would spend the rest of his life. And of course, I agreed.

"Both soldiers expressed gratitude that they hadn't been killed like some of their buddies. They hadn't known each other before being hospitalized, but in the true army spirit, they were buddies who took care of each other no matter what or where.

"I told them that I was grateful I had met them and that they had helped me in what I considered to be a role reversal. I asked if I might do anything for them. Both asked if I would hear their confession so they could receive communion the next time they went to Mass, which neither had attended since they had been wounded. I told them I would be honored to do so, but I wondered why they had asked me, when there had been many opportunities in the past for other priests to hear their confession.

"They taught me another important lesson when they said that any priest who would hear such a joke and laugh with them was a real priest with whom they could identify. They thought that humanity was a prerequisite for being a good priest. I laughed at their statement, but after that incident, both attended daily Mass and received communion each time until their discharges from the hospital. Clearly, by acting true to who I really am and to what I was feeling naturally, I had connected with them. What a great lesson that was for me, and I've never forgotten it. I hope people regard me as a real human being who has a calling to serve other humans.

"I receive a card from each of the former soldiers every Christmas. The one with the leg prostheses is married, has two children, and is employed as an accountant. The other had the second operation, can see with glasses, is also married to a wonderful woman, has a son, and works as an office manager.

"Mary, I truly believe those two soldiers were God's gift to me in answering my prayers for guidance. They showed how powerful is the human spirit and how I had no right to question God, when they had much more reason to do so but clearly did not. They lifted me from my feeling of self-pity and near despair into a deep love for God's people. Who was I to question God's will? I was reminded that faith and hope are two of three gifts needed for finding solace in God. The third, of course, is love. All I could do, as one of God's representatives, was bring the solace, emotional comfort, and grace of Jesus and the Holy Spirit to those who were suffering.

"I think I really became a true priest during my service as the Catholic chaplain for the army hospital. Another person in the army hospital who taught me much about service and life was the Jewish chaplain Rabbi Solomon Levine, lovingly known by the soldiers of all faiths as Rabbi Sol. He had been a hospital chaplain for over twenty-five years when I met him at dinner one evening early into my service, several weeks after my encounter with the two soldiers.

"During that dinner, it was so easy to talk to him that I asked if I might take advantage of his obvious caring nature to answer a question. With his easily gained permission, I asked how he had been able for so long to deal with all the suffering encountered in any hospital but especially a military hospital.

"He responded, 'Dan, first, please call me Sol so I can call you Dan. Next, to answer your question, I decided long ago that there are two ways to approach life. One way is to view it as a one-color jigsaw puzzle; the other is to view it as a puzzle of a beautiful garden filled with God's creatures of flowers; animals; butterflies and other insects; and, most importantly, all sorts of people representing mankind. The latter multicolored puzzle is much easier to solve and provides joy in viewing the world as it really is.'

"That was typical of the way he answered any question or situation I put to him. His responses made me contemplate the true meaning of my questions and his answers. Further, he had a Yiddish accent, having been born in Israel, and that always made me smile because his responses were like part of an entertaining play. He became my sort of guidance counselor. I thought that was surely a sign there is one God but more than one way or religion to serve him.

"When Rabbi Sol passed away, I attended his funeral—or, rather, the service they had planned for him. I had fully intended to do so but was truly moved when the rabbi who officiated at the service called me the day Sol died and said Sol wanted me to be there. Needless to say, the synagogue was packed with many people whom he had touched with his wisdom and love.

"When I returned to the diocese here in 1967 at the ripe old age of twenty-nine after serving in the army, I was assigned to St. Joseph's Hospital, and I have remained here since. I will soon celebrate my fiftieth anniversary of service to St. Joseph's."

After sitting back deep in thought, Dan said, "Good heavens, where did all that time go?" He sat back for a minute or so, obviously in deep thought again, before he said, "And that, my dear Mary, is my story."

Mary replied, "And a beautiful story it is, Dan. I hope you will be my friend and continue to teach me, as you have just done."

Dan replied, "I'd rather we be friends and teach each other."

And that was exactly what happened

CHAPTER 3

ADOLESCENT WITH LEUKEMIA

▷ FEBRUARY 5, 2018

At six thirty on the morning of Monday, February 5, 2018, following her usual routine, Mary parked her car in the doctors' lot and entered the hospital. She went to the mail room and collected her mail, messages, and assignments for the day. Then she went to the doctors' locker room and changed from street clothes into her scrubs and white coat. Next, she went to her assigned fourth-floor unit with the special VIP room and received the patient report from her colleague hospitalist who had been on duty from 11:00 p.m. to 7:00 a.m.

She then went to Mass in the hospital's chapel, where she served as a eucharistic minister for Father Dan. After Mass, she stopped in the cafeteria for coffee and a muffin, which she ate at the nurses' station while discussing patients on that unit with the nurses. There were to be three discharges and four admissions that day. None of the discharges required much beyond visiting to make sure there were no problems and writing discharge notes and prescriptions as requested by their admitting private doctors. The other unit to which she was assigned had a similar number of admissions, discharges, and patient needs.

The admissions had not yet arrived, so she took care of the discharges and went on to visit the patients who would remain in the hospital at least for another day. The nurses expressed no special problems with any of the patients who would remain in the hospital but were sad and concerned about a thirteen-year-old girl, Christine Silver, who had been admitted from the ER Sunday night because of severe menstrual bleeding. The pediatric unit only accepted children less than twelve years old, so all teenagers were admitted to the fourth-floor unit. The hospital always tried to admit those adolescents to the special private room so they might have some privacy away from the adult patients.

Christine's private doctor had not yet seen her but would be in soon before he began seeing patients in his office located in the building adjacent to the hospital.

Mary was finishing with another patient, when Christine's doctor asked to see her. He asked Mary if she would keep a special eye on Christine because he was worried that she probably had leukemia. Her hematocrit and platelet count were very low, and she had petechiae on her skin, an enlarged spleen, and enlarged lymph nodes in her neck. He'd ordered blood and platelet transfusions and a consult with his colleague Dr. Jeremy Penn, an oncologist who would be in to see her in the afternoon. Mary promised to leave Christine for last so she could spend more time with her.

By the time Mary finished with all other patients, it was a few minutes past three o'clock. She went to the nurses' station and signed out to her colleague who would cover the 3:00 p.m. to 11:00 p.m. shift. Despite the time, which never really meant much to her, Mary wanted to visit Christine before she left for the day.

She went to the room to find Christine sitting on the edge of her bed with an IV in her left arm. Her mother was sitting in a chair near the bed, talking to her. They stopped talking as soon as they saw Mary at the door.

Taking Christine's hand, Mary said, "I'm sorry to interrupt. I'm Dr. Mary Defazio, but most people call me Dr. D, as I hope you will. I am the hospitalist—that is, the doctor—who will be here every weekday from seven to three o'clock or so. You have been so busy today with other doctors and tests that I waited until now to introduce myself." She then shook Christine's mother's hand and asked if she might do anything for them before she left for the day.

Mrs. Silver responded, "Dr. D, I am so happy to see a woman doctor. This whole thing is so frightening to Christine and to our entire family. Her dad will be here as soon as he leaves work, and we will not leave her alone while she's here. She says that we don't have to stay, but I think that's best. What do you think?"

Knowing better than to take sides and possibly alienate either the patient or her mother, Mary responded, "Why don't you compromise by staying tonight and seeing how things go thereafter? Would that be OK with you and"—she looked at the patient—"with you, Christine?"

Both nodded and smiled.

"Is there anything else I might do now?"

They shook their heads.

"OK, I'll see you tomorrow morning."

As Mary walked out the door, Christine's mother followed her. She said she'd told Christine she was going to get some coffee in the cafeteria, but she asked if she might talk to Mary as they walked down the hall. Mary readily agreed.

Mrs. Silver then told Mary how worried she was about Christine. She said she'd read a lot about her symptoms and knew that Christine had a bad illness. After all, in addition to all the other tests, the doctors had done a bone marrow biopsy after lunch.

Mary told her that it was best to wait for the results of the tests before she jumped to conclusions. "There are a number of things that could be the cause of Christine's signs and symptoms. Also, many of these possible diagnoses have quite good prognoses, and she could do very well." While she didn't want to usurp the role of the private doctor when informing a patient or parent, she also wanted to provide some hope and comfort.

Mrs. Silver seemed to be appeased with the encouragement of a possible good diagnosis, agreed to wait, and thanked Mary for her response.

When Mary arrived on the unit the next morning, she read Christine's chart as soon as she could. Most of the test results, except for the bone marrow biopsy, were charted; and as she'd suspected, Christine most likely had acute lymphocytic leukemia, also known medically as ALL. Because the illness was curable with the right treatment, which Mary knew would be provided, she felt some relief.

When she went to see Christine, Mrs. Silver was there, having stayed all night. The first thing Christine said was "Dr. D, would you please tell my mother to go home? I am not a baby."

Mrs. Silver, who was shaking her head, said, "Dr. D, teenagers are impossible. They think parents are stupid and don't understand anything."

Mary responded, "Mrs. Silver, I am no expert on this topic, but I think all you have to do is wait until teenagers reach twenty-one or so, and parents suddenly become smart and understanding again."

Mrs. Silver looked worried and said, "But what if they don't react that way when they reach twenty-one?"

Mary knew Mrs. Silver was really asking if Christine still would be alive at age twenty-one. So she said, "Please believe me that there is no reason to think Christine will act differently." To her relief, her response seemed to placate Mrs. Silver and made Christine roll her eyes and smile. Mary hoped she was correct.

Dr. Penn, the oncologist, had asked for a conference with Christine's parents in his office in the medical office building adjoining the hospital at 4:00 p.m. on Tuesday afternoon, so Mr. Silver could attend after work. Mrs. Silver asked if Dr. Defazio could also join them, to which the oncologist and Mary readily agreed. Mary didn't mind staying the extra hour or so, because she could work on other things while waiting for the meeting.

At four o'clock, when they were all seated in Dr. Penn's office, he gently told them that the bone marrow biopsy confirmed Christine had acute lymphocytic leukemia, or ALL. He then explained that while no one wanted to have such an illness, ALL was a good kind of leukemia because in the vast majority of cases, it was curable with proper treatment, which he would provide.

Mrs. Silver started to cry with relief, and Mr. Silver reached over and held her. Mary had witnessed many incidents like this and was certain Dr. Penn had witnessed many more. She admired the gentle way he spoke to the parents. It was always important to leave patients and their families with some hope. Fortunately, in this instance, that was possible.

Mary then asked if Dr. Penn or Christine's parents wanted her to join them in telling Christine. Her mother said, "No, Dr. D, we do not want Christine to know. We asked you to join us because you have been so kind, and Christine really likes you."

Mary was shocked at the decision not to tell Christine her diagnosis. She asked them how they were going to explain her treatments. They said the term *leukemia* was too frightening, and they wanted her to be told only that she had a medical problem that would go away with some treatments. They looked at Dr. Penn and Mary and asked them to please tell Christine what they wanted her to hear.

Dr. Penn said he did not think that was a good idea but would follow their wishes. Mary sighed and thought about it, stating that she never lied but also would not betray the parents' wishes. She would need to think about how she might approach Christine so she might accomplish both.

Fortunately, over the next two days, Christine seemed happy that her mother agreed to visit for only an hour or so in the mornings and in the evenings with her father. She was obviously feeling much better with the blood and platelet transfusions and was to be discharged Friday after her first IV chemotherapy treatment, which she was told was a special medicine for her undisclosed medical problem. The rest of the chemotherapy treatments were to be provided on an outpatient basis in the medical office building.

On Thursday afternoon, after she had signed out, Mary visited Christine, as had been her routine, so she could spend some time with her before she was discharged in the morning. This time, she found her sitting in a chair, looking out the window, with tears streaming down her cheeks. Mary went to her and put her arms around her. Christine turned around and, sobbing, hugged Mary.

Mary asked what was wrong, and Christine responded, "I know I have leukemia and am going to die, but my parents, Dr. Penn, and you won't tell me. I'm very scared and want to talk about it but can't because I'm not supposed to know. I know how to use the internet, and it wasn't hard to figure out what I have."

Mary sighed loudly, handed Christine a tissue, and said,

"Christine, excuse me for just a few minutes. I need to go down the hall, but I'll be right back I promise you and we can talk. OK?" Mary hoped Christine would think she was going to the bathroom down the hall.

Christine nodded, and Mary left the room. She went down the hall and called Dr. Penn's office, and thankfully, he came to the phone immediately. Mary explained what had just happened and asked if he could come over or, if he couldn't, if she had his permission to speak honestly with Christine.

He told Mary he was in the middle of a diagnostic visit and couldn't come for at least an hour but would get there as soon as he could. He told her he had known that was going to happen and asked her to get permission from the parents before she spoke with Christine. He told her to let him know their response.

Mary agreed, and after she hung up, she called Mrs. Silver and explained the situation. Christine's mother started to cry and said she had been trying to protect her child but should have listened to Mary and Dr. Penn. She said she was sorry and asked Mary to please wait for the twenty minutes it would take her and her husband to get there before she spoke to Christine. Of course Mary agreed.

Mary went back to Christine's room. Christine was still looking out the window, but the tears had disappeared. Mary sat next to her, held her hand, and told her that her mother and father were on their way so they all could talk. While they waited, Mary asked what Christine had read on the internet about leukemia and what she was thinking now.

Mary was impressed at how facile a thirteen-year-old could be in using the internet, especially when the search involved a medical problem. In addition, in this case, the problem was personal and depended on the person's personality and what support she might have from parents or friends. Of course,

Christine and her peers had grown up with the internet, while older folks like Mary had not. *What might the next generation use to easily access essentially all the world's knowledge?* she wondered. *Or is all that actually available now?* On the other hand, she thought these youngsters were missing out on the personal social interactions not possible with the constant use of Wi-Fi to interact with one another. *The human touch is so important to the health and well-being of people.*

Another problem with the use of the internet to gain information, especially medical information, was that it could easily be misinterpreted. She said to Christine, "You know that it is not good to make a medical diagnosis based on what you understand from information read on the internet. You probably don't know the work of the poet Alexander Pope. He wrote something very wise: 'A little knowledge is a dangerous thing.'"

Christine interrupted and said she knew that saying.

Mary smiled and continued. "Yes, but do you know the next line? It is very important: 'Drink deep, or taste not of the Pierian spring,' which is the mythical source of knowledge. In this case, it means you need to be properly educated before making a diagnosis. Or put another way, leave it to the doctors to make the diagnosis."

Christine was puzzled by the response but decided to wait for her parents' arrival to find out what Dr. D had said.

When Christine's parents arrived, Mary explained to everyone that Dr. Penn would be there as soon as he was finished with another patient. However, he had asked Mary to speak with Christine and her parents before he got there, because he might be held up for a while and didn't want them to wait.

She then explained—mostly to Christine, because her parents already knew—that Christine had acute lymphocytic leukemia, which was the best kind of leukemia to have, as it was curable with the treatment Dr. Penn would provide.

The look on Christine's face was one of relief and happiness. She hugged her parents and Mary and started to laugh and then cry, releasing her anxiety. As Mary got up to leave, Mr. and Mrs. Silver rose and hugged her, saying they were grateful to her.

Mary said, "That's why Dr. Penn and I went to medical school. I am grateful to have provided the care I was taught to give, as I am sure is also true of Dr. Penn." As she left them, Mary felt that it had turned out to be one of the days she'd dreamed about while in medical school, when all the hours spent learning and gaining experience had become well worth the effort.

The next morning, she said goodbye to Christine and her mother, who had come to take her home. That afternoon, as she drove home, Mary was looking forward to a weekend that she hoped would be unexciting and peaceful.

CHAPTER 4

CHIEF MEDICAL OFFICER

▷ FEBRUARY 9, 2018

S t. Joseph's Hospital's medical staff of eleven doctors had met a number of times over the years, mostly at 3:00 p.m. so at least two shifts of them could attend the meeting. The younger hospitalists had been adamant about the importance of naming a chief medical officer, or CMO, who could represent them to the bishop, who was the chief executive officer of St. Joseph's. They wanted Mary to be the CMO because of their respect for her and because in the past, she had convinced the bishop to allow the physicians to make some decisions on their schedules. They knew she would represent their requests while being fair to the hospital.

Mary had often displayed her negotiation skills with them and other staff members of the hospital. She seemed able to always react to problematic issues and people with calm understanding while displaying a confidence that the problems could be resolved. Her sense of humor, patience, and gift of listening to people always provided them with confidence that she would do her best to help them solve their problems.

The staff wanted to write a letter to the bishop, requesting that she be appointed as the CMO. Mary said she was honored by their confidence in her and would be happy to serve in that capacity if the bishop approved. The letter was drafted and signed by all ten doctors, with Mary declining to sign because it involved naming her to be the CMO. She thought signing the document would have been arrogant, which she was not.

When he read the letter from the medical staff, the bishop received the suggestion with a big smile and great relief. Up to that point, he had been responsible for making the doctors' work schedules and had to handle all questions and other issues that arose regarding the medical staff. He had essentially delegated that responsibility to his diocesan secretary, a young priest who had no medical background and often needed the advice of Father Dan to resolve medical issues. The bishop was also delighted to name Mary as the CMO because he greatly respected her and knew she would be perfect for the position.

Soon after receiving the letter, the bishop responded to the medical staff in writing, met with Mary, and told her how happy he was to name her as the St. Joseph's Hospital CMO. He told her he would like her to take responsibility for, in addition to the doctors, the hospital's pharmacists and laboratory technicians, who drew blood specimens and inserted IVs. She readily agreed, telling him she would do her best to make him proud of how she managed the new position. He smiled, knowing how successful she would be based on her reputation and his previous interactions with her.

He responded by telling Mary he believed there were basically three types of individuals: innovators, implementers, and maintainers. Like good leaders, she veered toward the innovator and implementer types, but she also was able to ensure maintenance of what was implemented, because of the way she interacted with people.

He also told her that as she assumed the new administrative responsibilities, except for emergencies, she would only work the 7:00 a.m. to 3:00 p.m. shifts, with no weekend coverage. He knew she likely would continue working well after 3:00 p.m., sorting out clinical and administrative issues that arose. In addition, she would spend two of the five days a week working on administrative issues, receive a 10 percent salary increase, and be able to eat for free in the hospital's cafeteria. The latter was the same as Father Dan's arrangement for the cafeteria. The arrangements delighted Mary, and she thanked the bishop for his generosity.

Thereby, a CMO position was born, and the entire hospital staff—physicians, nurses, pharmacists, medical and laboratory technicians, maintenance personnel, ancillary staff, and private-practice physicians—were delighted. The doctors had no problem with Mary's working only the day shifts, because many of them preferred to work the less busy evening, night, and weekend shifts. They liked to use the weekend shifts to study for upcoming recertification exams, catch up on medical journal reading, or simply relax while reading an interesting novel between caring for patients.

Like all the hospitalists, Mary had been scheduled to work five weekends—or ten weekend days—per year. However, for the past few years, Mary had given up two of her four weeks of paid vacation, or ten days, so she would only work one weekend day, which she and the other doctors thought was fair. She liked to have Sundays free so she could attend Mass and have dinner with her mother, her brother, and his family.

She was happy having only two weeks of vacation to travel or do whatever she wanted. She already had taken her mother to Italy, which had required a great deal of persuasion because her mother was a homebody, and Mary had no desire to travel widely, preferring short trips to cities in the United States that had some significance to her. Her trips usually involved a medical conference to augment the continuing medical education she routinely gained via the monthly conferences sponsored by the private doctors' group. A certain number of continuing medical education hours was required to maintain her medical license, and she easily met that requirement.

One of the responsibilities of the CMO was to prepare the material for the upcoming Joint Commission on Hospitals (JCOH) evaluation necessary for the essential accreditation of the hospital. Mary wanted to do this as soon as possible as a means of getting fully acquainted with her new responsibilities as the CMO. The bishop sent over all the material he had for the past accreditation process and a recent document sent by the JCOH. Mary read the information and discovered that a new requirement was to include a history of the hospital and the current layout of the hospital building. She wondered why that was a new requirement, because she could not understand how anyone could have understood or judged the institution without having a clear view of how it was structured and laid out.

She certainly knew the layout of the hospital and was confident she knew the history, but she made an appointment with the bishop and spent an hour going over the details of the history. That weekend, she put together the documentation and filed it for future reference when she needed to complete the JCOH evaluation materials.

St. Joseph's Hospital

St. Joseph's is a private, community-based Roman Catholic hospital founded in 1910 and managed by nuns of the Daughters of Charity until 2010, when the management was taken over by the local bishop's office. The relationship with the Daughters of Charity nuns remains strong, and all medical care for the nuns is provided free of charge by St. Joseph's Hospital and its doctors and staff.

The hospital is in a community of about five thousand situated just outside a city of sixty thousand in Pennsylvania. It has 110 beds, with many active medical, nursing, and ancillary services that serve primarily adults but also some children patients.

Ninety-five beds are for medical or surgical adult patients. There is also a small five-bed obstetrics unit with a nearby small nursery of six bassinets, to care for twins if necessary. On the same floor as the nursery is a unit of ten beds allocated for children under the age of twelve, with most of these rooms being occupied by surgical patients. Only the children occupy semiprivate rooms; all other patients are admitted to private rooms.

The hospital's building is four stories high, with a fully functional basement that houses the maintenance, storage, housekeeping, heating-cooling, mail, and medical record units. The small emergency room (ER), all administrative offices, the kitchen and cafeteria dining room, the pharmacy, the gift shop, and a small telephone unit are located on the first floor.

The obstetric and pediatric units, the nursery, and an adult patient unit of thirty rooms are located on the second floor. The third floor has two units, each containing twenty patient rooms. The fourth floor has one unit of twenty-five beds; the doctors' call room with two beds, a shower, and a bathroom; and the doctors' locker room. One patient room on the fourth floor is larger than the others and is decorated a bit nicer than the others. This is the room where special patients, such as members of the board of trustees, donors to the hospital, priests, and nuns, are admitted.

There are two side-by-side elevators that serve the basement and all floors. Also, each floor has a bathroom and a maintenance room in the hallway outside the patient rooms. All floors are accessible by two sets of stairs located on each end of the long corridors that line the patient rooms.

The chief executive officer (CEO) of the hospital is the diocese bishop, who also serves as an ex officio member of the board of directors, which is essentially an honorific group who primarily are involved with financial matters. Therefore, all board members are financially well-to-do, influential individuals—mostly men but also some intelligent women who preside over large businesses—who ensure the financial health of the hospital. The board members sponsor an annual money-raising dinner and auction affair with well-to-do invitees, which provides extra money to ensure the financial health of the hospital.

St. Joseph's is a full-service hospital with hospitalist doctors; nurses; pharmacists; laboratory technicians; orderlies; and secretarial, record-keeping, and maintenance staff who are employed by the hospital.

The hospital's well-trained medical staff consists of nine hospitalists and two emergency medicine physicians who work full-time for the hospital. This ensures there is at least one full-time doctor in the hospital, though there are usually two or more, to care for the patients admitted by private doctors.

In addition, anesthesiology, radiology, pathology, nursing, laboratory technician, record-keeping, secretarial, and maintenance staff are employed by the St. Joseph's Private Physicians' Group, who work out of the hospital-owned four-story private medical office building adjoining the hospital.

The pharmacists work in the hospital and in the medical office building, with active pharmacies in both locations. The hospital pharmacy is open from 6:00 a.m. to 10:00 p.m., and the medical office building pharmacy is open from 9:00 a.m. to 5:00 p.m. Cross coverage by pharmacists is provided as necessary.

For convenience of the hospital staff and the private-practice doctors who admit their patients to St. Joseph's, there is a covered bridge connecting the hospital and the medical office building on the second floor.

There are two fully equipped operating rooms and a recovery room on the second floor of the medical office building, which are also managed and staffed by the private doctors' group. Patients who require hospitalization postoperatively are admitted directly from the recovery room via the second-floor annexation bridge to the hospital.

The private-practice doctors who provide primary care and specialty care pay an annual rental fee to the hospital for the space in the office building. They also provide the hospital with a certain percentage of the profits earned by their services. This arrangement is to ensure the financial health of the doctors and the hospital. It also allows the private doctors to have St. Joseph's hospitalist doctors cover their patients at all times.

The full-time staff have a key to the hospital entrances embodied in their ID cards, but for protection, when others seek entrance, there is always a guard on duty at the main entrance to the hospital and the emergency room entrance. A guard also is at the single entrance to the office building from 7:00 a.m. to 9:00 p.m., after which time the office building is closed. The guards who service the hospital and office building are provided by the local police department, which is paid by the hospital and private-practice group for this service.

St. Joseph's has an active ER staffed by well-trained physicians and nurse practitioners hired by the hospital. From 7:00 a.m. to 11:00 p.m., the ER is staffed usually by a physician trained in emergency medicine. From 11:00 p.m. to 7:00 a.m., it is staffed by a specially trained nurse practitioner backed up by the hospitalist physician, who primarily cares for medical problems that arise in hospitalized patients. There is always another hospitalist doctor on call from home at night if needed, which seldom happens because of the large city hospital located a relatively short five-mile distance from St Joseph's. That hospital has a large, active ER.

The ambulance service is provided by the city hospital, and all trauma patients and acutely ill individuals are taken to the city hospital. The only ambulance patients taken to St. Joseph's are those called to the ambulance service by private physicians who provide specific instructions to take those patients to St. Joseph's, which rarely happens.

From 7:00 a.m. to 11:00 p.m., St. Joseph's ER is busy because it serves as a backup for the private-practice group doctors, who often send patients there who do not have an appointment that day or call after office hours but need to be seen right away. These private-practice doctors are so busy they seldom have time to see these unscheduled patients, so the ER doctors and nurse practitioners care for them. The private physicians send their patients to the ER at any time, knowing that they will receive very good care and that the private physicians will be well informed about what happens.

If necessary, a phone call is made immediately by the ER doctor for consultation with the private physician, but that rarely is necessary. Usually, the private physician receives a call in the morning, and a copy of the patient's ER record is placed in the private physician's mailbox located in the basement of the hospital. Most of the private doctors pick up their mail, messages, and copies of any admissions in the morning before they go to see their admitted patients. If they have no patients in the hospital, they pick up any mail or messages before they leave for the day.

That kind of service and coverage encourages private-practice physicians to admit their patients to St. Joseph's. Although the majority of admissions are from the private-practice group whose offices are in the medical office building connected to the hospital, there usually are one or two patients who have been admitted by other private-practice doctors from the community or city.

The private-practice group is growing as community-based and even city-based doctors experience the convenience of admitting to the hospital and the excellent care provided by St. Joseph's hospitalist doctors and nurses.

Although no patient is ever turned away, almost all admitted patients have medical insurance. The hospital's reputation ensures that except for on weekends, the hospital is usually occupied to capacity, allowing for emergency admissions. One great asset is that the hospital's budget is always in the black, requiring only the board's annual dinner and auction donation to ensure financial health.

With the CMO position, Mary assumed responsibility for making up the schedule for doctor, pharmacist, and laboratory technician coverage, much as the director of nursing did for nurses. The director of nursing was also responsible for housekeeping, maintenance, and orderly staffs. It was essential for Mary and the director of nursing, Nancy Darcy, to have a close working relationship. Fortunately, that was not an issue because they already had a long-standing friendship. Mary would also be the main liaison person to the private-practice physicians who worked in the adjoining medical office building.

Almost immediately after Mary assumed the CMO position, Dr. John Bosko, the hospitalist physician who had been there the longest, alerted her that he was going to retire soon. He told her he had been planning to do so for a while but wanted to make sure that first she was in the CMO position, so she could choose his replacement. She told him he was such a great physician no one could really replace him, but she was grateful for his confidence in her to find a good doctor to fill the position. To her relief, he said he didn't want to retire until September, when he would spend more time after the summer with his wife and grown children, who lived away. That would give her plenty of time to recruit another doctor.

Mary decided that over the next few weeks, she would meet with each of the individuals for whom she was responsible—the doctors, pharmacists, and hospital laboratory technicians. She would set up weekly meetings with Nancy Darcy and monthly or so meetings with Dr. James Allen, chief of the private-practice physicians.

In addition, to become familiar with various issues that might arise, she would review the hospital's records of patient care, including numbers and types of patients served and outcomes of various diagnoses. Little did she know the terrible problem that would result from this research.

CHAPTER 5

_____

A SNOWY WEEKEND

O n Friday morning, February16, Mary packed three sets of underwear and toiletries in her briefcase, anticipating that she might have to spend the weekend and Monday at the hospital. The night before, a winter snowstorm warning had flashed every hour or so on the TV and radio. The weather report called for up to two feet of snow to fall between early afternoon on Friday and late afternoon on Sunday. Such a February snowfall occurred periodically in Pennsylvania, so natives knew how dangerous it would be to travel on the roads and even the sidewalks until they were cleared.

The first month's doctors' call schedule for which she was responsible as the CMO would be March, so she didn't remember which doctor had been scheduled to be on service that coming weekend. However, she did know that if the scheduled doctor had a family, especially young children, she would cover the weekend for him or her.

While she didn't like to leave Mom alone on a snowy weekend, she knew her mother would be fine because the neighbors looked out for one another. She also knew she could always count on a fifty-year-old friend who lived a few houses from them to look after Mom. Mary had helped him several years ago when he was trying to decide whether to come out of the closet and admit to being gay. He had wanted his partner to move in with him but had been afraid of what the neighbors would think and how they might react. She and Mom had made sure the neighbors knew their personal feelings by hosting a welcome-to-the-neighborhood party for the gay partner of their friend.

In addition, the seventeen-year-old twin sons of Louise Edgars, Mary's friend and classmate from grade and high school, would be out clearing snow on their block. Two years ago, the enterprising youngsters had begun earning money by shoveling snow for several houses on the block. They had saved their earnings from that year and purchased a snow blower at an end-of-the-season sale, and now they cleared snow for all fourteen houses on each side of the block. The boys always ended their snow clearing by stopping at the Davinos' house, where Mom gave them hot chocolate and homemade cookies, including a bag of cookies to take home. Their older sister was married and lived in New Jersey, so they had their parents to themselves and loved it. They were high school football stars, but they were polite and good-hearted boys and not at all spoiled.

They cleared snow for the elderly couple who lived across the street from the Davinos and did not want to accept payment, but the gentleman refused to allow them to clear the snow unless he paid like everyone else. The boys were smart enough to understand the gentleman's pride, so they charged him five dollars, and he always gave them a dollar tip. Mary loved the boys' kindness and respect for the elderly gentleman's pride, and she quietly made up for the difference in their actual cost when she paid the boys for clearing snow from the Davinos' walk and driveway.

The boys also volunteered to walk the elderly couple's dog so they would not have to venture out in the snow and walk on icy sidewalks. The couple's dog was a handful and not easy to manage, but the couple loved him, and he watched over them. Mary had once told Mom that she thought the dog was dyslexic, because he thought he was a god, not a dog. That had made her laugh, but she'd agreed.

Also, Mary would call home every few hours to make sure all was OK, and she knew it would make Mom happy to hear that Mary was also doing well.

When Mary left the house that morning, Mom was preparing to go to the church's soup kitchen, where she and her friend Sarah volunteered. She told Mary not to worry, because she and Sarah, who drove Mom to and from the kitchen, would be finished by one thirty in the afternoon at the latest and would be home before the snow started. However, as expected, she wanted Mary to call periodically so she would know Mary was safe at the hospital if she had to stay the weekend.

When Mary arrived at the hospital, she went to her assigned units on the fourth floor after she had changed into scrubs and picked up her mail and messages. No patients were scheduled to be admitted that day, and all patients able to be discharged from all units were already gone or soon would be. She then went to Mass and, afterward, returned to her assigned units to check on all patients remaining in the hospital and to discharge all others. There were no patients on the pediatric or obstetric units or nursery.

When she finished on the fourth floor, she went to check all the other units and found there would be only forty-one patients remaining in the hospital over the weekend. Many were elderly patients who could not be transported by ambulance to their own homes or to nursing homes, because those were nonemergencies, and all ambulances were on call for the impending snow emergency. Others were patients who required chemotherapy, IV antibiotics, or other IV medications or required close watching because of their diagnoses or treatment requirements.

As she was finishing her rounds on the second floor, she saw Dr. Jim Allen, the director of the private doctors' group, who, after discharging his hospitalized patients, was on his way to his office in the annexed medical building. Mary wanted to find out how the private doctors were going to manage the snowstorm situation and asked if she could walk with him to his office. She did not want to delay him in seeing the few patients he probably had scheduled for visits that morning.

As they walked across the annexing bridge, Jim told her that no patient visits were scheduled by the private doctors after 11:00 a.m. that day, and there were only two patients scheduled for bronchoscopies, one at 8:00 a.m. and the other at 9:30 a.m. Therefore, all patients and doctors could be out of the building long before the snow started.

When they entered the hallway outside the bronchoscopy suite, Mary heard the distinctive high-pitched sound of breath intake—a whooping sound—after a prolonged cough. She was puzzled and said to Jim that she'd thought there were no children in the offices that day. He told her there were no children scheduled that day. Then she heard the same distinctive cough and realized it came from a woman who was sitting up on a stretcher outside the bronchoscopy suite. The patient looked exhausted and had tears running down her cheeks from having coughed so much. A nurse was tending to her, trying to offer comfort.

Mary told Jim she was pretty sure the woman had pertussis, or whooping cough, and wondered why she was going to have a bronchoscopy. Jim thought about what she'd said and suggested she wait there to discuss her thoughts with the patient's physician, Dr. Kim Jackson, a pulmonologist who was probably finishing up with her first patient. Jim needed to go to his office but was sure Kim would be happy to hear Mary's proposed diagnosis. Mary agreed to wait because she knew Kim and in the past had found her to be willing to discuss possible diagnoses at clinical conferences sponsored by the group.

A few minutes later, Kim came out of the suite, greeted Mary with a big smile, and said, "Mary, what a pleasant surprise to see you. To what do I owe this visit?"

Mary responded with her own smile and explained her thoughts about the patient awaiting bronchoscopy. She made it clear that she was not a pediatrician, but she remembered that distinctive cough from medical school, having cared for an adult with pertussis during her residency.

Kim told her that the patient had had the cough, which often was so severe that she vomited, for eight weeks and was exhausted. Her x-ray, CAT scan, and chest MRI were unrevealing, so Kim thought bronchoscopy was the next step. Mary said she did not want to be presumptuous but only wanted to provide Kim with her thoughts.

Kim decided to present the idea to the patient and offer her the option of either going ahead with the bronchoscopy now or instead having a culture taken from the back of her throat with a swab passed through her nose and waiting for the result. If that test was negative for the bacterium that caused pertussis, they could reschedule the bronchoscopy for next week.

The patient opted for the test. She wanted to get home before the snow started and said she had put up with the "damn cough" for so long that a few more days would be fine, especially if the swab test might eliminate the bronchoscopy. So that was what they did, and Kim dropped off the specimen at the city hospital labs, which she passed on her way home.

Mary went back to the hospital units, where she discovered that John Bosko was scheduled to cover the weekend starting at 3:00 p.m. She was pleasantly surprised when he showed up early at 2:00 p.m. Mary thanked him for his early arrival and suggested he first go to the units for sign-out by the doctors who had children, so they could get home soon. She also told him she was willing to get the sign-out and cover the weekend so he could go home to be with his wife during the snowstorm. In response, he rolled his eyes, laughed, and said, "Are you kidding?"

When Mary asked about his response, he told her that his wife had gone to her sister's house just outside Philadelphia early that morning to spend the weekend with her. He was happy that he would have company all weekend with people he liked and that he would eat well because the hospital chef always made special meals for weather like that on weekends. Also, he wouldn't have to clean up his mess after trying to cook unhealthy meals for himself. He had brought a good novel he wanted to read, knowing he'd probably have time to read it with only a relatively few patients in the hospital.

With that response, Mary laughed and decided it would be fine for her to go home. She had already told all unnecessary personnel to leave as soon as it started to snow. John asked her to please go home so he wouldn't have to worry about her and to call him when she arrived home. It had started to snow at about two o'clock and was now really coming down hard. He promised to call her if he needed help; they both knew that the police and snowplows would ensure she could make it back to the hospital if necessary.

As soon as she had changed into street clothes, Mary called Mom and told her she was on her way home. That delighted Mom because she had been home since one forty-five, before the snow started. It took Mary twice as long as usual to drive home because the snow was piling up in the streets, and traffic was slow-moving. She was happy she had an all-wheel-drive car that did well in the snow.

When she drove up to her house, Mary saw that the Edgars boys had just plowed the driveway up to the garage and cleared a pathway to the front door of the house. She figured Mom must have called them to report that the doctor was on her way home, and they had started the task immediately. The boys were on their way home but smiled and waved to her as she turned into the driveway. She waved back and yelled a hearty thank-you out her open car window before she parked her car in the garage.

Mom was all smiles when Mary came in the door. She had just given the boys a big bag of cookies and half a cake she'd made the night before. They had also delivered some cookies and cake to the elderly couple across the street. Mary changed into sweatpants and a sweatshirt and planned to spend the weekend working on some administrative issues. She also planned to catch up on some reading.

Mom had a delicious stew with biscuits prepared for dinner, after which they said the rosary, which, for Mary, was more a time for meditation. They then watched the news, which mostly covered the weather report, and an old movie on TV. Mary was always amazed how wonderfully so many people made the best of a snowstorm. One TV station celebrated a one-year-old child's first encounter with snow. The child was bundled up in a snowsuit and sitting beside her mother in the snow as it fell. The child's reaction to the snow, with funny faces and giggles, was pure joy to watch.

Mary and Mom found the snow falling and accumulating beautiful and restful because they were safe, warm, and dry inside the house. Mary thought about the homeless people who were not as fortunate and was grateful for the shelters sponsored by the various churches and the city.

To entertain Mom, Mary told her about one icy winter storm that had occurred when she was a resident in Baltimore. She'd lived in an apartment that required her to park her car and then walk up a small hill to get to the door of her apartment building. Because the hill had been icy, she'd kept slipping and falling, until another resident of the apartment building had told her to take off her shoes and socks and put the socks over the winter shoes she was wearing. To her happy surprise, the traction of the socks on the ice had allowed her to walk only slightly gingerly up the hill. That experience had taught Mary to keep an extra pair of socks in her car during winter months.

The story made Mom laugh, and she told Mary she always had thought Mary kept a pair of heavy socks in her car in the winter for warmth. She said, "It's interesting how wrong we can be about things, and that's why we should ask if we're not sure about something." They both agreed on that wisdom.

Over the weekend, Mary did a lot of administrative work and managed to read for several hours. She called John Bosko a few times a day and found there were no special problems with the patients. John was happy making rounds periodically and interacting with the nurses, who also were happy. To their delight, the hospital chef had made free pizza and ice cream sundaes for the staff. Mary was well aware that simple acts of human kindness could go a long way.

So the weekend essentially was uneventful and peaceful, except for the existential unease Mary felt more frequently and profoundly lately. She found herself thinking about the meaning of her life and whether she was doing what God had planned for her. At first, these feelings had come primarily when she awoke in the middle of the night, when all her defenses were down. However, recently, they occurred during the daytime and concerned her. She planned to discuss them with Dan and hoped he could help her deal with the struggle.

In any case, she knew she was going to be so busy with her new responsibilities she might not have as much time to think about the issue. Time would tell.

CHAPTER 6

MEETINGS WITH MEDICAL STAFF

Mary decided to begin her individual staff meetings with the doctors, whom she knew from working with them but not in a supervisory role. The entire full-time medical and nursing staff had access to the hospital at all times. Mary had seen some of the doctors in the hospital on their off-duty days to get something out of the doctors' call room library or to check on a patient for whom they had provided care recently.

Being well organized required her to have a calendar for her scheduled meetings. She was delighted to have the help of an administrative assistant she shared with Dan and with the bishop for his hospital-based services. The arrangement presented no greater burden for the administrative assistant because essentially, all the bishop's hospital-based work would be assumed by Mary.

Her new office was in the first-floor administrative suite and consisted of a front reception room, where the administrative assistant had her desk, and three offices. The bishop's seldom-used office was in the center, with Father Dan's on the right and Mary's on the left as one entered the suite.

The administrative assistant, Martha King, had worked at the hospital for many years. It seemed to Mary that Ms. King had been there since the hospital opened, because she seemed to know everyone and everything about the place. Mary knew her only as someone who frequently attended weekday morning Mass in the hospital's chapel, sitting in the back. Clearly, she was someone who could be of great help to Mary.

While Mary had had little personal contact with her in the past, Martha had a reputation for being a smart, well-organized woman who refused to take sass from anyone, including the bishop. She abhorred arrogance and would not tolerate anyone who abused his or her position in the hospital. Mary knew they were going to get along well because she felt the same about arrogance and abuse of power.

When they first met, Mary called her Ms. King, which made the assistant smile and say, "Dr. Defazio, please call me Martha."

Mary responded, "Only if you'll call me Mary or at least Dr. D."

Martha looked at her with pursed lips and a pretend scowl and said, "Dr. D is enough of a nickname for me to call you at this point; perhaps in the future, I will call you Mary." Then she smiled broadly.

Mary straightened up, saluted, and responded, "Yes, ma'am." They both laughed.

Mary planned to spend up to an hour with each of the doctors, so she could get to know them much better than she currently did. She asked Martha to set up an appointment with each of the ten physicians, using five hours of the time reserved for administrative issues on Tuesday and five on Thursday. That way, she would have the doctors' meetings completed by the following week while allowing time for other administrative issues. She also asked Martha to set up a meeting with Dr. Allen and with Nancy Darcy.

Mary reviewed the curriculum vitae of the ten hospital-based doctors, of which three were women. Not surprisingly, she found that all of them were well educated and trained. Six of them were trained in internal medicine, two in emergency medicine, and two in family medicine. The oldest had been at St. Joseph's for thirty-two years and the youngest for three years. All had easily managed the care required for even the most complex patients, including those in the emergency room. Of course, it helped that all major trauma patients were taken by ambulance to the city hospital, bypassing St. Joseph's.

The first interview was with Dr. Mark Andrews, an internist who had worked at St. Joseph's for ten years. He was married and had two boys. His wife was a nurse who also worked at St. Joseph's. Both had family in the area and wanted to settle close to them. His hobby was woodworking, and most gifts he gave to his family were things he'd made. He was known for his intellect, especially in diagnosing infectious diseases.

The second interview was with Dr. Andrew Flynn, who was trained in family medicine and had been at St. Joseph's for fifteen years. He mostly covered pediatric patients, including newborns. He was married and had two teenage daughters, who he claimed were driving him crazy because they thought he and his wife, who worked from home as an accountant, were stupid.

Mary told him to wait until his daughters were twenty-one or so, and suddenly, he and his wife would become smart. He told Mary he'd thought he, not she, was supposed to be the one with some training in adolescent medicine. She only smiled and told him about her experiences with her niece and nephew and as a nurse dealing with many teenagers. He asked if he and his wife could consult her about their problems with their daughters, to which Mary responded that her mother would be a much better consultant for that, and they both laughed. He told Mary that in his spare time, he played the cello to try to maintain his sanity.

The third interview was with Dr. John Bosko, an internist and the oldest of the physicians, who had worked at St. Joseph's for thirty-two years. He had served in the marines for six years prior to coming to St. Joseph's. He was the physician to whom the other physicians came with questions, especially about the behavior of male patients. He claimed to have seen it all and then some while a marine.

Some found it amazing because of his background in the marines, but—probably because he was married and had two daughters and, thereby, a house full of women—he would not tolerate any man being disrespectful toward women. He was adamant that men must treat all women—whether doctors; nurses; technicians; housekeepers; or those who worked in the kitchen, dining room, or anywhere else in the hospital—as if they were their mothers, sisters, or daughters. Because everyone greatly respected him, that was a rule faithfully followed.

His wife was a retired nurse, and their daughters and grandchildren lived in other cities, so the couple had a so-called empty nest. He already had told Mary of his desire to leave in September in order to spend more time with his family. She told him again how grateful she was because that gave her time to get oriented to her new position and recruit another doctor.

The fourth interview was with Dr. Michael Paluski, an internist who had worked at St. Joseph's for twelve years. His wife and he had three children—two boys and a girl—all in school and active in sports. His wife was a full-time mother, coach, housekeeper, cook, and laundress and did all the other things necessary to keep the family healthy and together. He loved to talk about how much his wife and kids meant to him, which endeared him to Mary. He was especially interested in cardiac problems, having spent an extra year of training in cardiology.

The fifth interview was with Dr. Peter Lewis, who was specially trained in emergency medicine and had worked at St. Joseph's for three years. He was married to a nurse who was an anesthetist who worked with the private-practice group in the adjoining medical office building. They had no children, but he told Mary they were working on it, to which she smiled and wished them luck. He smiled back and said his family and his wife's family lived in the community and were cheering them on so they could have a grandchild.

The sixth interview was with Dr. Annette Reynolds, who also was trained in emergency medicine. She had worked at St. Joseph's for fourteen years. She was athletic, having played soccer in college, and was a strong advocate of women's liberation. She suffered arrogant or macho men badly. She had a great sense of humor, having once shown up for an evening meeting of the medical staff around Christmas wearing a sweatshirt that read, "Three wise men? Surely you jest."

Her husband was a political science professor at the community college, and they had a nineteen-year-old daughter who was away at college and a thirteen-year-old son at home. The family were frequent campers and recently had purchased a new van outfitted for sleeping overnights.

She told Mary she was grateful to Peter Lewis because he allowed her to work more 7:00 a.m. to 3:00 p.m. ER shifts than he did. She was especially happy when she worked that shift, because her husband could get her son breakfast and take him to school. The shift allowed her to make dinner and get her son to bed. However, she was prepared to work any shift, because she and Peter were friends, and she loved her work.

The seventh interview was with Dr. Emily Marino, who

was trained in family medicine and shared caring for the pediatric patients with Andrew Flynn. She had worked at St. Joseph's for twenty years. Her husband was a pathologist in private practice who worked in the adjoining office building. They had one son, who was a premed college student. Emily was a good violinist and frequently played for the patients when she was off duty.

The eighth interview was with Dr. Jane Chen, an internist with a special interest in rheumatology. She'd spent an extra year of training in that specialty. She had worked at St. Joseph's for twenty-two years. Her husband was a pharmacist who worked in the pharmacy in the adjoining office building.

They had two sons, one in medical school and the other in graduate school, studying computer science. She loved working with elderly patients, and because none of the private physicians who admitted to St. Joseph's had any special training in geriatrics, they frequently admitted their elderly patients when they knew she would be on duty. She also played the violin and sometimes joined Emily Marino in playing for patients when off duty.

The ninth interview was with Dr. Peter Hanraty, an internist who had worked at St. Joseph's for eleven years. He was married to a grade-school teacher, and they had a son and a daughter, both of whom attended the school where his wife worked. He was especially interested in endocrine problems and had spent an extra year training in endocrinology. He played the viola.

The tenth and final interview was with Dr. Louis Provo, another internist, who had worked at St. Joseph's for eight years. He was known for his general knowledge about adult medicine, having spent two years in private practice running a diagnostic clinic in the adjoining office building. He was well known to the physicians in the community and sometimes even those who did not have offices in the adjoining building but admitted their patients with multiple problems to St. Joseph's in order that he might be able to shed some light on the diagnosis. He was married to a nurse who worked in the adjoining office building, and they had one daughter and another child on the way.

When she had finished interviewing the doctors, Mary was more impressed than ever with the caliber of excellence in the doctors with whom she worked. She also told Martha she was going to ask Drs. Flynn, Marino, Chen, and Hanraty, who formed a string quartet, if they might play at hospital parties. Martha thought that was an excellent idea.

Mary's meeting with Nancy Darcy was a joy. Both women were happy to have much of the administration back in the hands of women, who they felt were better at getting things done with the least bother. They immediately agreed to meet weekly over lunch in one of their offices to save time. Efficiency was queen to them.

Nancy had worked at St. Joseph's since she graduated from college thirty-five years earlier. She had worked in the operating rooms and studied for her master's degree in administration at night over three years. She had become the director of nursing twenty-seven years prior. She was married to an engineer, Bill Darcy. They had three children—two boys and a girl—all of whom had graduated from college, were married, and had provided Nancy and Bill with six grandchildren. All of them lived within fifty miles of the community, so they got together frequently.

Mary's meeting with Dr. Jim Allen was also enjoyable. She had known Jim for many years and respected him as a physician and a decent human being. He was a cardiologist by training and a devout Roman Catholic whose kindness to Mary when she'd worked at St. Joseph's as a nurse while still a novice nun had been important to her. She would always be grateful to him for how much he taught her about patient care and just being a nice person to everyone.

He was married to a retired nurse, and they had two adult sons and five grandchildren. Both of their sons were doctors who'd married other doctors, and all of them worked in the city hospital. Theirs was another close-knit family.

Jim asked Mary if she would like to serve as a member of the private physicians' board, and she immediately accepted the offer. That would provide her with the opportunity to attend their monthly meetings and keep up with potential issues that might cause a problem for the hospital. As a member of the private physicians' board, she might be able to attend to those issues before they became major problems. She and Jim decided to meet on a need-to basis. She hoped those meetings would be as pleasant as was this one.

Mary next met with the nine pharmacists who worked at the hospital and the medical office building. All were well trained, but only a few had worked at St. Joseph's for longer than a few years, so she did not know them as well as the doctors, nurses, and other staff.

Many pharmacists made a relatively early departure because the need for pharmacists at the city hospital and regional pharmacies associated with CVS, Rite-Aid, and Walgreens was great, and the pay was higher. In addition, most of them were young and married and moved away from the area. All the current pharmacists were women, with six of them being Caucasian, two Hispanic, and one Afro-American. Mary spent a half hour with each of them and was happy with the results. None of them expressed dissatisfaction with her job, which made Mary happy.

Finally, Mary met with the nine laboratory technicians, of whom seven were women. All had been trained at St. Joseph's and were good at what they did. Six of them were Hispanic, and the other three were Afro-American. They were a cheerful, kind group who always received excellent ratings from the patients.

With the meetings completed, Mary could now get on with educating herself about the items she planned to investigate. Little did she realize what a complex and troubling adventure that was going to be.

CHAPTER 7

MEETINGS WITH THE HOSPITAL SUPPORT STAFF

▷ MARCH 6, 2018

B efore she met with the support staff and started gathering data and information about the hospital, some of which would be necessary for the Joint Commission on Hospitals evaluation that would occur in a year or so, Mary wanted to discuss the data-gathering process with Father Dan. So she asked him if they might share lunch in her office that day, and he agreed. She then asked Martha to arrange for the hospital cafeteria staff to prepare something for Father Dan and her for lunch.

When Dan arrived at her office, he was greeted with a roll-in table buffet set with a plate of tuna salad with vegetables and a large platter of his favorite ham and cheese, tuna salad, and chicken salad sandwiches, accompanied by potato salad, potato chips, and apple pie. Mary shook her head and said, "I didn't expect a feast, because when I meet for lunch in our offices with Nancy Darcy, we have a tuna or chicken salad with some vegetables. No dessert because we like to keep the calorie count down for lunch."

Dan laughed and replied, "Well, they know what I like and that I don't care about the calories, so I guess they wanted to please both of us."

Mary smiled and said, "Obviously, that was their goal, and they accomplished it with four stars. I think Martha will know what to do with what we don't eat, so it won't be wasted."

They began to eat, and after a bite, Mary explained to Dan that she wanted to know the important administrative things that had happened at the hospital over the past five years or so, of which she had little or no knowledge. She told him that some of the data she was going to gather would be necessary for a data-driven Joint Commission on Hospitals evaluation planned for the near future. Dan knew that accreditation by the commission was important for the hospital's rating and reputation but told her he was surprised she was preparing for it so early. She told him she wanted to be prepared as early as possible so she could take care of anything that might need to be fixed. Preparing for the commission while familiarizing herself with other administrative issues would kill two birds with one stone, so to speak.

While eating, Dan asked, "How might I help you with this process? I've never been part of it in the past, so I'm not sure what I can do."

Mary responded, "Well, I've never been part of this process either. I will read past reports, and that should help. Also, I expect the bishop will have some helpful advice, because he was here for the past two evaluations and is ultimately responsible for the evaluation. However, I want to make sure the report I prepare is exactly what is needed for a top rating. What I need from you is a sounding board if I have questions or find potential problems that need to be fixed. Would you help me in that way?"

Dan laughed and said, "If you promise to have lunches like

this served, of course I will be delighted to help. In fact, why don't we also meet to have discussions related to our shared experiences and issues involving our religion? Would that be OK with you?"

Mary responded, "That would be wonderful. I have so many questions about the Catholic rules and practices but never about my faith. That makes for some very confusing thoughts sometimes and causes me to struggle existentially with God."

When Dan left, she decided to begin gathering the information she needed. Because she wanted to accomplish the task in the most organized way, she began with a list of what would be necessary for her to be well informed about the hospital's functions. The list began with a complete organizational chart, so she'd be aware of who was responsible for whom and what. Of course, at the top of the chart would be the CEO, Bishop Ambrose O'Conner, and the board of directors. She thought she knew the rest but didn't want to be surprised.

Next—and, to her, most importantly—were the results of patient care. How well the hospital cared for patients was the prime criterion for true excellence. She believed the other information she needed would come as she studied the first two items on her list.

She asked Martha to please get her the organizational chart for the hospital, and Martha pursed her lips, looked toward the ceiling, and replied, "You must be kidding. You want me to share the chart that now includes the chief medical officer—that is, Dr. Mary Defazio?"

Mary looked concerned and replied that she was serious and wondered why that might be a problem.

Martha laughed and told her she was only kidding. "You see, I also have a sense of humor, Dr. D."

That delighted Mary, which she immediately told Martha.

With that interaction, she knew they were going to get along well.

Mary next went to the office of the head of the medical records room in the basement, where she asked Mrs. Gill, the coordinator of medical records, whom she knew well, for any information that might be available on the annual discharge diagnoses of all patients, including any mortality or serious morbidity that had occurred. She wanted the information for the past five years, which she figured should be sufficient to get her well informed generally and for the commission evaluation.

Mrs. Gill told her that even though all the data were in the main hospital computer in some form, it would take a few days to gather the information in the format she requested.

Mary knew Mrs. Gill was efficient and reliable and had a good staff. Even though the records room was officially directed by an information technology so-called whiz kid supervisor, everyone went to Mrs. Gill for information because the supervisor seemed to be a recluse who stayed in his office and didn't like to interact with anyone. So be it, as long as the necessary information flowed. It would be interesting to see on the organizational chart to whom the supervisor ultimately reported, she thought. The chart was becoming even more important than she had originally believed.

Mary also knew it would be a good idea to walk through the entire hospital each week on one of her administrative days so she could get to know as many support-staff individuals as possible and see how everything functioned up close and personal. She had a good knowledge of the various patient floors and the staff who worked there during the 7:00 a.m. to 3:00 p.m. shift, when she worked as a hospitalist most often, so she planned the walk-throughs to occur on both day and evening shifts for the first floor and the basement but only for the evening 3:00 p.m. to 11:00 p.m. shift for the other floors.

This was not a big deal because she seldom left the hospital before five o'clock.

Her administrative days were Tuesdays and Thursdays, so on the next Thursday, she began her visits on the top floor and worked her way down to the basement, making sure to greet everyone with at least a smile. She tried to remember the name of everyone so she could greet everyone personally. She knew that was going to be difficult but possible because everyone wore a name tag in addition to his or her ID card. That would mean getting close enough to each person so she could read the name tag.

She was familiar with almost all the physicians and nurses, so the patient floors went quickly. However, the first floor and basement of the hospital were going to take more time because except for the guards at the entrances and the pharmacists, she seldom saw those who worked there, including the telephone operators and the people in the gift shop. She knew almost no one in the basement.

The telephone operators she knew only by voice, and because everyone had a cell phone, an operator was heard only on the rare occasion when she or he called on the overhead speaker a fire drill or a code red that a patient had need of the emergency medical team. The operators on duty were happy that the chief medical officer was visiting them in person. Mary thought that was sad and promised to visit them every week, much to their delight.

The gift shop was a special place managed by the spouses of the private-practice doctors, and all proceeds went to the hospital, mostly for the chapel and to buy toys and supplies for the children on the pediatric unit. She knew visiting with them was going to be an enjoyable experience and an opportunity to get to know some of the spouses of her private doctor colleagues.

Except for the records room, the basement was a mystery to Mary. There she met the maintenance, housekeeping, and mail room staff. She only knew two of them: Pedro Gonzales, a maintenance man, and Elana Gomez from housekeeping. She knew both from weekday Mass in the hospital's chapel, where she—and, on occasion, Pedro—served as the eucharistic minister for Father Dan. Both Pedro and Elana were at Mass almost every day during the week and sometimes on the weekend.

Mary knew that Elana had been born in the United States, was happily married, and had two children, of whom she was very proud. She worked to ensure that each of her children would have a good education, including college.

Mary was especially fond of Pedro, who, because of his kindness to everyone and especially to the patients, had become a favorite member of the hospital's family. It was not unusual for him to present flowers from his small garden to a patient who seemed especially lonely or distressed.

Mary and Pedro had shared lunch several years ago when he had a day off and asked if he could meet with her because he had a question. His question was whether he could keep the out-of-date medical textbooks from the doctors' call room. He had been reading the books in the call room for years but only for an hour or so after he came off duty. Of course, Mary was delighted to give him the books after she discussed it with her colleagues, all of whom were happy to oblige.

During that past meeting, Mary had asked about his family. He had been born in Mexico, and his mother had taught herself and him English after his father was shot and died in a robbery at the store where he was a clerk. Pedro had been three years old at the time, and his mother had begun working as a housekeeper for a family from Texas who lived in Mexico, where the father directed a business. Pedro's mother had taught him to speak English, and he'd attended the same English-speaking Catholic school as the Texas family's children. He'd graduated when he was eighteen years old, and he spoke excellent English and Spanish. His mother had remarried when he was fifteen, and his sister had been born a year later.

After graduating from high school, he had come to the United States to help care for an elderly uncle who lived near the hospital. Pedro had wanted to work so he could help support his family in Mexico and applied for a job at St. Joseph's Hospital because he was interested in medicine. The only position they'd had for him at the time was as a maintenance worker who covered the night shift. He'd readily accepted. He'd kept that job after his uncle died, because he loved working with the people at St. Joseph's, and the job provided him with a good salary, benefits, and a pension. It also provided him with time to take some courses in English literature at the community college, because he loved to read, especially biographies and mystery novels.

In addition to Pedro and Elana, every person she met in the basement had a reaction similar to that of the telephone operators: sheer delight that the chief medical officer had come to visit them in person. Mary knew the weekly walk-throughs were going to be uplifting to her and to the staff. She was amazed at how little it took to make people happy. Simple acts of kindness and consideration were highly rewarding.

CHAPTER 8

PATIENT WITH DOWN SYNDROME

▷ MARCH 19–20, 2018

On Monday, March 19, Mary was happy to have a clinical day of seeing patients, with no planned administrative duties. Per usual, at 6:15 a.m., she went straight to her office after collecting her mail and messages and changed into scrubs and a white coat. She then went to the fourth-floor unit and the other unit where she was assigned for that week and signed in with her colleagues who had been on duty the night before. As was usually the case on Mondays, there were no pressing patient issues on any of the units she was covering, so she went to the chapel to assist Dan with Mass.

After Mass, she went to the cafeteria for two coffees and two blueberry muffins to share with Martha. She left Martha's goodies with her and went to the nurses' station on the fourth-floor unit so she could eat her breakfast while discussing patients with the nurses. There were only eight patients on the unit who had remained in the hospital over the weekend, but eight more were scheduled to be admitted that day. The other unit for which she was responsible had no pressing problems because the admitting private physicians already had taken care of everything.

According to the messages left for her by the admitting doctors, the only patient who needed extra care was Amanda Peters, a fourteen-year-old girl with Down syndrome, who was scheduled to have a cardiac catheterization the next morning.

Amanda was also the only patient mentioned as a possible problem by the nurses on the fourth-floor unit. They were accustomed to adolescent patients because the pediatric unit only admitted children up to age twelve. However, this adolescent would not be functioning at her fourteen-year-old chronological level. The nurses were concerned because they wanted to be sure they could provide the best care for her, having had no experience with younger children as patients.

Mary assured them they were well equipped to manage the patient, because all of them had children of their own. She kidded them that even though she personally had no children, she felt secure because of her experience with her niece and nephew as they were growing up. In addition, she had had two months on a pediatric unit during medical school. Mary told them she was just happy Amanda was not a two-year-old, saying that a two-year-old would have acted like a schizophrenic little imp with a superb prognosis. That made them laugh and feel better about the situation.

Mary spent the rest of the morning and afternoon caring for patients, including the new admissions. She deliberately left Amanda until last because she wanted to spend as much time as possible with her. Amanda's doctor, Jim Allen, had called Mary and told her he had been the cardiologist who assisted the pediatric cardiac surgeon who cared for Amanda when she was an infant. He had already seen Amanda that morning and written the admission note to make it easier for Mary. As her cardiologist, he knew Amanda's long, complicated medical history.

He provided any information he believed would help Mary to care for her. Unfortunately, Amanda had been born with tetralogy of Fallot, a serious congenital cardiac defect that had required surgical repair when she was nine months old. Dr. Allen, along with her pediatrician, who was not part of the private-practice group, had been following her since infancy. He needed to perform a cardiac catheterization now because she was having some spells that might have been related to her heart. The cardiac surgeon had been alerted and was ready to see her if necessary.

Dr. Allen also reported that Amanda's parents were wonderful individuals who had tried for years without success to have a child. Then, to their surprise, her mother had become pregnant when she was forty and the father was forty-nine years old. They loved their child and provided excellent care for her, including special tutoring because Amanda's functioning was now at the level of a six-year-old.

Mary thanked Dr. Allen and told him she was grateful for the history. She promised to take special care of the child.

By the time Mary finished with the other patients, it was 2:15 p.m. She had skipped lunch, which was not unusual, so she grabbed a power bar, a supply of which she always had in her desk, and ate it as she walked down the hall to Amanda's room.

When she entered the room, she saw Amanda sitting on the bed with her mother, who was reading a picture book to her. As soon as she saw Mary, Mrs. Peters slipped off the bed, and Mary put out her hands to take both of Mrs. Peters's hands and introduced herself.

Mrs. Peters said, "Dr. Defazio, I am so happy you are going to care for Amanda while she is in the hospital. She does much better with women."

Mary smiled, went to Amanda, and said, "Amanda, I am happy to care for you while you are here. Now, what can I do for you before I listen to your heart?"

Amanda looked at her with a scowl and immediately said, "I am scared and want to go home."

Mary responded, "Well, you will go home as soon as a very special heart test is done tomorrow morning. How about both of us listening to your heart so you can hear what it is telling us?"

Amanda looked at her with wide eyes and said, "My heart can talk?"

Mary responded, "Yes, in special heart talk. Let's listen to it, OK?" Mary put her stethoscope on Amanda's chest, listened to what she needed to hear, and then took the earpieces out of her ears and placed them in Amanda's ears.

Amanda's face broke out in a wide smile, and she squealed, "Mommy, my heart is talking to me!" She bounced up and down in the bed, which made her heartbeat even faster, and that made her even more excited.

After a minute or so, Mary removed the earpieces and said, "See? I told you your heart can talk. Now, tomorrow morning, the other doctors need to listen and even to see your heart with a special machine sort of like my stethoscope but for the eyes, not the ears. And you won't even know, because you will be sleeping, having nice dreams."

Amanda said, "But I am scared of the other doctors and their machine. And I don't want to go to sleep. I want Mommy." She started to cry, and her mother came over to hold her, looking at Mary with tears in her eyes.

Mary looked at Mrs. Peters and then at Amanda and said, "Honey, Mommy can't come into the room with you tomorrow, but how about if I come with you then and hold your hand until you go to sleep? I will make sure no one hurts you, and I'll be there when you wake up, and everything will be over. I will then take you back to Mommy. OK?"

Amanda stopped crying and said, "Do you promise you will hold my hand when I am with the other doctors and their machine and take me to Mommy when I wake up?"

Mary responded, "I promise."

Amanda said, "OK. But I won't go anywhere if you're not there with me." She hugged Mary.

Mary smiled and said, "That's a deal. I will see you tomorrow. Now I'd like Mommy to walk with me down the hall, but she'll be right back."

Amanda replied, "OK, but she better come right back."

When Mrs. Peters and Mary were outside the room, Mrs. Peters said, "Dr. Defazio, how can I ever thank you? Will you really be able to take that time to be with Amanda?"

Mary said, "Mrs. Peters, I would never promise something I couldn't deliver, especially to a child. In the morning, I will be here to walk with you and Amanda to the radiology suite, and I'll go in with her to hold her hand until she's asleep. They'll call me before they wake her, so I'll be there holding her hand when she wakes up. I will then walk along her stretcher to where you will be, in the recovery room, and you can take it from there. Now, get some sleep tonight, and don't worry. I'll see you in the morning."

Before she left for the day, Mary called Dr. Allen, who was delighted that Mary would be there in the morning and immediately arranged for her to be in the radiology suite with him and Amanda.

Early the next morning, which was an administrative day, Mary arrived as promised, and everything proceeded as planned. After the child's cardiac catheterization was over and Mary had taken Amanda to her mother, Amanda hugged Mary and said, "I like you a lot."

Mary hugged her and smiled, saying, "I like you a lot too."

Mrs. Peters was happy and relieved. She asked if she could speak with Mary later because she had an important question to ask her, but it would take some time to explain. Mary agreed and told her to have the nurses call her office when Mrs. Peters was ready to discuss whatever she needed to discuss. Little did Mary know that the most difficult part of Amanda's care was about to come.

Later, Martha told Mary that Mrs. Peters had called and asked if they might meet someplace other than Amanda's room. Mary asked Martha to tell Mrs. Peters they could meet in her office. About ten minutes later, Mrs. Peters arrived, and Mary invited her to sit at the table in the office. Mrs. Peters told Mary that Amanda was sleeping and doing well and would go home in the morning because the cardiac catheterization showed nothing unexpected or dangerous.

Mary told Mrs. Peters she was pleased with the report, and after Martha brought them coffee, Mary asked what issue she wanted to discuss.

Mrs. Peters sighed and said, "Dr. Defazio, this is very difficult, but I know you are a former nun and a eucharistic minister as well as being a superb doctor. I need your advice. You see, Amanda has had her menstrual cycle for the past two years, and this presents a problem at times. She has had several embarrassing accidents when she was at her special school, because her cycles are not regular, so I can't always be prepared to manage the situation. It is also very difficult to explain to her why she has bellyaches, as she calls menstrual cramps. The menstrual blood frightens her so much it takes a lot to calm her down, because she thinks she's going to bleed to death.

"I worry because while I know Amanda will probably not live a long life because of her heart, I don't know what will happen if she outlives my husband and me. I am now fifty-four, and my husband is sixty-three years old. We have no relatives young enough who could take care of her. We have set up a trust for her care, but most of the very good places where she would be well taken care of won't take any developmentally disabled person who can't provide most self-care. Amanda can eat, bathe, and dress herself with no problem, but the menses is a big problem for her.

"Also, Amanda is a very loving person, and as you probably noticed, she hugs people she likes. We worry that a bad man might take advantage of her, and she might get pregnant. That would be horrible for her heart and in general, as you can imagine."

Mrs. Peters had tears in her eyes. "Because of this, my husband and I would like for her to have a hysterectomy, and her pediatrician is all for it, but he is Jewish, and we are Catholic. We chose a Jewish pediatrician because he was highly recommended especially because of his reputation for caring for children with intellectual and other disabilities. He has been wonderful, and we would never change from him. Now I need to ask what you think we should do as good Catholics."

Mary felt as if someone had just punched her in the stomach. Of all possible things Mrs. Peters might have asked, she was completely unprepared to answer this question.

She said, "Mrs. Peters, I know what my gut reaction is, but I'll need some time to research this before I respond as you have requested—that is, as a Catholic. I will be in to see Amanda before she is discharged tomorrow, and I will try to get what I need to respond by then. Would that be OK with you?"

Mrs. Peters responded, "Of course. Any advice you can give will be greatly appreciated."

All the way home that evening, Mary mumbled to herself. *Dear God, why me? What do I know about this? Is this another example of your being the Great Comedian, as Dante noted? If so, I think your sense of humor is sometimes very weird.*

Oh well. I guess I know what I'll be doing tonight, because I can hardly ask for Dan's advice on this question. I hope to learn something that will agree with what my gut response would be.

That evening, after watching the 6:00 p.m. news with Mom, Mary went to her computer and searched "hysterectomy in a Catholic girl or woman with Down syndrome."

She was happy to find an excellent published article that provided an answer, and to her delight, it agreed with her gut response to the question. The article, "Sex and Trisomy 21" by Sister Renee Mirkes, OSF, MA, had been published in 1990 in *Ethics and Medics: A Catholic Perspective on Moral Issues in the Health and Life Sciences.*

She thought, *Thank God for nuns, especially the one who published this article.* The article stated that essentially, a hysterectomy was sanctioned by the Catholic church if it was performed for therapeutic and not contraceptive reasons—that was, the removal of an organ whose continued functioning would have been a threat to overall well-being. Surely that was the case with Amanda.

Mary was happy that this Catholic doctrine made sense and was different from what she had found with Julia, the young woman who'd died in her arms from sepsis resulting from a self-inflicted abortion. Mary was against abortion, but surely God recognized there were certain situations in which it was understandable and not worthy of being damned to hell. She felt so strongly that her view had resulted in her leaving the convent. Perhaps it had been a test of her true calling, but she had never regretted that decision. At any rate, that would not be a problem for her in this case.

The next morning, Mary went to Amanda's room to discharge her and not only told Mrs. Peters what she had read but also gave her a copy of the article she had printed for her. Mrs. Peters profusely thanked Mary and asked if she would be willing to take care of Amanda again if they decided to have the hysterectomy at St. Joseph's Hospital, which she thought was likely.

Mary responded that she would be happy to care for Amanda if she was on duty that day, which was a good possibility because she only took vacation two weeks a year. If Mrs. Peters would call Mary before she scheduled Amanda's procedure, Mary could tell her whether that was a good time for her. Mary then gave her cell phone number to Mrs. Peters, who promised not to use the number except as planned. Mary told her she could call her if she had a question Mary might be able to answer but not one that should be answered by Amanda's doctor.

Mrs. Peters said she understood, again thanked Mary, and then left with a big smile on her face. Amanda gave Mary a big hug and left with a grin on her face.

Some days it feels so wonderful to be alive and able to help someone, Mary thought. That day had been such a day for her.

CHAPTER 9

GATHERING DATA

After Mass on March 19, Pedro asked Mary if he could speak with her, and of course, she agreed. He told her he had decided to retire and return home to Mexico, his place of birth, where he would live with his sister, who was younger than he, and be with some of his childhood friends. He told Mary he had heard the doctors talking about asking the bishop to make her the chief medical officer, and he'd wanted to be at St. Joseph's when that happened. He said she truly deserved that honor, and now that it had happened, he could go to Mexico.

He had given notice to his supervisor, nurse Nancy Darcy, the previous afternoon and wanted to tell Mary in person. He thanked her for her kindness to him over the years and promised to pray for her every day. He handed her a small gift-wrapped package, which she unwrapped to find a rosary made in Mexico. He told her that Father Dan had blessed it for her. Mary was moved by Pedro's gift and what he had said and told him she would also pray for him.

That afternoon, she met with Nancy, and together they planned a farewell party for Pedro to take place the next Friday evening.

To show their affection for him, all the staff who could showed up to the party to say a sad goodbye and wish him well. They had all chipped in to buy him the latest editions of the main medical textbooks for adult and pediatric care and a sweatshirt from St. Joseph's Hospital. More than fifty doctors, nurses, and other staff had signed a card for him. Mary hugged him and told him again that she would miss him. They both had tears in their eyes as they bid each other farewell. Mary knew Pedro would be happy back home with his family and childhood friends.

Beginning the following Monday, Mary spent the mornings of most of her five administrative days from March 20 to April 3 looking at the hospital data for the past five years, which had been provided by Mrs. Gill from the records room. First, she found there had been an average of 3,200 patients admitted annually for an average of 3.7 days each. Next, she looked at the discharge diagnoses and found that cardiac problems, cancer, infectious diseases, stroke, and surgery were the top diagnoses, accounting for about 70 percent of diagnoses. There was nothing unusual in any of the diagnoses. None of that was a surprise to her because most of the seriously complex problems and diagnostic dilemmas were admitted to the city hospital. The diagnoses recorded were within the realm of expectation for any community hospital, such as St. Joseph's.

She next looked at the morbidity—minor and nonlethal problems—including side effects of various medications and other treatments. They consisted primarily of an expected number of almost all nonserious infections, and there were no serious or unexpected side effects from the medications or treatments. Fortunately, no patient had fallen or been injured because of negligence. In essence, she found no significant problems out of the normal expectations for a hospital the size of St. Joseph's.

Finally, Mary looked at the patient deaths that had occurred in the hospital. She carefully reviewed each record individually. Thankfully, there had been relatively few deaths each year, and almost all of them had been in patients with end-stage malignancies and very elderly patients who had heart attacks, strokes, or pneumonia presenting on admission or developed soon after being admitted for broken hips or other bones resulting from falls. Most of the latter patients had been admitted from local nursing homes. The elderly, others with malignancies, and the remaining patients with cardiac problems and strokes accounted for all but five deaths.

Those five patient deaths in the hospital were of special concern to Mary, and she reviewed their charts especially carefully. One patient was a seventy-eight-year-old missionary priest who had just returned from rural India and was staying at the rectory of St. Ann's parish, across the street from St. Joseph's. Apparently because he did not want to be hospitalized, he told no one about his problem of having several days of severe bloody diarrhea and an inability to eat or drink anything, including water. One of the priests went to his room when he failed to come to breakfast after also missing dinner the night before. That priest was concerned because the missionary priest had looked ill since he first came to the rectory four days ago. He was found unconscious in his bed and barely breathing. He was rapidly carried to St. Joseph's ER.

Unfortunately, despite all efforts to get the priest out of the coma, he could not be revived and died within twelve hours of admission. At autopsy, the medical examiner found several blocked coronary arteries, inflammation of and bleeding in his gastrointestinal tract, and severe malnutrition. The official cause of death was listed as myocardial infarction, or heart attack, and a severe gastrointestinal infection with copious blood loss.

The second patient who died was a twenty-year-old woman who took a massive overdose of drugs and was found unconscious in her bed by her mother. Because she lived one block from St. Joseph's and the devout family wanted her to be in a Catholic hospital, they drove her to the ER. She was treated there, including an attempt to eliminate her stomach contents. Apparently, she had taken the drugs the night before, and there was little in her stomach. The doctor even tried to wash out what might have remained in her stomach, with little result.

She was admitted, but despite all efforts, including cardiac resuscitation when she arrested, she died nine and a half hours after she was admitted. Because her blood levels of illegal drugs were so high, the medical examiner found no reason to do an autopsy, and the official diagnosis of death due to drug overdose was made.

Mary remembered how devastated the parents had been to lose their only child and how kindly Dan had dealt with them. Out of respect, Mary and several other doctors and nursed had attended the funeral mass celebrated by Dan.

The third patient was a vagrant man who lived on the streets in the city but for some reason was found near St. Joseph's. The police who found him unconscious in an alley drove him to the ER, where he was found to have had a myocardial infarction, as well as pneumonia and scabies, and he was emaciated and dehydrated.

After washing him and administering IV medications and nutrients, the hospital admitted him. A cardiac catheterization was scheduled for as soon as he was in sufficiently reasonable health to tolerate the procedure, hopefully within the next day or so. However, he did not respond to treatment; had another, this time massive, myocardial infarction; and died the day after admission. At autopsy, the medical examiner found three blocked coronary vessels, liver cirrhosis, and severe malnutrition.

The fourth patient was Matthew Crenshaw, a sixty-four-year-old man who was a benefactor of the Catholic church in general and especially of St. Joseph's Hospital. He owned three restaurants—one in the community and two in the city—and was considered a pillar of the community. He was a member of the board of directors of the hospital, and his death caused great consternation with the bishop, the clergy, the hospital staff, and the city and community.

Even though she had not been directly involved in his care, Mary remembered many of the details of his death, which had occurred in May 2017.

He was admitted in apparently good health except for some nonspecific chest discomfort. He was scheduled for a cardiac catheterization the next morning to check the condition of two coronary artery stents that had been placed two years prior to this admission. There was no problem when a nurse checked on him after the change of shifts around eleven thirty at night or when a laboratory technician drew some blood and inserted an IV around four thirty the next morning. However, that morning at 6:45 a.m., when an orderly arrived to transport him to the catheterization room in the radiology suite, he was found to be unresponsive and cool to the touch. Nothing could be done, and he was pronounced dead at 7:16 a.m. by Dr. John Bosko, who had been covering the hospital from 11:00 p.m. to 7:00 a.m. the previous night and had not yet gone off duty before signing out to the 7:00 a.m. to 3:00 p.m. doctor.

Because of the nature of his demise, an autopsy was performed, at which the medical examiner could find no obvious explanation for his death. In fact, the two coronary stents were patent, or not occluded, as were the other coronary arteries. Blood toxicology showed only a very low level of chloral hydrate, which had been given to him the night before to help him sleep. The official cause of death was recorded as "non-specific cardiac arrest."

The fifth patient was Calvin Wilkes, a sixty-two-year-old man who also was a wealthy benefactor of the Catholic church and St. Joseph's Hospital. He owned a great deal of real estate in the city and was another so-called pillar of the community. He too was a friend of the bishop's and also a member of the hospital's board of directors, having recently served as its chair. His death in November 2017, just six months after that of Matthew Crenshaw, caused even more consternation with the church, the bishop, the hospital staff, and the community.

Again, Mary had not been directly involved in his care, but she remembered the details of his demise because it had occurred only five months ago.

He was admitted in apparently good health except for some nonspecific chest discomfort. He was scheduled for a cardiac catheterization the next morning to check the condition of the two coronary stents that had been placed two and a half years prior to this admission. He was in good spirits when the nurse gave him his sleeping pill at 9:00 p.m. and was asleep when checked by another nurse around eleven thirty. He was drowsy but smiled when a laboratory technician drew blood and inserted an IV at 4:25 a.m. Wilkes had been set up with a continuous heart monitor for his vital signs of blood pressure and pulse, as ordered by Dr. Allen, the same private cardiologist who had taken care of Matthew Crenshaw. The monitor was a special precaution because of what had happened to Mr. Crenshaw.

At 5:15 a.m., the monitor set off an alarm, which alerted the so-called crash emergency team consisting of a physician, nurses, and a technician, who immediately ran to Wilkes's room and began cardiac resuscitation procedures. However, despite several attempts at resuscitation, including electric shock to stimulate his heart into beating, he could not be revived.

He was officially pronounced dead at 6:05 a.m. by Dr. John Bosko, the hospitalist on duty for the 11:00 p.m. to 7:00 a.m. shift.

Mary was struck by the coincidence that Dr. Bosko had been directly involved with both Matthew Crenshaw and Calvin Wilkes. However, John Bosko had worked the schedule prepared by the bishop, so it should not have been all that surprising.

Because of the nature of Wilkes's demise, an autopsy was performed, with essentially the same result as Matthew Crenshaw's autopsy. The same medical examiner who had performed the autopsy on Matthew Crenshaw again found no obvious cause for the death of Calvin Wilkes. His two coronary stents were patent, as were the other coronary arteries, and the blood toxicology report showed only a very small amount of chloral hydrate medication, which had been administered by a nurse the night before to help him sleep.

The medical examiner was perplexed because in his twenty-seven years as county coroner, he had never encountered two successive cases from the same institution with essentially the same results on two similar patients. The official cause of death again was "nonspecific cardiac arrest."

The last two cases concerned Mary because two unusual deaths under similar conditions had occurred within six months of each other. Perhaps she had seen too many mystery movies on TV with Mom, but what if the pattern continued, perhaps every six months? If so, another similar death might happen in a month or so. Was there a serial killer in the hospital? She shook her head at the thought; surely she was being ridiculous.

The two deaths had caused consternation for many because

of the two very important persons involved, but her concern had nothing to do with their VIP status. She knew another similar death at St. Joseph's would be horrible for the dead patient and would likely reflect badly on the hospital's reputation. Therefore, she planned to discuss the situation with Father Dan at their next meeting.

Almost as a second thought, she decided to see if it would be possible to get a list of the patients who had been on the same unit the nights of Crenshaw's and of Wilkes's deaths. Both men had died in the special VIP room on the fourth-floor unit. She wanted to be sure there had been no major problem with other patients who might have been disturbed by the ruckus that occurred, especially the attempted resuscitation of Wilkes.

Because it was a special request for something that might cause a great deal of work, she decided to personally go to the records room to ask Mrs. Gill if she could supply the patient information. She did not want to be seen as someone who took advantage of her position to ask for things that might cause a great deal of extra work or consternation for the medical records room staff. This was especially important to her because everyone had been so kind and accommodating to her, and she wanted to maintain their goodwill.

Fortunately, because all hospital information was digitalized, Mrs. Gill told her the request would be possible. However, unless it was an emergency, the information would take at least a week to obtain, because the record staff were involved in a major maintenance issue to guarantee the accuracy of what they produced. Mary told her she would be grateful to receive the information at the convenience of the staff.

Mrs. Gill said, "Dr. D, I wish everyone was as nice as you. We will get this for you soon."

Mary thanked her, not knowing where the request would lead.

CHAPTER 10

CONFIDENTIAL DISCUSSION WITH DAN

▷ MARCH 21, 2018

O ne evening, after finishing dinner in the cafeteria, Dan was walking to the hospital chapel, where he always ended his day with a prayer before he retired to his room in St. Ann's rectory across the street. He heard his name called out and turned around to see someone rushing toward him. After catching up, the person asked Father Dan if they might go somewhere quiet and private where the person could tell him something important.

Dan wasn't sure why the person was in that part of the hospital at that time, but he smiled and replied, "Of course. I am on my way to the chapel, which is usually empty this time of day. We can certainly speak privately there."

On the way to the chapel, the person told Dan that the priest's word of honor was essential; he could not divulge their discussion to anyone unless the person speaking was dead or gave specific permission for the disclosure. Dan thought that was an unusual request but not much different from how Dan treated anything divulged to him in the sacrament of penance, so he agreed.

When they were seated in the empty chapel, in a short explanation, the person admitted to having taken the lives of Matthew Crenshaw and Calvin Wilkes. When finished, the person reminded Dan of his promise not to divulge the information to anyone.

Dan was shaken by the information, but he reassured the person that as a priest, he considered his word under God sacred. He sat quietly for a few minutes, considering the situation, and then suggested there was something the person could do for him before they separated. The person agreed to Dan's request, and afterward, they both left the chapel and hospital, going their own way.

While Dan walked down the hall, he thought deeply about what he had just been told and tried to understand why the person had admitted to him the taking of two lives. Certainly, that had not been necessary; the person could have kept the secret with no chance that it would have been revealed.

As Dan was crossing the street on his way to his room, he prayed he would never have to worry about the information he'd just been given. After all, both deaths had been investigated by a medical examiner, and the causes of the deaths of Matthew Crenshaw and Calvin Wilkes seemed to have been resolved.

Little did he know just how much worry and angst that knowledge would cause him over the next few months.

CHAPTER 11

MARY AND DAN'S FIRST SPECIAL MEETING

▷ APRIL 5, 2018

Mary asked Martha to set up a luncheon meeting with Dan as soon as possible. She had learned it was not wise to set up her own meetings. When Mary had done so before, Martha, though she'd remained her usual polite self, clearly had been miffed. When Mary had asked her what was wrong, Martha had made it clear that setting up and managing Mary's meetings was her job, not Mary's. That was necessary to ensure Mary did not double-book or miss meetings because she became busy with all the other work she had. It would also ensure that appropriate refreshments were ordered if called for by protocol.

Martha believed that if a meeting was missed or appropriate refreshments were not served, it would and should reflect badly not only on Mary but mostly on Martha, her administrative assistant. There was no disabusing her of that belief. Besides, the arrangement was a great relief to Mary, and she thanked Martha profusely. Martha replied with a big smile on her face, "That, my dear doctor, is my job, and I take pride in doing it well."

The meeting with Dan on April 5 occurred over an even more sumptuous lunch than the one they'd had during their first meeting getting to know each other. It was an early April spring day that seemed to be trying to mimic late fall with rainy and generally miserable forty-degree weather. Therefore, the hospital chef included hot chicken noodle soup with the sandwiches for Dan and the salad for Mary. They both found the soup to be a wonderful addition to their lunch.

Mary said, "These delicious hospital meals, with their caloric load, are almost as fattening as my mother's dinners. I'll have to add an extra exercise day to my schedule."

When Dan inquired about her exercise schedule, Mary explained that she routinely worked out on exercise equipment in the finished basement of the house she had grown up in and now lived in with her mother. Her father had been an excellent carpenter and general fix-it man who completed the basement of their house with a workroom and a bathroom and shower near the furnace, set off from a large room that had served as a playroom and then a recreation room and now was an exercise and TV room. It contained an elliptical machine, a treadmill, and a stationery exercise bike. All were situated so that whoever was using them could see the large TV set situated in front of a couch and chairs. At least three times a week, she used the exercise equipment, and occasionally, her brother, Frank, and Mom used it. In addition, she and Mom watched TV there in the evenings and on weekends.

Dan said, "So that's how you keep your figure; I wondered how you did it."

She replied with a grin, "Well, you don't seem to have any trouble maintaining your weight, so don't gloat."

Between bites, Mary told Dan she wanted to speak to him about two things. First, she wanted to begin their discussions on what she described as her existential crisis, which was getting worse and becoming a recurring problem for her. Simply put, she seemed to be in a constant search for the meaning of her life and how she was supposed to be serving God. She remarked on the irony of the word *crisis*, when it was really a chronic problem for her.

Dan nodded and said, "Well, your so-called crisis is probably better described as a struggle. Let me ask this: Have you always felt this way, or is it more recent?"

"Well, I never felt like this when I was married to Tom. With him, I never thought about the meaning of my life. I felt joyous almost all the time. We both were involved in work that helped people and supported each other. We shared pretty much everything and were very happy. Oh, we had a few mild spats, but they never lasted very long and were always over silly nonsense.

"There was only one time when we were arguing about something that really angered me. It was so silly I can't even recall what the argument was about. But even though I, like Tom, seldom raise my voice, I was shouting at him and wouldn't stop. He reached into his pocket and took out his cell phone. That stopped me, and I asked him what he was doing.

"He responded quietly, 'If you don't stop this, I am going to call Mom, as he called my mother, and ask her to please come over right away because I need her help and to bring her wooden spoon because you are acting like a spoiled brat.'

"That made me laugh, and I realized he was absolutely correct. I apologized, and we never had another real argument again."

Dan said, "That's a wonderful story. I wonder why you have never married again. I know you dated in the past, but you seem to have stopped."

"I was so in love with Tom and so fulfilled. I've never found that kind of relationship with any other man. Tom and

I were soul mates, and I've never found that kind of feeling again. There were a few lesser relationships with men with whom I remain friends, but I never date them anymore. After a while, I simply stopped dating anyone and decided my life was meant to be spent as a dedicated physician and decent person. I really do enjoy caring for patients and trying to help whomever I can. Also, spending time with my family, meditating, praying, being a eucharistic minister, attending Mass almost every morning, and reading help a lot, but it's not the same as when I was with Tom. Someday I'll tell you more about that but not now."

Dan replied, "Mary, sometimes it takes a lifetime of contemplation to find the true meaning of life. I'm still searching, but it has become a part of who I am, and I've accepted that I might never have that transcendental moment or experience. I think we both need to think about this and perhaps help each other.

"Existentialism is not an easy thing to understand. Theologians and philosophers have spent many years trying to understand and even to write about it. How about our discussing what we've read on the subject and who, especially Tom, might have helped a little the next time we meet?"

Mary agreed and said, "We have some time left, and I'd like to discuss another topic. It's about something I discovered when gathering data and information about the hospital."

Dan replied, "Now, that sounds interesting to me. What did you discover?"

"Well, I am very confused and concerned about two deaths that occurred at St. Joseph's last year. As you know, I've been collecting data and information for my own edification and for the Joint Commission visit, which will occur in a year or so. As I believe I told you, I want to be very well prepared for that visit.

"Among other things, I have gone through all hospital deaths that occurred over the past five years. There were five that were not readily explained and required a close reading of the medical records. Two were easily explained, but three involved the county coroner, otherwise known as the medical examiner. His role is to provide information explaining the cause for each death. However, at autopsy, the medical examiner could not find any obvious reason for the deaths of two of the three patients he examined. So he called the deaths the result of nonspecific cardiac arrest, whatever that might mean. I have never heard of that diagnosis before by a medical examiner."

Dan asked, "Why are you concerned about that diagnosis for these two deaths?"

"I think you might be aware of the two patients involved and will better understand my concern if I'm more specific on who they were. One was Matthew Crenshaw, who died in May 2017, and the other was Calvin Wilkes, who died in November 2017, just six months later."

Dan sat up and felt his heart skip a beat. Trying to mask his concern, he quietly replied, "Oh yes, I well remember the shock and consternation of almost everyone here who knew them and in the city and community. But I thought things calmed down after the medical examiner's autopsy reports."

Mary replied, "That's true, but something just doesn't sit right with me."

"Why?"

"Well, both of these men were wealthy so-called pillars of the community, special friends of the bishop, extravagant donors to the church and to St. Joseph's, and members of the hospital board of directors, with Wilkes even having been the chair of the board at one time."

"You know God doesn't consider such things when he decides to take us from this earth."

"True, but I guess my concern really centers on how both these men, especially Wilkes, were not exactly well liked by the medical staff or nurses here in the hospital or by those in the private medical offices. Both were extremely arrogant and demanding of the staff in both environments. They also were noted for being, shall we say, obnoxious to women. The cardiologist who cared for both tolerated them because they treated him and his staff very well and were on best behavior in his presence.

"Both were especially disliked by the women staff and nurses, who would do almost anything not to deal with them. Fortunately, I had few interactions with either of them, but I always felt ill at ease in their presence. I try to believe it was simply my reaction to the rumors, but I really know better. A woman knows."

Dan asked, "What rumors, Mary?"

"It was known that both men would tell obscene—not off-color but downright dirty or even filthy—jokes in the presence of women. They also had roaming hands and fingers just shy of being obvious to others."

"Weren't they married?"

"Crenshaw's wife died several years ago, and his children are grown and lived away at the time of his death. Wilkes's wife divorced him many years ago after they had been married for only a few years. They had one daughter, who was about a year old at the time of the divorce. His wife was granted full custody of the child, and they moved away. The church hierarchy here didn't seem to have a problem with Wilkes since his wife sued him for divorce and not the other way around."

Dan felt and looked concerned and remained thoughtfully silent for a long while. Then he asked what Mary was planning to do about her concerns.

Mary said, "I'm not sure—this all might be my overreacting

to a bad issue. However, I've thought about looking further into the situation surrounding both deaths by thoroughly reviewing their medical charts. I want to know who was on duty at the time, the specific actions taken by the medical and nursing staff, and so on. What do you think? Am I overreacting?"

Dan furrowed his brow and thought about her questions for a while. Despite his fear of what might result from her investigation, he wanted to be fair to Mary, so he responded, "I think you must follow your conscience and do what you think is best."

"Thank you, Dan, because that's what I've already done. Please forgive me for asking you only now after I already looked at the charts. I respect your opinion very much, and if you had told me I shouldn't review the records, I'm not sure what I would have done. Please know that I understand if you are angry with me for leading you to believe I had not yet reviewed the charts. I was worried that you are so kind you might not give me your true opinion on something I had already done."

Dan shook his head and said, "Mary, I am not angry and understand why you asked me in this way, but please don't ever do that again, because if you do"—he stopped and briefly inhaled—"I will call your mother." He laughed.

Mary blushed and promised never to do it again. Then she said, "On a much more pleasant note, Mom wants to know if you'd be willing to join her; my brother; his wife, Megan; and me for dinner this coming Saturday evening at around six o'clock."

Dan replied with a wide smile, "What a great invitation! I can now meet your family. I can't wait. I'm sure it will be a wonderful evening."

"Just so you know, Mom arranged for Frank and Megan to arrive a half hour later so she would have time to dote on you. Also, please eat a very light and early lunch because Mom will stuff you. I'll try to hold her to six courses, but I can't promise anything."

Dan's eyes widened. "Six courses? I'm accustomed to the jokes about an Irish seven-course meal consisting of a six-pack of beer and a boiled potato, but really? Six courses?"

"Well, there is antipasto, soup, salad, pasta, a meat course, and dessert. I already convinced her to eliminate the usual seventh fish course because it's not Friday, and you will have had fish the previous day."

Dan laughed and said, "Who told you that?"

Mary also laughed and said, "Well, whatever. We'll see you Saturday at six."

CHAPTER 12

DINNER WITH THE DAVINO FAMILY

▷ APRIL 7, 2018

Father Dan felt alert and happy when he awoke on Saturday, because he was so looking forward to dinner that evening with the Davino family. He said the usual 7:30 a.m. mass, assisted that morning by Elana because Mary wanted to stay home to help her mother prepare dinner for his visit. Now that Pedro was gone, it was not unusual for Elana, who was now trained as a eucharistic minister, to fill in for Mary on Saturdays, and she always filled in on Sundays because Mary attended church at St. Ann's parish with her mother, her brother, and his family. Dan enjoyed Elana's devotion in assisting him at Mass. She was as enthusiastic as Pedro had been. He thought it might have been in the Mexican genes.

After conducting Mass and hearing a few confessions, mostly from patients and their family members, he ate breakfast and then visited all the patients in the hospital and distributed the Host to those who requested communion but were unable to attend Mass in the hospital chapel. Because of Mary's warning about her mother's dinners, he ate a light early lunch and then went shopping for some flowers and chocolates for Mrs. Davino. His mother had taught him well, so he knew to arrive with gifts for Mary's mother.

On the drive to the Davino home, he noted the simple, lovely houses in the neighborhood. He arrived at the house at 6:00 p.m. and parked in the driveway, as Mary had instructed him. He was impressed with how well kept the house, lawn, trees, and flower beds in front were. The house was a simple two-story structure probably built in the early 1950s but well maintained over the years. There were no flowers planted yet, but he could imagine how beautiful the beds might be in the later spring, summer, and fall.

He walked up the stone walkway to the front door, and before he could ring the doorbell, the door opened, and he was greeted by two smiling women. Mary introduced him to her mother, Beth, who held out a hand, and when he reached out to shake hands, she took his hand in both of hers and welcomed him to their home.

Mary was dressed in black slacks and a green cotton blouse that brought out the green in her hazel eyes. Mrs. Davino wore a colorful dress and a full apron. Both women wore obviously comfortable flat shoes. He always had thought Mary was beautiful, but he was surprised how beautiful her mother was. There was a definite resemblance between the women, except Mrs. Davino had brown eyes and shorter hair that was peppered with gray. Mary had no gray hairs.

Dan immediately noted the delicious aromas emanating from the kitchen. He handed Mrs. Davino the flowers and candy, and she beamed—he had scored OK on that one. She excused herself and immediately went to the kitchen to put the flowers in a vase, which she then placed on the set table in the dining room, replacing the flowers that had been there. As she did so, Mary winked at him and whispered, "You have made her evening. And you'll be happy to hear I convinced her to skip the soup course."

When she returned, Mrs. Davino told Dan how blessed they were to have him there for dinner and for Mary to have him to watch over her at the hospital. He smiled and said, "I think Mary watches over me as much as I do over her."

Then Mrs. Davino told him how proud she and the family were of Mary. She gushed about how bright, kind, and energetic she was. It was Mary's turn to blush and say, "Mom, please stop that."

But Dan interrupted her and said, "Mrs. Davino, I agree with you. Mary is wonderful."

Mary exclaimed, "Dan, you are not helping!"

Mrs. Davino looked sternly at her and said, "Mary Elizabeth Davino Defazio! It is *Father* Dan, not Dan. You know better!"

Mary smiled, looked at Dan, and said, "*Father* Dan, you know, there was a time when those words and that look would send chills down my spine." Then she went to her mother's side; put her arms around her back, giving her a side hug; and, smiling, said, "But not so much anymore."

Dan replied, "I can easily identify with that. With me, the words were 'Daniel Patrick Murphy,' but the killer look was the same." They all laughed. Dan was moved greatly by the obvious love shared between the two women.

They then asked Dan if he would like a tour of the house before Frank and Megan arrived, to which he happily agreed. As he walked through, he was impressed by the woodwork throughout the rooms, all done by Mary's father. His attention was drawn to a beautiful vase and to three wedding pictures on the credenza in the living room. Mrs. Davino told him the vase had been given to her by her grandmother, who had carried it all the way from Italy to the United States.

He told them he was impressed at how well it had been preserved over time and was surprised to see Mrs. Davino look sideways at Mary, who put her head down as her face turned red. He wondered what had happened to cause that interaction but decided, because it seemed to be something private, to let it go. He turned to the pictures. The first one was obviously that of a young Mr. and Mrs. Davino. He could see a resemblance between Mary and her father, especially in the eyes. The second photo was of a young Frank and Megan. The third was of Mary and Tom, and Dan noted how handsome Tom was. He was tall and well built and had a wonderful smile. Mary looked as if she were filled with joy in the picture.

When they had just finished the tour of the first floor, the doorbell rang, and in came Frank and Megan, bearing three bottles of wine, as Frank had been instructed to purchase and bring for dinner. Mary had warned Dan not to buy wine, because her mother had chosen special Italian wines to match what she planned to serve, hence his choice of flowers and chocolates.

To his delight, Megan was truly of Irish decent, with auburn hair, blue eyes, and a broad smile. She wore dark brown slacks and a copper-colored blouse that augmented her complexion and auburn hair. She also wore flat, comfortable shoes. Frank was dressed in a dark dress suit with tie. After introductions and handshakes, Frank said, "Father Dan, Mom insisted I wear a suit and tie, but would you mind if I took off my jacket and tie?"

Dan responded, "That would be wonderful because then I can take off my jacket too. I know you are a judge, and I'm a priest, but here I hope we will just be friends."

They both looked at Mom, who was beaming and nodded, so they removed the jackets and tie, which Frank hung in a closet. Mrs. Davino then invited them all to sit in the living room around a large coffee table. On the table were an enormous platter of Italian meats, cheeses, and olives and a basket of Italian bread Mrs. Davino had made that morning. She said Mary thought it would be nice to eat the first course in the living room. Frank poured the wine, and Dan happily agreed to begin with the chilled pinot grigio.

Mrs. Davino told Father Dan she usually served artichoke hearts with the antipasto dish but never with a good wine because artichokes were a natural sweetener and ruined the taste of a good wine. Dan smiled broadly and responded that he had not known that fact but couldn't recall ever drinking wine while eating artichokes.

As they ate, Frank and Megan were filled in on what had already transpired. Megan said she was pleased to have a fellow Irish American in the house with her finally. They all laughed.

While the other three sat there, Mary and her mother retired to the kitchen to finish preparing dinner. Megan explained that she would help with the dishes and general cleanup after dinner but would have been lost in the kitchen with Mary and Mom. Even though Mom was kind and had taught Megan to cook some Italian meals, Megan said she could never compete in the kitchen with Mom and Mary.

When they were asked to sit at the dining room table, Mrs. Davino made sure the men sat at the two ends of the table. Mary sat near Dan, and Megan sat near Frank. Mrs. Davino sat in the chair nearest the kitchen. She asked Dan to please say grace as they all held hands, and he did, with a special blessing for everyone involved in preparing and serving the dinner.

Over a lot of happy talk, the next two hours were filled with incredible food, including a salad, homemade linguine pasta with red clam sauce, delicious veal Milanese with vegetables, and great Chianti and Sangiovese wines. The salad was made of fresh greens and sweet grape tomatoes, which didn't taste like cardboard, as most tomatoes did at that time of year. As she handed Dan the dish of pasta, Mrs. Davino explained that she had chosen clam sauce because Mary had convinced her to eliminate the usual fish dish from the menu.

When Dan looked at the long strands of linguine in his dish, he glanced around the table and saw that the others were rolling the pasta around their forks. He was worried because he didn't know how to do that and had always cut pasta strands into small pieces so they could easily be scooped up with a fork. He felt he could not do that in the Davino house. Fortunately, Mary and Megan saw what was happening, and when Mary winked at Megan, she got up and went over to Dan.

Megan said, "Dan, you look like I did the first time I ate long strands of pasta in this house. Now I will show you what Mom taught me." She proceeded to show him how to roll the pasta around his fork, and by his third attempt, he was able to do it. He felt like a little kid who had just learned something special and smiled to himself all through that course.

Dan later told them he loved the pasta and had never seen or tasted a veal dish like the next course. The veal melted in his mouth. Mary told him Mom had instructed Mr. Marienelli, the butcher, that she needed special veal cutlets because she was making veal Milanese for Father Daniel Murphy. Mr. Marienelli and his wife both had been patients at St. Joseph's Hospital, and he still remembered how kind Father Dan had been to him, his wife, and his family, so he had gone into the back of his shop and come back with special very thinly cut, lean veal cutlets.

Dan smiled and shook his head at the story, saying he was sure it was because he was a priest. Mary shook her head in disagreement and said, "Part of the reason for the special treatment is because of respect for your being a priest, but the biggest reason is because of the kind of priest you are."

He just sighed and hoped that was true.

Dan was relieved when Mary asked if he'd like to have dessert in the living room, because that would allow some time before more food would be served. He was happy to have missed the eliminated fish and soup courses, because he felt stuffed after the veal dish.

Mary had told him that Mom volunteered three days a week in the cathedral's community center, where they served lunch to the poor every day except Sunday. She cooked soup in the community center's kitchen, and Dan could imagine how delicious that soup must have been. Mary was grateful Mom's friend Sarah, who was another volunteer, would pick up her mother and drive her to and from home. Otherwise, she knew, Mom would have taken the bus to get there and back. Despite Mary's objection, Mom had refused to own or drive a car after Tom had been killed in an automobile crash, but Mary had convinced her to maintain an active driver's license just in case.

In the living room, the coffee table had somehow been cleared except for clean cloth napkins, a bottle of grappa, glasses, and dessert dishes. Dan asked if there was a good fairy who cleaned and cleared things magically. Mary, Frank, and Megan simultaneously looked at Mrs. Davino and said, "Yes. Mom!"

Mrs. Davino smiled, obviously happy with the accolade. Then she brought in a plate of parsley and a large platter of homemade cannoli, and Frank brought in a tray of coffee, cups, saucers, spoons, forks, sugar, and cream. Everyone took some parsley and chewed on it, so Dan followed suit, looking puzzled. Mary laughed and explained that Mom cooked with fresh garlic, and the parsley, which was a good source of natural chlorophyll, was better than mouthwash. No one wanted to offend non–garlic eaters, so parsley was customarily served after a garlic-laden dish.

Dan somehow found room to eat two incredibly delicious cannoli completed with coffee and a small glass of grappa. Unbelievably, after three glasses of wine and the grappa, he felt completely alert—probably because the entire meal had lasted more than three hours. It was now 9:30 p.m.

He insisted on helping to clear and clean the tables and fill the dishwasher. All the pots, pans, and big bowls were nowhere to be seen. Mom obviously had been at work again. He now understood where Mary had gotten her unbelievable organizational skills and energy.

While they were cleaning, Mary motioned for Dan to come near to where she was standing in front of a drawer. She said, "Remember when I told you that you'd always know you were in an Italian kitchen because all the spatulas were orange? Well, look." She opened the drawer to reveal four orange spatulas, which had been dyed over time by the red pasta and other tomato sauces. They all had a good laugh at that. Dan thought it was wonderful that people could laugh at themselves and their heritage.

With all five of them working, the entire place was back to normal by ten o'clock, when Frank and Megan told them they wished to leave if it was OK. Dan thought it was also time for him to leave. So they all hugged and said good night to one another, with a special thank-you to Mom, who handed Dan a large bag of leftover food, including several large sprigs of parsley, which, he found out, had come from Mom's windowsill garden planted for consumption during the months when the outside garden was not available. God forbid he should have bad breath or starve on the short drive home.

As Dan was about to go through the door, Mom stopped him and said, "Father Dan, since I hope you will be coming back here for dinner often, please call me Beth. That would make me feel very good because that's what my friends call me."

Dan responded with a big grin, "OK, Beth. Now we are friends for sure. So will you call me Dan?"

She responded with feigned shock, "Never," and smiled broadly.

Dan hugged her and said, "Beth, you are a wonderful old-school Catholic woman, and I know better than to argue with you on that issue."

As he left the house, despite his age, Dan practically skipped down the walk to his car, as he was so happy. What a special day it had been. He doubted he would ever forget it.

On the drive home, Dan thought about how much he appreciated the women he'd been with that night. The delightful fragrance of lavender that emanated from Beth was the same he'd noted from Mary when he was in close contact with her. Despite being a priest, after all, he was a healthy man and appreciated beauty, especially of certain women. He smiled, recalling the old joke about a priest who went to heaven and found out the rule for priests was *celebrate*, not *celibate*. However, he was thankful he hadn't succumbed to the alluring temptation and had never broken his vow of chastity.

His love for the three women was spiritual and gratifying.

CHAPTER 13

MONDAY AFTER DINNER
WITH THE DAVINOS

▷ APRIL 9, 2018

T he Monday after dinner with Dan and her family, Mary arrived at her office at the usual 6:30 a.m. to allow time for sign-out from the doctor who had been on duty the previous night and to attend the 7:30 mass in the hospital chapel. Before Mass, as she was helping Dan to don his vestments, he told her he was still filled from the dinner and again raved about the food.

She asked if he would like to share dinner with her family about once a month or so on a Saturday night or Sunday afternoon, when Mom, Frank, Megan, and she could all make it.

He grinned and said, "Are you kidding? I would love that. When Pedro and his sister were still here, I often shared with them dinner that his sister cooked. We ate in Pedro's apartment. I really miss that kind of family gathering. Please tell your mom she's made me a very happy man."

Mary was pleased that he was a happy man and told him so.

The dinners became a tradition everyone enjoyed, especially Mom, who would spend hours planning the menu and cooking the meal. However, at Dan's and everyone else's pleading, except for on special occasions, such as a holiday, she only prepared a three-course Italian meal each time.

Mary was looking forward to spending the day caring for patients, which she did on Monday, Wednesday, and Friday of every week. As she entered the reception area of her office, she was greeted by a smiling Martha, who said, "Father Dan told me all about dinner at your home last Saturday. The dinner sounded like something prepared in heaven. Father Dan called it 3D Day—that is, Devine Davino Dinner Day. He told me that the following day, he ate what he had taken home with him for lunch and dinner. Your mother must be a fantastic cook."

Mary said, "Yes, she really is. Do you like Italian food?"

Martha replied, "Are you kidding? Who doesn't like Italian food?"

"Well, how about if on Mondays, I bring you something from our usual Sunday dinners that you can have for lunch?"

Martha said she would be grateful for such treats. Thereby began a routine that solidified a close friendship among Mary, Martha, and Mom. To Mary's delight, she thought that plan would also take care of the monotony of Monday's dinner always consisting of Sunday's leftovers.

As was her routine, Martha had prepared a list of the patients who had been admitted after 4:00 p.m. on Friday and the patients scheduled for admission that morning to the units that were to be Mary's responsibility that day. There seldom were many admissions over the weekend, and almost always, they had been admitted from the ER, as was the case that Monday.

After Mass, Mary began her rounds on the patients admitted to the floors to which she was assigned that day. Sign-out from the doctor who had worked 11:00 p.m. to 7:00 a.m. included a five-year-old boy who had had an uneventful emergency laparoscopic appendectomy on Sunday morning and a forty-year-old man who'd had a myocardial infarction and been admitted on Saturday evening from the ER. He was scheduled for a cardiac catheterization that morning. In fact, he was already in the radiology suite for that procedure when she started her rounds.

Mary started with the pediatric unit, where she greeted the nurses, who were always happy to see her. They told her she should have been a pediatrician because she was so good at dealing with children.

She told them she loved children and was sorry not to have had some of her own, but God had a different plan for her. She told them sometimes she thought that her having no children was proof that God was a man, because if God had been a woman, she would have had at least one child and probably several children. But then she said that if she'd had a child or children, she might not have become a doctor, and considering not being a doctor made her sad. She said, "So whatever God's gender, he or she has a good plan for everyone, and who am I to question that plan—or God's gender?"

That made the nurses laugh and tell her that she had a great sense of humor and sense of God. That gave her pause, but she responded, "I hope you are correct."

After she left the nurses' station, she went to the room of the five-year-old boy, Michael Landry. He had a small abdominal bandage and was walking around his room, telling his mother, who had stayed the night with him, that he was hungry and wanted to go home.

Mrs. Landry explained that he'd refused to stay in bed after he awoke, and he wanted more than the soft diet of oatmeal and apple juice he had been delivered earlier that morning. Mary thought, *Kids are amazing. No adult would be up and about and demanding solid food that soon after laparoscopic abdominal surgery.*

Mary asked the obviously tired and frustrated mother if he had held down the oatmeal, and she confessed that he not only had held down the breakfast but also had eaten a chocolate candy bar she had mistakenly left on the bedside table while she was using the bathroom to freshen up that morning. Upon questioning, she told Mary he had indeed passed gas, much to his delight—for a boy, the louder the better. That was something he had learned from his older brother.

Mary nodded and laughed knowingly and said to the boy, "Michael, I need to listen to your belly to make sure it tells me that you can go home. If it does, I will check your belly where the bad appendix that made you hurt was taken out. Then I'll put on a fresh bandage, and you can go home."

Michael immediately climbed onto his bed and said, "Does my belly really talk, or are you fibbing?"

Mary said, "No, I don't fib. No one should ever fib. Do you want to hear your belly talk?"

Michael loudly said, "Yes."

So Mary put her stethoscope on his abdomen and searched for bowel sounds, hoping they would be prominent. Her wish was fulfilled, because there were relatively loud rumbles. She put the earpieces into Michael's ears and put her index finger to her lips, telling him to be quiet and listen carefully. The wide-eyed look on his face told her he heard the sounds. He then shouted, "Mommy, my belly is talking!" Mary also offered Mrs. Landry the opportunity to listen, which she did, and she smiled broadly at the sounds.

Mary then inspected the small, clean wounds made by the laparoscopic surgery; changed the dressing; and discharged him. She told Mrs. Landry that the surgeon wanted to see Michael in his office in two days. She would give Mrs. Landry

material to change his dressings. The surgeon who had oper-
ated on Michael had left word for Mary to please discharge
him if everything seemed to be OK. The surgeon had an early
morning operation scheduled and didn't want the patient's
mother to wait for him to finish the surgery. Mrs. Landry
was so happy that she thanked Mary and quickly retrieved
Michael's clothes from the closet.

Mary went back to the nurses' station to write the discharge orders for Michael. She then walked down the hall to
check on the three other children who were in that unit, all
of whom were doing well and were waiting for their private
physicians to visit them later that day. None were ready to
be discharged. She loved seeing the children, who were so
resilient.

Mary next went to see the patients in the other units to
which she was assigned that day. She went to the nursery to
check on the newborns, all of whom were healthy and obviously hungry, because they were raising a fuss. As was her routine, she asked the nurse if she could take one of the infants to
his or her mother. The nurse, as always, was happy to see Mary
and asked her if she might ask a question. Mary responded,
"Of course."

The nurse asked, "Why do you call this nursery the miracle unit?"

Mary replied, "Well, consider the result of two single
cells—an ovum and a sperm—joining together. These two
joined tiny cells form an embryo and, ultimately, an infant.
Considering all the steps involved, it's amazing that a normal
tiny human results. A newborn is indeed a miracle, and this
is where newborns are placed until they go home with their
parents, so it's the miracle unit."

The nurse nodded, and Mary added, "Of course, you know
the reason it takes one ovum but thousands of sperm for one

sperm to find the ovum, right? The sperm, like everything male, don't stop to ask for directions."

When the nurse laughed, Mary added, "Seriously, I believe that every time a baby is born, it's proof that God hasn't given up on humans."

The nurse nodded again and, smiling, pointed to one of the howling infants and said, "She's all yours."

Mary picked up the infant and snuggled her close to her chest. She loved the fragrance and warmth of babies, so she held the infant for a minute or so before carrying her to her mother, who was waiting with open arms and a big smile on her face.

Mary checked on that mother and the others in the unit, all of whom were doing well and waiting to be discharged by their private doctors.

Then she went to check on all the patients in the other unit to which she was assigned that day. There was one patient who needed a brief exam, and some patients required discharge orders because their private doctors had left word for follow-up requirements, including medications.

Mary wrote the necessary notes and prescriptions for the patients about to be discharged and went to see the patients who were having problems. Most of them had problems Mary could easily solve with medical orders, usually involving pain medications.

The nurses told Mary they were concerned about one patient, a twenty-four-year-old woman named Alice, who had been admitted for a complete evaluation of a new diagnosis of adult-onset diabetes mellitus that would require insulin. They were concerned because Alice had been crying off and on since being told of her diagnosis the previous Friday afternoon.

Her blood sugar was now under control with the required insulin injections, and she seemed adept at giving herself the injections and checking her blood sugar level, as had been taught to her by the nurses. That was not a problem, but she would not tell the nurses why she was so sad. The nurses were happy Mary had been assigned to their unit, because they knew how well she did with sensitive issues.

Mary entered the patient's room, where she saw a beautiful young woman sitting in a chair by her bed. She was staring out the window and had tears running down her cheeks. Mary introduced herself and handed the woman a box of tissues. She then pulled over a chair and sat facing the patient. Mary asked why Alice was so sad and if she might help. Alice looked at her and, for a reason Mary couldn't understand but for which she was grateful, reached out her hands. Mary took her hands and, smiling, said, "Please tell me why you are so sad, and I will try to help you."

Alice then poured her heart out to Mary, explaining that she recently had become engaged to a wonderful man and didn't know how she was going to tell him about her condition. She was worried it might make him change his mind about wanting to marry her.

Mary said, "First of all, Alice, I think you just might be wrong about his reaction, but if your fiancé does feel that way, you are lucky to find that out about him now. I doubt you would want to spend the rest of your life with someone who felt that way about you. Am I correct?"

Alice replied, "I guess so, but I love him."

"I assume you haven't told him yet. When do you plan to do that?"

"He is coming to see me on his lunch break from work today. I don't know how I'm going to tell him. My parents know about my diagnosis, and they are very understanding. They want to learn all about diabetes so they can help, but I'm not sure about Paul, my fiancé."

Mary said, "Would you like me to help you explain diabetes to him?"

Alice responded excitedly, "Would you really do that?"

Mary said, "Of course. Just have the nurses call me when he arrives, and I will come here."

At 12:10 p.m., Mary was called by the nurse on Alice's unit, and she went directly to her room. She had deliberately kept herself relatively open after noon, expecting the call. She had busied herself with completing young Michael's online medical record and the never-ending insurance forms that doctors hated.

When she arrived at Alice's room, she was introduced to handsome young Paul, who was holding Alice's hand and didn't let go when Mary came into the room. That was a good sign to start. Mary introduced herself, and the three then sat with her facing them. With Mary's encouragement, Alice told Paul of her diagnosis, saying Dr. Defazio was there to answer any questions he might have.

He sighed deeply and, with tears in his eyes, revealed that he had been worried about her and was relieved she didn't have cancer or something as bad. He had many questions about diabetes, mainly concerning the treatment and prognosis. Mary explained to both about insulin pumps, which she was sure Alice's doctor was going to suggest.

She told them people with diabetes lived long lives as long as their blood sugar was kept in a reasonable range, which was possible by using an insulin pump and eating well. That meant having a reasonable diet, mainly low on carbohydrates, which would be a good diet for them both to follow. With sugar substitutes and sugar-free desserts, there was no longer a reason to eliminate tasty ice cream, cakes, pies, cookies, and so on.

A dietician was scheduled to visit Alice later that day, and at her discharge, she would be given a book containing details about diabetes. A diabetic diet was included in the book.

Mary also answered questions about the risk of their children having diabetes. Because neither of Alice's parents was diabetic, nor was there any diabetes in Paul's family history, the risk was probably low. However, more specific details would be provided by the endocrinologist who was going to care for Alice.

When they were finished, Mary asked if she might provide them with anything else. Paul took Alice into his arms and hugged her, telling her they were going to do just fine and not to worry. Alice was obviously relieved and happy, and they both thanked Mary profusely. As she left them, Mary thanked God and thought how lucky she was to be a doctor who could help people in so many ways, often simply by providing advice.

She then went to see the patients who had just been admitted and those who would soon be admitted. Most of them did not require much from Mary because their private physicians had already dictated the histories, physical exams, orders for tests to be made, and medications, which were in each patient's chart. She only had to introduce herself to each patient after she read the pertinent material in his or her chart and be sure there were no problems she needed to solve.

Finally, she checked on the patient who had returned from the cardiac catheterization, who was doing well and would probably be discharged in the morning.

By the time she had finished with the patients, it was time to sign out to the doctor who would take over responsibility for the patients for the 3:00 p.m. to 11:00 p.m. shift. She considered the day to have been successful on many accounts, and she would be home in time for dinner with Mom, which did not always happen on Mondays. That would make Mom and Mary happy.

CHAPTER 14

MORE DATA AND INFORMATION

▷ APRIL 10 AND 12, 2018

On the first Tuesday following her meeting with Dan, Mary wanted to spend all the time she could during the upcoming administrative days further pursuing what had happened with the hospital mortalities of Matthew Crenshaw and Calvin Wilkes. Despite what others thought, she believed the circumstances surrounding their deaths were still open to question. She felt anxious about pursuing the issue, knowing it had been put to rest by all others involved and administratively required nothing further from her. However, she knew she would never be rid of the question in her mind if she didn't proceed with investigating the deaths further.

She had not slept well the night before, despite having had a happy, peaceful evening with Mom. She even had been able to get home from work in time to say the rosary before dinner.

She, her parents, and Frank had said the rosary together before dinner every evening when she was growing up. By her early teenage years, she'd found it difficult to keep her attention on the prayers. During how many repetitions of the Hail Mary prayer could she be expected to stay tuned in? But she had known better than to say that to her parents. It had bothered her a great deal because she wanted to be a good Catholic like her mom and dad. Although she'd thought Frank might have had the same problem, she hadn't discussed it with him either. *No use looking for trouble.*

Being an avid reader even in her teenage years, she had borrowed a book on Christian meditation from her parochial school library and decided she could use the repeated rosary prayers as a mantra when her thoughts started to drift away from the prayers. That had solved the problem for her at that time and throughout her time in the convent, and she continued the practice to that day.

The previous night, she had gone to bed at the usual 10:00 p.m., but as had occurred on other recent occasions, she'd awakened around one thirty and been unable to go back to sleep. Upon awakening like that, with her natural defense mechanisms down, her first thought had been about how much she missed Tom. That always made her sad. After he'd died, she'd given all his clothes away except for four of his T-shirts she had taken from the laundry basket of items to be washed, because they held his fragrance.

She'd carefully folded and stored two of them safely in a bag and placed them in a drawer. She'd used the other two as pajamas until they had been washed to shreds. After that, she had taken out one of the other two and slept in it, preserving the other one. When the third one had turned to shreds from washings, she had taken out the last one. After all those years, she still had that one, which she wore only on their anniversary. As silly as she knew it was, wearing his T-shirt made her feel as if she were in Tom's embrace, and that gave her great comfort.

Despite not wearing his T-shirt because it was not their anniversary, as always, when she awoke like that, he was her first thought. She said a prayer that he was with God, and that made her thoughts go to her struggle with her religion. Spiritually, she knew her doubts were not unusual. It had given her great comfort and confidence when she'd read that even the saintly Mother Theresa had had moments of doubt. Surely then there was hope for her.

She now was fully alert, and her thoughts turned to how she was going to handle the issue of the two deaths in the hospital. After tossing and turning while trying to decide what to do, she finally fell asleep.

She awoke to her alarm at 5:30 a.m. It was rare that she needed the alarm, but she always set it just for such disturbing nights. In her mind, it would have been a catastrophe to be late for work. Mom, another early riser, likely would have made sure that didn't happen, but it would have embarrassed her if Mom had to wake her up.

When she got to her office that morning, after her usual morning agenda, the first thing she did was to carefully reread the medical charts for Matthew Crenshaw and Calvin Wilkes. She had retained both charts in her office, in a locked desk drawer.

For each incident, she recorded all the staff who might have had access to both patients around the times of their demise. She found that the two patients had had two different laboratory technicians, two different orderlies, and two different maintenance men. That made it unlikely those staff members had been involved in the deaths.

Further, of the several nurses present in the hospital during both incidents, only one had been directly involved with both patients: Arlene Filbert, an excellent Afro-American nurse who had worked at St. Joseph's for many years and was still working on the same unit where the incidents had occurred. Mary planned to ask Nancy if she would join her in discussing the situation with Arlene.

The physician who'd signed the death certifications in the medical charts for both patients was John Bosko. He had been on duty for the 11:00 p.m. to 7:00 a.m. shift when Wilkes died despite all efforts to resuscitate him. As per protocol, he'd pronounced Wilkes dead at 6:05 a.m.

She remembered that John Bosko also had been on duty for the 11:00 p.m. to 7:00 a.m. shift the day Crenshaw was discovered by an orderly at 6:45 a.m. Even though he had been on the night shift, which ended at 7:00 a.m., Bosko also had pronounced Crenshaw dead and recorded the death in the medical chart, at 7:16 a.m. Because Bosko had not yet officially signed out to Annette Reynolds, who had been there for the 7:00 a.m. to 3:00 p.m. shift, he had been the doctor who pronounced Crenshaw's demise and signed the chart and document.

This last discovery caused Mary great discomfort because she respected and admired John and considered him a friend. But he officially had been on duty when both Crenshaw and Wilkes died. She knew she had to be careful in how she approached and carried on any discussion with him and others about the situation.

She asked Martha to set up separate meetings with Dr. Reynolds and Dr. Bosko at their earliest convenience sometime on or after April 24. Preferably, she wanted to meet with Reynolds before Bosko. By that time, she wanted to be sure she and Nancy had met with nurse Arlene Filbert. She wanted Arlene's description of what had happened before she spoke with Bosko and Reynolds.

When Martha asked her what the meetings were about, knowing that both doctors would ask, Mary said to tell them she needed their advice on a delicate situation. She hoped they would trust her enough to be satisfied with that explanation. Martha looked at her quizzically and perhaps with a hint of skepticism, so Mary said, "This is going to be a tough one, Martha, and I need you to trust that I know what I'm doing."

Martha said, "Dr. D, I always trust you, no matter the situation. I just have a feeling you are embarking on something that will cause you much grief. Please know that I will always support you and that I have a strong, soft shoulder. I have a feeling you are going to need it and a lot more to get you through this matter."

Mary said, "Martha, you are a godsend to me, and I view you as a special blessing, especially now."

Martha responded, "A blessing I am not; someone you can trust I am."

"Indeed, you are."

Mary then called Nancy Darcy and asked if she could meet with her sometime before their usual weekly scheduled meeting. Nancy asked if they could meet now because she was about to take a coffee break. They planned to meet in Nancy's office, and Mary would pick up coffee for both in the cafeteria.

With two coffees in hand, Mary entered Nancy's office. When they both were seated, Mary briefly explained that she had been looking into the hospital deaths of two patients, Matthew Crenshaw and Calvin Wilkes.

Nancy shook her head and said, "Uh-oh, I do believe here comes trouble."

Mary agreed but told her that she felt compelled to do some further investigation. She told her what she had found thus far and asked if she and Nancy could meet with nurse Arlene Filbert, who had been present at both deaths. Mary wanted to see if Arlene might be able to shed some light on the situation.

Nancy agreed but said she would like more information before she set up a meeting. Since she and Nancy were to have their weekly meeting in two days, Mary thought it was wise to wait until then to further explain, because they would have much more time then.

When they met in the morning two days later, Mary explained her concerns in detail and what she thought she might do about them. She admitted that she might have been overreacting to a sad situation. However, she did not divulge to Nancy what she had found concerning Dr. Bosko.

Nancy told her she was happy about the further investigation of the hospital deaths, because she also had been disturbed by what had happened. They then discussed how to approach Arlene so as not to raise undo questions or concerns.

Nancy asked her secretary to set up a meeting for the following Tuesday morning at 7:30 a.m., after Arlene had signed out for the day. The secretary was to tell Arlene Filbert that Nancy and Dr. D needed to discuss something she might be able to provide some insight on. Also, Nancy would pay for the overtime hour or so and would provide breakfast.

Nancy wanted first to meet alone with Arlene over breakfast for a half hour because it was time for her annual review, and she could kill two birds with one stone. Arlene was a terrific nurse, and her review was always a joy for Nancy. The timing was perfect for Mary because it allowed her to serve as eucharistic minister at the 7:30 a.m. mass.

Mary went back to her office and decided to spend most of the rest of that administrative day completing schedules and other paperwork that needed her attention. The amount of paperwork necessary just to keep the hospital in compliance with the various insurance and other agencies was a real chore but had to be done.

Before Mary started on the routine paperwork, Martha came into her office and handed her the report from the records room, which contained the names of patients who had been on the fourth-floor unit on the nights of Crenshaw's and

Wilkes's deaths. The report was only a few pages long, so she looked at it immediately. It contained the names of fourteen patients excluding Crenshaw's on one night and fifteen patients excluding Wilkes's on the other night.

As she left her office, she told Martha she was going down to the medical records room because she needed to look through twenty-nine patients' medical records, and it would be better to do it down there. Martha shook her head and said, "Well, there goes the rest of today. Do you want me to order a box lunch for you?"

"Thank you, but that won't be necessary. If I get hungry, I'll go to the cafeteria." Off she went.

When Mary arrived at the records room, she went directly to Mrs. Gill's office with a rose in a vase she had picked up in the gift shop. She held out the vase and rose and said, "Mrs. Gill, I bring you something you can throw at me if you'd like, because I have another request."

Taking the vase and rose and smiling, Mrs. Gill said, "And now what can I do for you, dear Dr. D? Please don't worry about my throwing anything at you, especially not such a pretty vase and rose."

Mary explained that she wanted to look at the medical records of the twenty-nine patients listed in the report Mrs. Gill had sent to her office. She had come to the records room because she hoped that would make it easier for the staff.

Mrs. Gill smiled and said, "Dr. D, you forget that all patient records are digitized and can be accessed from any computer in the hospital as long as you have the correct password, which I know you have. Also, because I thought you might want to look at these records, I have them ready to send to the computer in your office."

Mary laughed and said, "Mrs. Gill, how can I ever thank you? You are an angel, and I could hug you."

Mrs. Gill replied, "I love hugs."

Mary hugged her and left, laughing and saying, "I promise never to bother you again—until the next time."

When Mary returned to her office, Martha shook her head as Mary explained what had just happened. Mary then went to her computer and began looking at the report, which listed twenty-eight patient records. Perplexed, she looked carefully at the list she had, which listed twenty-nine patients, and noticed for the first time that one patient had been in the unit when both incidents occurred. The patient's name was Ross Stewart, which sounded familiar to Mary, but she didn't know why. She decided to leave his record for last.

She spent the next two hours or so looking through the twenty-eight medical records and found no notes that any of the patients had said anything to the staff, aside for a few asking the nurses what had happened. None had stated distress, only sympathy.

While eating her favorite sandwich, cheese and tomato with fresh basil, Mary looked carefully at Mr. Stewart's record. Martha had brought the sandwich from the cafeteria when she returned from lunch, despite Mary's having told her that was not necessary. Obviously, Martha knew Mary's habits well.

In reviewing the record, Mary discovered, among other things, why his name was familiar.

Mr. Stewart was the fifty-six-year-old owner of a small family-owned contracting company in the city. He and his two sons had great reputations for honesty and excellent workmanship, especially in renovating houses and businesses. His daughter was an accountant and managed the business office. His wife, Melanie, was a nurse who had retired a few years ago after working for twenty-five years at St. Joseph's, mostly on the unit where her husband had been admitted.

Mary felt rather stupid for not immediately recognizing

the name, because she thought Melanie had been one of the finest nurses with whom she had ever worked. Of course, Stewart was a relatively common name in the city and community, so there was some excuse for her lapse of recognition.

Mr. Stewart had been in the hospital at the same time as Crenshaw because he had sustained a laceration on his leg that had become infected and required a few days of close observation and IV antibiotics. He had been discharged the day after Crenshaw's death.

He had been in the hospital at the same time as Wilkes because he'd had elective surgery for bilateral inguinal hernia repairs. He had requested to be the last surgical case, which had required his staying overnight in the hospital. It was not clear why he had requested the late surgery, but the procedure had been successful, and he had gone home the next day—the day after Wilkes died on the 11:00 p.m. to 7:00 a.m. shift.

Mary was not sure what to do with that information but decided to keep the notes she had made about his two admissions.

By 3:30 p.m., she was tired of reading and was happy to visit all the units and the personnel in the basement and on the first floor of the hospital. She made a special stop to thank Mrs. Gill again, knowing that she never left at 3:00 p.m., when her shift was over. Many of the staff worked like that. Thankfully, there were few, if any, clock-watchers.

The interactions with the medical, nursing, and support staff were always a delight for Mary. During the visits, she often was able to solve minor issues before they became major problems. Sometimes she could resolve them herself, and sometimes she would inform Nancy of issues that involved nurses and other staff for whom she was supervisor. It never ceased to amaze her how effective teamwork was.

By 5:00 p.m., she was ready to drive the four miles to her home, listening to her favorite classical music station on the car radio while mulling over what had happened that day. She hoped that by the time she reached her driveway, she would have the day's issues straightened out sufficiently so she could have a quiet evening with Mom and get a good night's sleep.

CHAPTER 15

MARTHA KING

F riday, April 13, was the usual slow clinical day on the fourth floor and other units. By one o'clock, all patients to be discharged had left, and Mary had cared for the remaining patients on the fourth floor and all those on the other units for which she was responsible. The nurses encouraged her to get some lunch and said they would call her if she was needed.

She had an idea and called Martha to ask if she had eaten lunch already. She was pleased that Martha had not eaten because she was just finishing some work she had performed for the bishop. Mary asked her what she would like from the hospital cafeteria and said she would pick it up along with her own usual salad so they might have lunch together. Martha thought that was a great idea.

Mary arrived in her office suite and asked Martha to join her in her office so they could discuss something while eating lunch, including split pea soup and a ham and cheese sandwich for Martha. Mary would leave her office door open so they could hear Martha's phone in case anyone called or came into the reception area.

When they were seated in Mary's office, she said, "Martha,

I know you and my mother have become friends, so you must know more about me than you ever wanted to know. Am I correct?"

Martha laughed and responded, "Well, when I called to thank her for the delicious food, your mother told me a lot about you but not more than I wanted to know."

Mary shook her head and said, "Well, in any case, you know a lot about me, but I know very little about you, and that doesn't seem fair to me. Now, I know you are a very private person, but because we work so closely together, I really want to know you better. Would you tell me about yourself, at least to the extent that you are comfortable?"

Martha smiled and nodded. "Of course. I am comfortable telling you pretty much anything you want to know about me. I assume you want to know about my family and how I came to St. Joseph's. So let me begin at the beginning. I was born in 1958, and that makes me sixty years young.

"My parents, Robert and Martha King, were relatively old when my sister, Robin, and I were born two years apart, with me being the older one. They were delighted with our births, having tried to conceive for many years. We were both named after our parents—that is, Martha and Robin. My mother was forty-one and my father was fifty when I was born. My father was a master vehicle mechanic by experience, and my mother worked as a clerk in a supermarket.

"I had a very happy childhood, and Robin and I were very close. When I graduated high school, I went to the community college to obtain my two-year associate's degree in business. I was hired by St. Joseph's Hospital as soon as I graduated in June 1978 and worked as a secretary for the bishop at that time and Father Dan, who had been the chaplain at St. Joseph's since 1967. I attended night school year-round and obtained my bachelor's degree in business after four years. Several years later, I was promoted to an administrative assistant, and I continued to live with my parents, as they requested.

"That same year, my sister's boyfriend, Gil, graduated from the one-year master vehicle mechanic trade school program he had started the year before. He had been a year ahead of Robin in high school, had been a protégé of my father for many years, and wanted to follow in his footsteps, so to speak. He and Robin had been together since her freshman year in high school and planned to marry as soon as Gil graduated from mechanic school.

"So in September 1978, they were married. Gil's parents and his two younger brothers immediately moved to Texas, where his father had been offered a very good job. Gil and Robin moved into an apartment two doors down from my parents' house.

"In October 1978, only a month after Robin and Gil were married, my father suddenly died of a massive heart attack. And that began the worst year of my life. He and my mother were very heavy smokers. They both tried to cut back and stopped smoking in the house when my mother became pregnant with me. They also had all the carpeting replaced and had the entire inside repainted.

"We were all very saddened by my father's death, but things seemed to get much better a few months later when Robin became pregnant, with a due date of October 1979.

"Unfortunately, that rosy outlook turned dark when my mother died of lung cancer in May 1979, just six months after my father. For many years, she'd had a terrible smoker's cough, but she paid no attention to it until she began coughing up blood. Unfortunately, by then, it was too late.

"We were devastated by the deaths of my parents so close together but still had the new baby to look forward to, so we tried to concentrate on that. At point, I wanted Robin and Gil to move into my parents' house, and I would move into their apartment. Another option was to sell the house, and they could use their half of the sale toward the mortgage on a different house. But they wanted to wait a while to sell the house, so they would have saved enough money to add to the house sale's money so they could buy their own house outright. Besides, there was nothing they liked on the market at that time.

"Then, in October 1979, a week before her due date, Robin began to bleed profusely. We called an ambulance, which took her to the city hospital. She had placenta previa, and the placenta had become detached from her uterus. An emergency C-section was performed by the obstetrician on call. But something went wrong, and they were only able to save the baby girl but not my sister."

Martha had tears in her eyes, and Mary reached out and took her hands in hers, saying, "Oh, Martha, what a horrible thing to endure." Both women then sat there silently for several minutes, choking down tears. Mary reached for tissues and gave one to Martha.

Now more composed, Martha said, "So in one horrible year, I lost the three most important people in my life. Gil was almost inconsolable, but we needed to care for the beautiful little baby girl, whom Gil named Robin after her mother. I was named her godmother, and Father Dan christened her.

"If not for Father Dan, I don't think I could have made it through that period or the following few years. He was like a ray of hope, always shining for me and encouraging me to carry on. He and the bishop allowed me to arrange my hours whenever necessary so I could help take care of little Robin.

"Robin and I lived in the house, and Gil remained in his apartment. Gil arranged his hours so he worked from ten o'clock at night to six o'clock in the morning every weekday. He was such a good mechanic the garage where he worked didn't care what hours he worked as long as his masterful work could be done. After work, he would get to the house by seven, and by then, I would have fed and changed little Robin and could get to work by seven thirty or eight if Gil was a little late. Gil ate the breakfast I'd prepared for him and cared for Robin until noon, when a wonderful older woman, Mrs. Litteri, who lived near the house, arrived to care for Robin from noon to five o'clock every weekday.

"After she arrived, Gil would go to his apartment and sleep until seven or eight at night. I would be home by four thirty or five and take care of Robin until the next morning. I made dinner for Gil and myself, and we both enjoyed playing with Robin until Gil left for work; then I went to sleep. Robin slept in a crib near my bed so I could feed and change her during the night until she was older. During the weekends, Gil and I would catch up on sleep and chores, spelling each other for long naps.

"The first year was the hardest. After that, it was a breeze. When Robin started kindergarten, Mrs. Litteri worked fewer hours and so on over the next years. She died when Robin was twelve years old. We all loved her and were very grateful to her because she had been a godsend. We really missed her, but thankfully, we knew we could now get on without her. We considered ourselves blessed for having had her help for so long.

"When Robin was fifteen years old, Gil married Olivia, a schoolteacher. She loved Robin, and Robin loved her. Olivia and I became friends almost immediately. Robin continued to call me Mommy and then Mom and called Olivia by her first name, which was fine with her.

"When Gil decided to marry, we sold the house, and Gil bought a house in the city for Olivia, Robin, and himself. I bought a condo near the hospital, where I now live. Robin graduated from college and is now married and has children of her own. She lives about forty miles away and calls or texts me every day. She still calls me Mom, and her children call me Nana and call Olivia Grandma. We all get together for holidays and birthdays whenever possible. And that's my story."

Mary sighed and asked if Martha ever thought about marrying.

Martha replied, "I really didn't have time to date anyone until Robin was in school. After that, I dated a few men, but I didn't think I wanted to spend the rest of my life with any of them. You might be surprised, but I still have some male friends with whom I have dinner or go to movies or the theater. I like my life as it has turned out. I am fulfilled as the mother of Robin and with my job here, and the rest is not important to me. Dr. D, I am very much like you in that you never married again, having been fulfilled with your wonderful Tom."

Mary nodded and said, "I guess we are really together in that." She thought for a few seconds and then added, "I have no idea how or why people are put together in this world, but I am very happy that we have been put in a place where we are able to know each other and work together. You make my life a lot easier and much more enjoyable, and I appreciate it very much."

Martha responded, "And I feel the same way about you, my dear doctor."

Mary then said, "And on that note, we'd better get back to work."

Mary returned to the unit and completed her work, and as she drove home that late afternoon, she felt at peace with herself, thinking how lucky she was. As an afterthought, she shook her head and laughed that she had thought how lucky she was on Friday the Thirteenth. *The Great Comedian at work again.*

CHAPTER 16

CHILD IN THE ER

▷ APRIL 14–15, 2018

Despite having been freed from weekend coverage as part of becoming the chief medical officer, Mary wanted to cover the last weekend she had been scheduled before she'd accepted that position. She thought it would not have been right to expect her physician colleagues to do an extra weekend to cover her. That was her responsibility, and she was happy to fulfill it.

Her weekend coverage began at 7:00 a.m. on Saturday, April 14, and concluded at 7:00 a.m. on Monday, April 16. Even though she would return to her normal schedule at 7:00 a.m. on Monday, at that point, after showering in the doctors' call room, she could change her scrubs and white coat she would have taken from her office to the call room and resume her normal routine.

If it turned out to be a usual weekend, there would be plenty of time to sleep, because normally, only an occasional patient was admitted, and the needs of those already in the hospital hardly ever took much time. Of course, there was always a backup doctor on call from home in case things became too busy for one doctor to attend to all the patients' needs.

On Saturday, she went to her office, changed from street clothes into scrubs and a white coat, and collected two messages from the mail room. Both had to do with Monday's planned admissions. There was no mail. At 6:45 a.m., she took report from her colleague, and she then went to the 7:30 a.m. mass. Afterward, she had some oatmeal with raisins and coffee in the hospital cafeteria.

From the cafeteria, she began visiting all the units, beginning on the fourth floor. None of the nurses reported any problems with patients on any unit, and she only needed to write pain medication orders for a few. The other chart notes were routine and not time-consuming.

She visited every patient and any family members who were in the hospital and answered questions or simply made sure there was nothing she needed to do for them. She finished by noon, when she went to the ER, which was quiet, as expected. It was unusual for anyone to use St. Joseph's ER on weekends, because all ambulance calls routinely went to the city hospital.

After a salad lunch, Mary went to her office, where she responded to her email messages and read a few journal articles. Around five o'clock, she visited all the patient units again. In the interim, she responded to only one call from a nurse, about a patient who wanted to sign out against medical advice because he was bored and thought he could go home.

In response, Mary first read that patient's chart and found that he was recovering from a serious infection and required two more IV doses of an antibiotic. He was scheduled to be discharged on oral antibiotics the next morning.

She went to his room, and from the doorway, she could see that he was obviously agitated. He was loudly arguing with a nurse because she wanted him to wait for the doctor who was on the way, but he wanted to get dressed and go home.

Mary took a deep breath, entered the room, reached a hand out to shake his, and said, "Mr. Ricco, I am Dr. Defazio. I want to help. Please tell me why you want to go home now."

He turned to her, smiled, took her hand, and said, "Doctor, I feel fine and am bored sitting here doing nothing. I have plenty of work to do at home, so why do I have to stay here until tomorrow?"

Mary responded, "According to your chart, there is no one at home who could administer the IV antibiotic you need. You had a very serious infection and need two more IV doses and then are scheduled to go home tomorrow on oral antibiotics. Your last IV dose is at midnight and will be given while you are asleep. However, if you wish, I can return at twelve fifteen to discharge you if someone can pick you up and take you home then."

He laughed and responded, "Hmm. Nice. I bet you really would do that. However, I can't ask my wife to pick me up then. She is a partner in a very busy legal firm in the city and would have a fit if I asked her to come here after midnight. So I guess I'll stay until tomorrow. How early can I leave?"

Mary said, "Name the time, and I'll be here."

He responded, "How about eight thirty?"

Mary smiled and said, "I'll be here. See you then."

As promised, she was in his room the next morning at 8:30 a.m. sharp to discharge him and meet his wife. When she arrived, he said to his wife, "I told you she'd be here."

Mary smiled, introduced herself to Mrs. Ricco, and then said, "I always keep my word. Now, please take him home, and make sure he behaves himself."

Mrs. Ricco pursed her lips and told Mary, "I know women have two intact X sex chromosomes, and men have one intact X chromosome and one chromosome with a piece missing that makes the X into a Y chromosome. I think all the common-sense genes are on the missing piece."

Mr. Ricco rolled his eyes and shook his head while both women laughed.

Mary left the room and went to the nurses' station to write a note in his chart. While she was finishing the note, the nurse from the man's room came up to her and said, "Dr. D, thank you very much. You sure knew how to handle him."

Mary responded, "Sometimes you have to put yourself in the other person's shoes and try to understand how to appease his or her anxiety. I got lucky."

She went on to make her rounds on all units. Then she ate a late lunch of split pea soup and a tuna salad sandwich, after which she went to her office, where she did some administrative work and read a few journal articles. She made another quick visit to all units to make sure she was not needed. At about ten o'clock that night, when she had finished with all units, she went to the doctors' on-call room to read and get some sleep.

Around eleven thirty, as she was just dozing off, she was called immediately to the ER. Because the on-call doctors slept in their scrubs, she was able to immediately rush there, and upon arrival, she was greeted by Olga Rushkin, an excellent nurse practitioner who had worked in the ER for almost thirty years.

As they swiftly walked down the hall, Olga said, "Dr. D, I'm surprised you are working the weekend, but it's so good to see you. We have an eighteen-month-old boy in the treatment room who is having trouble breathing. I have put an oxygen mask on him and put a pillow under him to extend his neck and help him breathe, which seems to have helped only a little. He also has a fever of thirty-nine degrees centigrade."

On entering the treatment room, Mary was greeted by a child, Nicholas Gerrity. He was obviously in respiratory distress, and his mother was silently crying, sitting by the stretcher on which he lay. She was holding his hand, and he was gasping for breath. Mary immediately asked Olga to get intubation equipment so she could pass a tube from the child's mouth into his trachea, so she could assist his breathing if necessary. That also would allow her to get a close look at the back of his throat.

Mary softly said to the mother, "Mrs. Gerrity, I'm Dr. Defazio. It would be best if you wait outside so I can take good care of your little boy. I promise you I will fill you in on what I have done, and I will do so as soon as I make sure he can breathe better and has received any other care he might need, OK?"

Olga handed Mary the equipment and walked Mrs. Gerrity out of the room, telling her that her child was in the hands of the best doctor she could ever have wished for. Mary prayed that Olga was correct in her being capable of managing this serious situation.

Olga immediately returned to the treatment room, where Mary was listening to the child's lungs, holding him with his head extended to straighten the airway as much as possible so he might breathe easier.

She said, "Olga, we don't have time for an x-ray to see what is obstructing the child's airway or to call an otolaryngologist, so I'll have to look and probably pass an endotracheal tube into his trachea."

Olga held the gasping child down on the stretcher, making sure to continue extending his neck. Mary made the sign of the cross and whispered, "Dear God, please help me." Then, with a laryngoscope, she observed a bulging abscess in the back of the throat, obstructing the child's airway. She asked Olga to hand her a fifty-cc syringe and a long number-twenty spinal needle, which, thankfully, were within easy reach.

After Olga handed her the syringe connected to the needle

while she continued to hold the child, Mary punctured the bulging abscess and withdrew twenty-two ccs of pus from it. She carefully removed the needle, swabbed the area with some gauze on forceps, and slowly withdrew the laryngoscope, prepared to immediately reinsert it if necessary. To her relief, the child relaxed and began breathing normally.

Mary stepped back, took a deep breath, and asked Olga to set up an IV, which she inserted. After drawing a blood culture in case the infection had spread to the blood, she started the IV and injected a strong antibiotic. She also ordered the pus from the throat abscess to be cultured for the type of bacteria and the sensitivity of the bacteria to various antibiotics to be sure the antibiotic she ordered was the right one. She then went out to Mrs. Gerrity and asked her to come see her child, who was now sleeping and breathing normally.

The mother turned and hugged her, saying, "Doctor, you are wonderful, and certainly the nurse was right when she said you are the best. Thank you."

Mary smiled and explained to the mother what the problem had been. She then took a proper history from her and did a thorough physical exam. She found nothing abnormal now. The child's lungs were clear, and air was passing normally. She admitted the child to the pediatric unit, knowing the nurses there would watch him carefully. She ordered the IV antibiotics to be continued.

Just in case, Mary accompanied the child to the unit. She planned to sleep in the doctors' on-call room two floors above, but it would be easy to get to the pediatric unit quickly if necessary. Mary always carried her cell phone to be available no matter where she was in the hospital.

After Mary was sure the child was safely admitted to the pediatric unit and sleeping soundly and breathing easily with Mrs. Gerrity sleeping in a reclining chair at his bedside, she returned to the ER nurses' station at about two thirty in the morning to write a note in the child's chart. Olga was also writing a note for the chart. She looked up when Mary came to thank her for being such a great nurse.

Olga immediately said, "I thought I had seen it all before, but this episode was a real zinger." She told Mary that while she knew she wasn't a pediatrician or an ER doctor, she truly was a great all-round doctor.

Mary told her she had been frightened by what she saw and by what she knew she had to do. But somehow, she'd had to get it done. "Thank God it all worked out."

Mary had decided to take her thermos of Mom's delicious coffee to share with Olga and stay with her for a while so they could get to know each other better. Olga was happy and told Mary she wanted to discuss the deaths of Mr. Crenshaw and Mr. Wilkes at St. Joseph's.

Mary looked at her quizzically and asked why she wanted to discuss that issue.

Olga responded that their deaths in the hospital were a topic much discussed among the nursing staff. She remembered both events because she had been on duty when Crenshaw and Wilkes died. Those two nights had required the ER on-call doctor, in both cases Dr. Reynolds, to be called in. A need for the on-call ER doctor to come in only happened five or six times a year, so it was easy to remember.

Mary now had been alerted to something she believed was important. She asked Olga if she could return the following night at midnight or so to discuss those nights with her further. She said she was now a bit sleepy and needed to check on the Gerrity child before she slept. She wanted to be fully alert when they had that discussion. Olga readily agreed.

The next morning, before she even showered and changed clothes, Mary checked on the Gerritys, who both were sound asleep. By that afternoon, the child's temperature was normal, and he was eating a soft diet. He was discharged on Monday by his private pediatrician, who thanked Mary for a job well done.

Of course, the story about what had happened in the ER made the rounds on the following Monday, and Mary's colleagues congratulated and teased her. That was routine for how the medical team dealt with encouraging one another. Martha greeted her with "Dr. D, I can't leave you alone for even a weekend without you doing something heroic. God bless you."

Mary blushed and said, "Martha, many times, a doctor reacts to an emergency situation by automatically recalling how to manage it. That plus luck can make you look like a hero."

Martha responded, "That plus knowledge, experience, and caring is what makes a heroic doctor, and that's who and what you are."

Mary said, "I am just grateful that everything worked out so well for that child and his mother." She didn't tell Martha about the discussion she'd had with Olga Rushkin, because she first wanted to think about it more.

PART 2

INVESTIGATIONS

CHAPTER 17

DISCUSSION WITH NURSE OLGA RUSHKIN

▷ APRIL 15, 2018

At a quarter past midnight on Sunday, April 15, Mary went to the ER to discuss the conversation she'd had the previous night. She found Olga Rushkin, the ER nurse practitioner, at the nurses' station, working on the computer. She looked up when she saw Mary and smiled. "I see you really did want to discuss the Crenshaw-Wilkes issue with me. Forgive me for sounding glib by calling it that, but that's how those incidents have been labeled among the staff."

Mary responded, "I know, Olga, and that's how I often refer to those hospital deaths too. Would you please tell me about those nights in question as clearly as you remember?"

Olga said, "Oh, I remember both nights very vividly. The night Mr. Crenshaw died, at about twelve thirty, I received a call from a mother who was frantic because her sixteen-year-old diabetic son had just passed out. She checked his blood sugar, and it registered forty-five, so she gave him a shot of glucagon. However, even though he soon woke up, she, her husband, and their son were on the way to our ER to make sure he was going to be all right. They lived only a fifteen-minute drive from here.

"I immediately called Dr. Bosko, who was the doctor in the hospital on the eleven o'clock to seven o'clock shift. He asked me to call in the ER on-call doctor because he was very busy with a patient he was treating for a myocardial infarction and who had been admitted at ten thirty. I called Dr. Reynolds, who immediately changed into scrubs and a white coat and was on her way here. As usual, she left her cell phone on speaker while she dressed and as she drove, so she could respond to me if necessary before she arrived here.

"The patient and his parents arrived first, but the boy was alert and seemed to have recovered nicely, except for the looks on his parents' faces. I checked his glucose, and it was ninety. His pulse and blood pressure were a little high for a sixteen-year-old, but I wasn't too concerned because of the circumstances, especially the look on his mother's face. I gave him a glass of orange juice, which he was drinking when Dr. Reynolds arrived. She spoke with the parents, examined the boy, and found nothing of concern. His blood sugar was now one hundred, and his pulse and blood pressure had returned to normal.

"The parents reported that their son had skipped dinner without telling them. He was trying to lose weight for an upcoming wrestling match. They were not very happy about that, and his mother guaranteed it would never happen again. Dr. Reynolds and I laughed at that, knowing the meaning of how she was looking at her son and how miffed both parents were with their diabetic son for skipping a meal.

"We waited another half hour and rechecked his blood sugar and vital signs, all of which were normal. So we discharged him at about two o'clock in the morning.

"Even though it was a chilly November night, Dr. Reynolds

went out to sleep in her new van, which she said was going to be her habit from now on when she was called in and was slated to work the next morning. Before she left, I asked her about the cold night weather, but she said she and her husband were avid campers and had outfitted their van with a small, thin mattress; pillows; blankets; and a quilt on the flattened back seats to make a cozy bed.

"She had parked her van in the space reserved for the ER doctor just outside the ER entrance. She had arrived in scrubs and her white coat, which was also customary for the on-call ER doctors because they always kept a set at home. She asked me to call her on her cell phone to wake her at six fifteen if she didn't let me know she was awake and in the hospital by that time.

"After sleeping in her van, Dr. Reynolds said she would come into the ER at six fifteen or sooner and go to the bathroom here to wash up, brush her teeth, comb her hair, and change into clean scrubs. We keep several sets of scrubs in the ER, each of which fit Dr. Reynolds or Dr. Lewis. She would then go off to check in with the eleven o'clock to seven o'clock doctor. They would meet on the unit she was scheduled to cover that morning. And that was what she did that morning after checking in with me at about six fifteen, as planned.

"The night Mr. Wilkes died, at about one o'clock in the morning, I received a call from an asthmatic man's wife saying that he was having trouble breathing and that they were on their way here. He had forgotten to refill his prescription for his nebulizers and had no asthma medications to take at home. I called Dr. Bosko, who again was in the hospital on the eleven o'clock to seven o'clock shift, but he was very busy with two patients who were having problems. He asked me to call the ER on-call doctor, which again was Dr. Reynolds.

"I did so, and she repeated the same scenario I already

described. She spoke with me on her cell phone while driving in. The patient arrived before her, but she had already told me what asthma medications and treatment to administer. I did what she prescribed, and by the time she arrived, the patient was breathing better. He was sitting up on the stretcher, holding his wife's hand. Both looked very relieved.

"Dr. Reynolds examined the patient, who sheepishly apologized for having forgotten to fill his prescriptions. Dr. Reynolds smiled and kindly told him that was why we were here, but she thought it was probably much better for him not to be here with us. We all laughed at that. After watching the patient for another half hour or so, she wrote prescriptions for asthma medications, and he was discharged.

"Dr. Reynolds left at about three o'clock to sleep in her van, asking me again to wake her if she was not in the ER by six fifteen. However, like the first time, she was here by six fifteen and went through the same routine."

Mary asked Olga if she'd observed Dr. Reynolds leaving the ER and getting into her van. She responded that she had not but wondered why Dr. D thought she should had done so. Mary said, "Oh, I was just curious that she didn't sleep in the on-call room. I guess she is more accustomed to sleeping in her van, undisturbed by hospital noises. Maybe I should keep that in mind for myself for the future." They both found that thought amusing.

Getting to what Olga wanted to discuss, Mary told Olga the Crenshaw and Wilkes affair seemed to be a curious mystery to everyone, including herself. Therefore, she was not able to provide any more specific information on the subject. Olga nodded and said she'd thought that was the case, but she still had wanted to ask.

Mary then thanked Olga for the nice discussion and left the ER to ponder what she had just learned. She also had asked

Olga whether the security guard had been in the ER when the patients were treated. Olga had said that as usual, he was in the ER with Olga and spoke with Dr. Reynolds to make sure she didn't need his help with anything, which she politely declined. Because he had been with Olga all the time except when she and Dr. Reynolds were in a room with the patients, Mary decided to forego discussing the issue with him. However, clearly, she needed to speak with Dr. Reynolds. Something about what she'd learned did not seem right to her, so she planned to ask Martha to set up a meeting with Dr. Reynolds.

CHAPTER 18

MARY, NANCY DARCY, AND ARLENE FILBERT

▷ APRIL 17, 2018

On Tuesday, April 17, Mary had two important meetings planned for the day: one with Nancy Darcy and nurse Arlene Filbert and the other with Dr. Annette Reynolds alone. When she arrived at the hospital, she skipped going to her office at the usual time right after Mass and instead went directly to Nancy's office to meet with her and Arlene Filbert. When she arrived there, she was greeted by two smiling women who obviously enjoyed each other's company. Nancy had reminded Mary that Arlene was a vigorous fifty-three-year-old Afro-American woman who had worked at St. Joseph's for almost thirty years.

Arlene's three children were all grown and had moved away to other states after graduating from college and marrying. Her husband was a truck driver, and for the past eight years and, before that, whenever he had been on the road, she'd worked the 11:00 p.m. to 7:00 a.m. shift, sparing the younger nurses that shift. That was typical of her kindness.

As soon as she arrived, Mary was offered a cup of coffee and a muffin, which she gratefully accepted because she had not yet eaten breakfast. Mary had had several interactions with Arlene over the years, so she expected it to be relatively easy to get into the reason for the meeting. Nancy had not told Arlene anything specific about the meeting, wanting Mary to take the lead.

When they were all seated at a small table, Arlene said, "Dr. D, before we begin, I want to tell you something that I doubt you know. Because of your blessed husband, Tom—God rest his soul—my husband and I were able to purchase and upgrade one of those houses Tom made possible through the real estate agency for which he worked. All the families who live on that block will be forever grateful to him."

Mary was taken aback and had to clear her throat and take a deep breath before she said, "Arlene, I didn't know that, and I really appreciate your telling me. Tom was an incredible human being, and I miss him very much, but God has his reasons for doing things. I only wish I was wise enough to understand them."

Nodding, Arlene and Nancy agreed with her regarding their lack of knowledge concerning God's reasoning.

After a brief silence, Mary sighed and said, "Arlene, I hope you can help me with an issue I'm working on for my own edification and in preparation for an upcoming Joint Commission hospital visit. I have reviewed various hospital data and information, including all deaths that have occurred over the past five years. I'd like to understand more about two of them, and you were present for both."

Arlene nodded and said, "I think you mean Mr. Crenshaw and Mr. Wilkes. Correct?"

Mary responded, "Yes. From what you remember, would you tell me what happened?"

Arlene said, "I remember both incidents very well, and I'll be happy to tell you about them. With Mr. Crenshaw, I was signing out to the seven o'clock to three o'clock nurse, when an orderly came running to the nurses' station in a huff. He excitedly asked us to please come quickly because he was pretty sure the patient he was supposed to take to the radiology suite was dead. Another nurse and I ran to his room, along with Dr. Bosko, who was still there from the night shift, and Dr. Reynolds, who had just come on duty. It was clear Mr. Crenshaw had died during the night, because he was not breathing, had no pulse or heartbeat, and was cool to the touch. However, no one had alerted Dr. Bosko during the night of any problem with Mr. Crenshaw, so we were all very surprised.

"Because Dr. Bosko had not yet signed out to Dr. Reynolds and therefore was officially still on duty, he pronounced Mr. Crenshaw dead. He wrote a note for the chart with the time of death and signed the death certificate. We were all in shock, but there was nothing we could do.

"I went home and was unable to sleep, because I kept thinking about it. That was only the second time in all my years as a nurse that a patient had been discovered like that in the morning. The first time had been in another hospital during my last year in nursing school.

"With Mr. Wilkes, I was in another room down the hall, checking on a patient, when the alarm went off at about five o'clock or so. I went running with the crash cart to Mr. Wilkes's room, where Dr. Bosko, who again was the night-shift doctor, had just arrived. He'd arrived quickly because he was nearby, having been making his usual rounds in all the units, as was the custom for the weekday-night-covering doctor. Those doctors did not sleep, because they were busy with patients or simply wanted to stay awake to cover any emergent problem.

"The patient's heart monitor was flat, and for about thirty minutes or so, we and another nurse tried to resuscitate him, using all means, including electrically shocking him twice, but to no avail. We could not even get a single spontaneous blip on the ECG. Dr. Bosko finally called an end to the resuscitation attempts, pronounced him dead, put a note with the time of death in the chart, and signed the death certificate.

"Because a similar thing seemed to have happened with Mr. Crenshaw just five or six months previously, we were all dumbstruck and were walking around shaking our heads. What on earth was going on? When we signed off at seven o'clock, we were still in shock, thinking about what had happened. And that's the best of my recollection. I'm still perplexed by what happened."

Mary thanked her and asked, "Was there anything at all that might have gone wrong from the hospital's perspective to help explain the two deaths?"

Arlene said, "I have thought about that a lot and can honestly say absolutely not. Everything possible was done. But one thing you probably should know, if it's possible you don't, is that both these men, especially Mr. Wilkes, were universally disliked, to put it mildly. To call them dirty old men would not cover it; they both were filthy old scumbags, if you'll forgive my language.

"None of the young nurses wanted to take care of them. Many years ago, when the young nurses first told me that these men spoke dirty to them and touched them in a way that made them feel creepy, I decided to fill in for them as often as I could.

"My first encounter was with Mr. Wilkes, who tried to touch my breasts. I grabbed his hand, and squeezing it, I told him that if he ever tried that again with me or any other nurse, we could make his hospital stays very uncomfortable.

"He at first grew angry and asked if I was threatening him, and I said no, I was warning him. He then said that he had not deliberately touched me but that I had come too close to him, and it was my fault. I just glared at him with the look I used on my children when I was very angry, and he backed off. However, he reported me to Nancy and wanted me to be fired.

"He must have warned Crenshaw about me, because I never had a problem with him."

Nancy said, "Fortunately, I was very aware of Wilkes's and Crenshaw's reputations, so I ignored the complaint against Arlene. Amazingly, he never pursued the issue with me. I guess he didn't want the bishop to hear about it."

Mary sighed and said, "Unfortunately, I am also well aware of their reputations. I want to sincerely thank both of you, and I wish there was something I might have done to help the situation." Then, smiling, she added, "However, please know that I would never want to get on either of your wrong sides." They all laughed.

After the meeting was completed and Arlene left, Nancy asked Mary if she could stay because she wanted to discuss something with her. Mary immediately replied, "Of course," and sat down again in the chair she had just occupied.

Nancy looked serious when she sighed deeply and said, "Mary, I'm not sure I should even tell you this, but I think you need to know about it. The incident I'm about to reveal to you happened to one of our nurses a few years ago, but I swore I would not reveal it in any way in which it could be associated with the nurse involved or her family. It would cause great embarrassment and hardship to the nurse and her family. However, because I know you, I trust that you also will promise the same as I have. In fact, I hope you will not have to tell anyone, but who knows what is going to happen with your investigation?"

Mary also looked serious and assured Nancy she would never do anything that would implicate or harm anyone, especially the nurse involved or her family.

Nancy, knowing that, nodded and continued. "The

incident occurred at a party for some doctors and their families sponsored by Crenshaw and Wilkes at one of Crenshaw's restaurants in the city. This nurse, who is a Muslim, and her fiancé and her brother, both of whom are doctors, were there as guests. At one point, she was returning from the ladies' room through an empty room adjoining the main dining room, where the guests were gathered, and was accosted by both creeps. One held her to a wall while the other hugged her. She screamed and kneed the groin of the guy hugging her.

"Her fiancé came running, followed by her brother, and they grabbed the guys and were about to beat them, when the bishop and the best friend of the brother, who had also arrived at the scene, stopped them. Ironically, the brother's best friend from high school through college and medical school was Catholic and admitted patients to St. Joseph's. He had also been invited to the dinner.

"The creeps apologized profusely, claiming they were drunk and recently had had anesthesia for cardiac catheterizations and probably should not have drunk alcohol at all. They claimed they had lost their senses because of the mix of alcohol and remnants of anesthesia. I'm not sure who they thought they were talking to, but that ridiculous excuse did not go over very well.

"However, the bishop convinced the family and the brother's friend that it would be best if they all kept the incident secret so as not to embarrass the nurse or her family. Because all the doctors saw patients at the medical office building attached to the hospital and admitted patients to St. Joseph's on occasion, they agreed out of respect for the bishop. But the doctors warned that if either or both creeps tried anything with any woman, especially a Muslim woman, they would make sure neither man was able to walk again.

"The bishop told Crenshaw and Wilkes each to make a

generous contribution to the mosque where the family worshipped, which they did. When the couple married a few months later, each creep sent a check for a large amount of money as a wedding gift. To no one's surprise, both checks were returned.

"I was told about this because the nurse was so shaken and wanted me to know why she became tearful one day when she was assigned to the unit where Wilkes was a patient. I comforted her and reassigned her to another unit that day.

"Mary, I'm not sure what you might do with this information. Fortunately, we have two female Muslim nurses, both of whom are married to doctors and have brothers who are doctors who see patients and admit to St. Joseph's."

Mary said, "That makes me feel better because I don't want to know the identity of the nurse. I'm also not sure what I'll do with this information, but I'm grateful you've told me. I only hope no other Muslim woman—or any other woman, for that matter—was molested by these creeps, as you called them. I can think of far better descriptive words for them, but *creeps* will have to do."

Mary then thanked Nancy for all her help that day. She was concerned by the incident with the Muslim nurse. However, she was pretty sure that after she met with Dr. Annette Reynolds alone later that day, she would have enough information to go forward to meet with John Bosko.

The meeting with Bosko was not something to which she looked forward, but she knew she must have it, or else she would never be able to stop thinking about the issue.

Her meeting with Annette Reynolds was on her agenda for lunch that day.

CHAPTER 19

DISCUSSION WITH DR. ANNETTE REYNOLDS

▷ APRIL 17, 2018

Mary had requested Martha to ask Dr. Annette Reynolds if she would kindly meet with her for lunch on Tuesday, April 17. Martha was to say that Mary needed to ask her questions about some patients. Reynolds readily agreed, and at noon, they met in Mary's office, where Martha had arranged for lunch. Both women requested a chicken salad and iced tea.

When Mary arrived in her office suite, she found Reynolds laughing with Martha. They looked at her and filled her in on a comical incident involving Annette's nineteen-year-old daughter. They all laughed at the teenager's antics, and Mary thought it was a great way to begin her meeting. When she had first entered her office suite, Martha had looked at her, smiled, and winked. Mary thought, *God love that woman—she really knows how to set up what might be a difficult meeting before it begins.*

When Mary and Annette were alone in her office, Mary told her that if the meeting required her to stay overtime to complete her work for the day, she would receive reimbursement for the time. Annette laughed and said that would not be necessary and then said, "Mary, what questions do you have for me? I am very curious to know."

Mary responded, "Well, I have questions for you about two different things. First, I need your help with a patient-based issue. I'm trying to become as familiar as possible with all the administrative items I need to know about for my own edification and also in preparation for the Joint Commission evaluation, which will occur in a year or so. I can cover both at the same time with my first issue. Let's start with that one."

Annette said, "I'll be happy to help in any way I can, but I can't imagine how."

Mary said, "One of the items I'm working on is a review of deaths that have occurred in the hospital over the past five years. There are two I'd like to understand better."

Annette nodded, smiled, and said, "I think you mean Matthew Crenshaw and Calvin Wilkes, right? They have caused a lot of trouble and consternation for many people over the years, and it looks like that's still happening."

Mary nodded and said, "You're correct. You were here both nights when Crenshaw and Wilkes died in the hospital, because you were called to the ER. Did you notice anything peculiar going on?"

Annette looked at Mary, wrinkled her face, and said, "Well, that night, I wasn't in the hospital other than the ER, and nothing peculiar was happening there, unless you consider anything happening in an ER not to be peculiar." Both laughed at that. "I know there has been a lot of talk about those two bastards, if you'll excuse my French, but I think the world is much better off without them.

"You know as well as I do that they were disgustingly filthy old men who dealt dishonestly with anyone crazy enough to do business with them. I had a patient who worked for Wilkes who told me he had raped her and said if she told anyone, he would make sure she never got another job in the community or city. She said he and Crenshaw had done the same to other women who worked for them. She swore me to secrecy, at least until a time when it would be safe to reveal what she'd said.

"My one personal encounter with Crenshaw was when he loudly told a filthy joke in front of some nurses, and I called him on it right then. He told me I had no business speaking to him in that tone of voice, and I told him my tone, unlike his joke, was clean and clear. He shouted that he was going to report me, and I told him I wished he would do that so I could repeat to whomever he reported me the joke he'd just told. He went off in a huff but never did report me, or at least not that I know of.

"My only personal bad encounter with Wilkes was when I had to examine him in the ER several years ago when he came in for some mild chest pain. As you know, our ER serves as the backup for the St. Joseph's Private Physicians' Group. Those doctors often send patients if the patients call in and need to be seen as soon as possible but the private doctors already are too busy with other patients in their offices to see them.

"Well, Wilkes took advantage of this arrangement at least several times a year. Peter Lewis and I thought that sometimes his private doctor deliberately sent him to the ER just so he wouldn't have to deal with him. He knew we would let him know if he needed to be directly involved. Clearly, I say *he* because no woman doctor wanted to care for Wilkes.

"On the occasion in question, while I was listening to his heart, Wilkes reached over and squeezed my breast. I grabbed his hand in both of mine and squeezed it until he yelled and had tears in his eyes. You know I am quite athletic and have good hand strength. He gave me a very angry look, but before he could say anything, I told him that if he ever tried that again on me or any female staff, I would break every bone in his hand. He said nothing, and I never encountered him thereafter."

Mary asked, "Weren't you worried that doing that might lead to or worsen a myocardial infarction? After all, he was to be seen for chest pain."

Annette responded, "I had reviewed his ECG just before I went to examine him, and it was perfectly normal, as were his vital signs. As usual, his so-called chest pain turned out to be indigestion from his lousy eating and drinking habits."

Mary said, "Annette, I know both these men were sexually pretty disgusting to women. I am certainly not naive, but I have a hard time understanding why men act like that."

Annette replied, "Mary, we both know that physiologically, the human body does not have a sufficient amount of blood to simultaneously supply the brain and the penis. Guess which one wins out every time in some men."

Mary laughed and responded, "Yes, but most men control it. All the men I personally have known—like my wonderful Tom, my dad, my brother, the men who work here, and those I've dated—have acted like gentlemen. I guess Wilkes and Crenshaw could not or simply would not."

Annette responded, "In their case, it's *would not*, and nobody made them."

Mary said, "I guess not, but now what about the issue with Crenshaw? Even though you did not pronounce him dead or sign the medical chart or death certificate, you were present when he was found by the orderly. Would you tell me what you remember about it?"

Annette said, "Of course. I remember it quite well, even though it occurred almost a year ago. It happened just before seven o'clock. John Bosko, who had been on from eleven to seven, was about to sign out to me, when an orderly came running toward the nurses' station, where we were. He was obviously very shaken and told us he thought the patient he had come to deliver to the cardiac catheterization room in the radiology suite was dead.

"John and I immediately ran to the room, which turned out to be Crenshaw's. He was cool and had obviously been dead for some time, so not surprisingly, he didn't respond to our attempts to resuscitate him. John was very distressed because he'd had no idea that Crenshaw had obviously died on his shift, and he had not been called.

"The night-shift nurse who was on the unit said she'd had no indication the patient was in trouble. She knew he had been fine when the laboratory technician put in the IV and drew blood earlier that morning, and she hadn't wanted to wake him again before it was time for the orderly to pick him up. Even though he was pronounced dead after seven o'clock, because John had not yet officially signed out to me, he was officially on duty and took care of the paperwork. That's the best I remember."

Mary asked if other than what Annette had reported, there had been anything unusual in the presentation of the patient when they found him or with anything else.

Annette responded, "Not a thing, Mary. But may I ask why you are going over the deaths of these two guys? I thought the autopsy reports resolved any questions surrounding their deaths."

Mary replied, "Because in the autopsies for both, the medical examiner could find nothing that might account for their deaths, so the official recorded cause of death for each was nonspecific cardiac arrest. I'm not even sure what that means exactly, except it's rarely the recorded cause of death. It just seems odd to me that this could have happened twice within six months at St. Joseph's, especially to two men who had been so involved with the hospital."

Annette looked at her with serious concern and said "Mary, I know you are a very smart, wonderful person with great integrity and want to do the fair thing no matter who's involved, but I don't know why you or anyone else is concerned about either of those guys. You should stop worrying about them. Good riddance. Let them go."

"Thanks, Annette, but at this point, I simply can't. But please know that I really appreciate your friendship, advice, information, and concern; and after I discuss the situation with John Bosko, I hope to be able to forget about it and get on with other matters."

Annette sighed. "I really admire you, Mary, but I think you are getting upset over something that should be left alone. As I said before, the world is a much better place without them."

Mary responded, "I understand how you feel, and I hope to get on with it soon. Now, may I ask a question about the second issue?"

Annette responded, "Of course."

"OK, my second question has to do with how you manage coming to the ER when you're the on-call doctor and on duty the next morning. I know you and Peter Lewis requested I only schedule you both to be the on-call ER doctor when you are to be on duty the next morning. But I am curious about why you don't sleep in the hospital until the next morning.

"I was discussing a number of things with Olga Rushkin the other night when I was the weekend doctor. That's the last weekend I will have unless someone asks me to cover for him or her or there is an emergency. She told me about the last two times you were called in, first for a diabetic boy and next for an asthmatic man. Olga told me that when both patients were discharged from the ER, you slept in your van and not in the on-call room. I wonder why you did that. Is there something wrong with the on-call room that I need to have fixed?"

Annette laughed and said, "Of course not. I just am very accustomed to sleeping in our new van. As I think you know, our family camps out a lot, and we equipped our new van so we can sleep comfortably overnight no matter how cold it might be. I sleep there because it is quiet, and I can get an extra forty-five minutes or so of sleep by staying in the van parked in the ER parking space instead of driving home." Then she looked seriously concerned and asked, "Is there something wrong with my doing so?"

Mary quickly said, "Not at all. In fact, what you say makes sense to me. Thank you for your help with these questions."

Annette then repeated that she thought Mary should stop worrying about Crenshaw and Wilkes and let the issue go. She shook her head, smiled, got up from her chair, gently squeezed Mary's hand in hers, and left the office.

Mary was concerned because she felt the issue with Annette was still not completely resolved. She thought, *I hope my concern is unwarranted, because Annette is such a great doctor and human being. I really need to discuss this with Dan.*

CHAPTER 20

MARY AND DAN'S SECOND SPECIAL MEETING

▷ APRIL 19, 2018

On April 19, the Thursday after her meetings with nurses Nancy Darcy and Arlene Filbert and Dr. Annette Reynolds, Mary met with Dan for their second special meeting. This time, they met in his office, which was not a big deal because their offices were in the same suite, on either side of the central office occupied by the bishop, although he rarely used that office. Dan's office and Mary's office each had a desk facing the door, with one swivel chair behind the desk and two visitor chairs in front. There also was a small table with two chairs on the side of each room.

Once again, the hospital chef had prepared so much food for them that it barely fit on the table where they sat. After some small talk between bites, Mary said, "I'm so happy we could meet, because I really need your guidance." She then told Dan she had decided to go ahead with her plan to investigate the hospital deaths of Crenshaw and Wilkes.

Dan felt slightly nauseated upon hearing that, because

he knew only too well the possible trouble that might result from her further investigation. However, to be fair, he nodded thoughtfully and said, "I'm not surprised you are going to do that. You are a determined woman with a great sense of responsibility—in this case, probably way beyond what is necessary. But who am I to judge? So what have you discovered?"

Mary explained what she had found thus far from the medical records and from her conversations with Nancy Darcy, Arlene Filbert, Olga Rushkin, and Annette Reynolds, all of whom Dan knew and greatly respected. She also related the incident with the Muslim nurse, stating only bare facts that in no way could identify the nurse and emphasizing the importance of confidentiality. Dan readily agreed with the need for confidentiality on all accounts. She told him she was unsure what she might do to further investigate the issue, because it seemed to be an impossible task.

She was going to meet with John Bosko the following Tuesday and was dreading the meeting, especially because she was worried that either he or Annette might have been involved in the deaths. Mary hated to think that but knew she had to further her investigation before she could be satisfied that they in no way had been involved in the deaths. However, she did not want to hurt them or endanger her friendship with them by discussing the Crenshaw and Wilkes deaths in a way to cause them any angst. She considered both to be dear friends and colleagues for whom she had a great deal of respect.

Mary also said she knew that all members of the physician staff had passes that allowed them full access to the hospital at any time, and they could go anywhere. She knew that some of them occasionally came to the hospital to check on something or to pick up something they had inadvertently left behind.

Dan thought about the dilemma and, still wanting to be fair to Mary, said, "Knowing you and your superactive conscience, I think at this point, you have to proceed with the investigation until you are satisfied. I know you will not rest unless you do so. I also know that you will proceed very carefully and with kindness because that is your nature.

"However, I hope that the meeting with Bosko, combined with the other meetings, will ultimately satisfy your pursuit of what happened and that you'll free yourself from any further investigations. I can't imagine that Bosko, Reynolds, or any of the physician staff would have done anything but provide the best care they could under any circumstances. Bosko and Reynolds just happened to be unluckily on duty when both curious deaths occurred."

Mary nodded and said, "I really hope you are correct, because I want this terrible burden to be off my list of concerns. I will let you know for sure."

Dan smiled. "I'm confident you will. But for now, let's discuss the issue of your existential struggle and constant searching for the true meaning of your life. As I told you, I share your search for meaning, but after many years of struggling, at my age, I am more comfortable with the struggle. You were going to tell me about Tom and why you didn't struggle with this when you were together."

Mary smiled and was silent for a minute or so while thinking about the best way to describe her life with her beloved husband, Tom.

She began by telling Dan about how she and Tom had met about a year after she left the convent: on a blind double date set up by a couple known to them. Unbelievably, she had fallen in love with him on that first date. He was handsome and well built, but that had not been what made her love him. He was kind and soft-spoken but with a great sense of humor and a contagious laugh.

That date had been the beginning of their magical life

together. They had gotten married within four months of meeting, much to the glee of their families and friends, who'd referred to theirs as a marriage made in heaven. Mary had agreed, and she was confident Tom had too.

Tom's father was the office manager for an American firm that had a major office in Rome, and that was where his parents lived, having moved there from their home in California.

"My mom and dad met them at our wedding, and they became friends immediately. Tom's parents treated me like a daughter, and my parents treated Tom like their son." Mary smiled, reminiscing. "After we were married, the only thing we had to get accustomed to was really funny. He had spent most of his life with men, so after he put the toilet seat up, he simply couldn't remember to put it back down. I had to learn to always check the seat because it was frequently up. I had been raised in a house where, because two women also lived there, my dad never left the seat up, and he taught Frank to do the same. And as you can imagine, that was never a problem in the convent."

Dan laughed and said he was guilty of the same male habit, but fortunately, it had never been a problem for him, as he'd spent most of his life living with men. That also made Mary laugh.

Mary asked if Dan would like to know how she'd solved that problem, to which he readily replied in the affirmative. She said, "Well, one Saturday morning, I got up and went to the bathroom, and as usual, the seat was up. I checked to make sure Tom was still asleep. I then put on jeans and a sweatshirt and went to the lobby outside our apartment, which was on the first floor. I waited about five minutes and then called Tom from a public phone in the lobby. Remember, we had no cell phones back then.

"When he answered, I said, 'Tom, I need you to come get me.'

"He said, 'Mary, where are you? I've been worried because I woke up and couldn't find you.'

"I responded, 'I'm in the sewer system, where I warned you I'd land if you kept the toilet seat up.'

"Tom said, 'What!' and at that point, I hung up the phone, rushed up to our apartment, came up to him from behind, and laughed at his expression when he saw me. Then we both laughed."

Dan shook his head and said, "You surely can be an imp, can't you?"

Feigning innocence, Mary said, "Me? Not really. I just think at times, you must use unusual means to accomplish some things. It worked, because he never left the seat up again."

Dan shook his head, laughed, and told her he thought she probably had been right, but so had Tom. She was still an imp.

Mary then said, "As I've told you, Tom had been in the seminary but quit after a year and instead went to college for a business degree. At first, and before we were married, I couldn't understand that decision and his working for a real estate company. He was very spiritual, and the job somehow didn't seem to suit his spirituality. Then I found out what he was doing with his job, and I understood his decision.

"You know that block of homes on the street just before the city limits that was converted from a group of poorly built, run-down houses into a small mixed-race neighborhood of beautifully renovated and kept homes? Well, Tom arranged for his real estate company to purchase the abandoned houses there and sell them at very low prices with low interest rates to people of modest means who agreed to certain conditions.

"He was able to get grants from some rich donors, and that money was provided to those who bought the houses, who could never before afford a house. They had to agree to use some of the money to renovate the houses and to live there for at least seven years.

"None of those renovated homes ever have been sold, because most families still live there, and the few who no longer live there have willed the houses to their families. Arlene Filbert told me she and her husband raised their family there, and they still live there. She told me Tom is considered a saint by the families who bought those homes. That didn't surprise me because I've always believed Tom is a saint.

"At his funeral, there were so many people in attendance, but I was so sad I really can't remember many of the hundreds who were there. However, I do remember many from that neighborhood. Obviously, he had found a way to have God's love flow through him outside the priesthood. That is what I am seeking for myself, but I have not yet found it without Tom to help guide me.

"We loved the simple things, like music, nature walks, movies, and dinners with family and friends. Our favorite poem was by E. E. Cummings. Would you like to hear it?"

Dan replied, "I'd like that very much, especially because I'm not much of a poetry reader."

Mary proceeded to recite: "I thank you, God, for most this amazing day—"

Dan immediately raised a hand and said, "Mary, I'm sorry to interrupt you, but I know that piece. I've always thought it was a prayer, not a poem. In fact, I begin every day with those very words.

Mary nodded and said, "The entire poem—or prayer, if you will—is printed on Tom's memorial card, on the side opposite his picture."

Dan nodded and said, "That is a beautiful, spiritual poem and is well placed on Tom's funeral card."

Mary nodded and said, "The only travel we did was on

our honeymoon in Italy. Tom had done a lot of reading and planned our entire trip. I read a great deal about Italy but left the planning and driving up to him. The Italians are crazy drivers, and I knew I could never manage the roads and drivers.

"Tom arranged to rent a car so we could tour Italy over two weeks, beginning with Perugia and spending the last three days in Rome. There we stayed with his parents while we visited the sights, and we spent a lot of time at the Vatican, including St. Peter's Cathedral and the Vatican Museum.

"We loved Saint Francis and the movie *Father Sun, Sister Moon*. When we landed in Rome from the US, we immediately rented a car and drove from there to Perugia on a Saturday evening. We wanted to experience where Saint Francis fought for Assisi before he gave up riches; worked with the poor; and, ultimately, became a saint.

"On Sunday morning, we drove the short distance from Perugia to Assisi for Mass. Tom knew to park in the lot on the hill above the Basilica of St. Francis. As we walked down the path from the parking lot to the basilica, the church bells began to ring, and a flock of birds flew overhead. We were so struck by the moment that we stopped and held each other until the bells stopped. It was a magical moment I will always cherish.

"There were so many other moments like that with him. When he died, I thought I'd lost at least part of my soul. He was truly my soul mate. My grief at losing the beautiful relationship I had with him was so intense I thought I'd never get over it.

"But I knew he'd want me live on, and therefore, I must. Even now, I miss him so much sometimes I feel like a shell and not a complete human. But I am so grateful for having had him, if only for such a short time, and I still have all the wonderful memories of our life together."

She then told Dan about sleeping in Tom's T-shirts so she

could feel as if he were hugging her. She also told him that listening to certain music, especially "Con Te Partiro (Time to Say Goodbye)" by Sarah Brighton and Andrea Bocelli or Ennio Morricone's Sergio Leone Suite played by Yo-Yo Ma, tore her apart. She could only imagine what Sartori and Quarantotto or Morricone must have felt when writing their music and lyrics or hearing the music played, how Yo-Yo Ma must have felt when playing it, and how Brighton and Bocelli must have felt when singing the words. She thought that surely it touched their souls as it did hers and those of so many other people.

Mary also told Dan about a poem by an unknown author she had discovered online. She'd printed it out, and she kept a copy by her bedside and in her wallet. It provided solace to her when she especially missed Tom. Dan asked if she might read her favorite part of it to him, so she took it out of her wallet and read:

> I heard your voice in the wind today …
> I held you close in my heart today …
> You may have died … but you are not gone.
> As long as the sun shines …
> the wind blows …
> the rain falls …
> You will live on inside me forever,
> for that is all my heart knows.

At this point, tears were streaming down her cheeks, and Dan got up and walked over to his desk for a box of tissues, which he handed to her. She wiped her eyes and face, blew her nose, and apologized, telling him she was embarrassed at losing control in his presence.

Dan said, "Why are you embarrassed? Do you think I have never cried? As Bishop Oscar Romero said, some things can only be seen through eyes that have cried. Only humans can cry with tears. Even hyenas laugh, but only humans cry. I consider crying a special gift from God. You are so fortunate, because it seems you have tasted the meaning of your life, but it was with Tom. Now you must find it without him; it must be just between you and God." With that, Dan reached out and hugged her, whispering, "You will find it."

Mary thanked him and asked if he thought angels cried. Dan, startled by the question, sat back and sighed deeply. After a long pause in which he looked concerned, he said, "Mary, I've never considered that question, so I'd have to think more deeply to respond responsibly. However, at this point, I don't see why they wouldn't. On the other hand, crying just might be a totally human response, so I really don't know. But now you have me thinking, so stay tuned."

Then they left the office to finish their day's work.

As she drove home that evening, Mary thought once again about the beautiful music that brought Tom so close to her, and she wondered how the composers or the artists who performed the music felt when composing or playing such beatific music.

In any case, she knew how fortunate she was to have a friend and confidant like Dan.

CHAPTER 21

MEETING WITH DR. JOHN BOSKO

Martha set up a lunch meeting for Mary with John Bosko on Tuesday, April 24, when he was scheduled for the 7:00 a.m. to 3:00 p.m. shift. It was the same arrangement as for the meeting with Annette Reynolds, except Bosko wanted a ham and cheese sandwich and soup for lunch.

The noon meeting was great timing for Mary because it meant she could assist Dan at the 7:30 a.m. mass. She was happy because she thought she needed all the heavenly help she might gain from the mass for the upcoming meeting. After clearing the altar and putting things from the mass in order, she stayed in the chapel for a few minutes to pray for guidance. Dan saw her and waited silently until she arose from kneeling before the altar.

He said, "Mary, my prayers and thoughts will be with you when you meet with John Bosko today. I hope you will find resolution of your concerns and will be able to get on with your life."

Mary sighed and replied, "As my Jewish friends would say, Dan, from your mouth to God's ears."

Dan nodded and smiled.

She had hoped to gain some insight from her meeting with Dr. Annette Reynolds to assist in the meeting with Dr. John Bosko. She wasn't sure why, but she was more concerned with this meeting than the one she'd had with Annette, even though she was still concerned about Annette's possible role in the deaths of Crenshaw and Wilkes.

Mary left the chapel and went to the mail room to collect her messages and mail, and at 8:00 a.m., she entered her office. She spent the morning working on the never-ending paperwork and administration issues until the scheduled 12:00 p.m. meeting.

At noon, Martha told Mary that John Bosko was in the reception room for their meeting, and she went out to meet him. He smiled broadly at Mary, and she smiled back, reaching out a hand, which he grasped for a warm handshake.

Behind him, Martha gave Mary a fingers-crossed sign with both hands, shook her head, and returned to her desk.

When they were settled at the small table in her office and began to eat, as with Reynolds, Mary told him if the meeting caused him to remain overtime, he would be reimbursed for the extra time. He laughed and said, "Surely you jest. We all, including you, never look at a clock when it's time for us to leave. It's no big deal, so forget about it. However, before we start, Mary, I want you to know that I spoke with Annette about your meeting with her last Thursday. I knew you had met with her, and I asked if she could tell me what it concerned. She made it clear that she didn't want to divulge anything that might endanger your friendship or stop you from confiding in her. She only told me your reason for wanting that meeting but nothing about what was said beyond that."

Mary responded that she was not surprised that had happened and was happy he had been filled in on the meeting, at least to the extent of what Annette had divulged. It saved her from having to explain the purpose of their meeting. Now she only had to explain why she was looking into the situation concerning the hospital deaths of Crenshaw and Wilkes. She asked him if he would please tell her what had happened with the two deaths from his perspective.

He responded, "Gladly," and proceeded to tell her almost exactly what she'd been told by Annette and nurse Arlene Filbert about the incidents. She knew John and Annette would never have discussed specifically what Annette had told Mary, so she had no question about collusion. She had to believe that since both of them and nurse Arlene Filbert had provided essentially the same story, it must have been what had happened.

Mary told him she hoped he understood why she was especially interested in his perspective, because he had been the doctor who pronounced both deaths and signed both death certificates and medical records.

John said, "Mary, I guess that on both occasions, I must have been in the wrong place at the wrong time. But regardless, may I tell you with complete honesty my emotions about the deaths of these two men?"

Mary nodded and asked him to please proceed.

John responded, "You know how I feel about men who take advantage of anyone, especially women, or who abuse women in any way. Those two creeps epitomized everything I hate about men like them. I think you know the stories about them and the way they treated women. I think they were so disrespectful with women that they might even have tried something with you, a very spiritual woman, which would show just how disgusting they were. It makes me angry just to think about that. If I had known that ever had happened with you, I'm not sure what I would have done."

Mary quickly said, "John, I really appreciate your kind

concern, but they never tried or said anything off base with me." Smiling, she added, "Further, I might be spiritual, but I know how to defend myself with men like that. Remember that my father was very protective of me, and when I was twelve years old, he taught me how to quickly kick my knee to the groin of any man who tried anything. I learned a few more things as a woman doctor, so please don't ever worry about me."

John laughed and said, "I should have known that about you. I think many of us who know you believe that beneath that gentle veneer of yours lies a tigress. However, their horrible behavior didn't stop with how they treated women.

"You might not know about their business practices and how they cheated and used people for financial gain. They, especially Wilkes, cared only for themselves. One incident that personified their greed made me so irate I almost physically went after Wilkes.

"It involved the wonderful real estate project your incredible husband, Tom, was working on that resulted in the special small neighborhood of renovated homes. Wilkes went to the city managers and wanted them to block the sales of those houses to Tom's real estate agency, which planned to use the houses for Tom's project that helped so many. Wilkes wanted to buy the houses at very low prices and upgrade them using inferior materials and his own workers, many of whom were illegal aliens whom he paid less than minimum wage. Then he would sell the houses at a high profit. That was how he worked with other properties he owned.

"Fortunately, the city managers had such great respect for Tom that they refused to block the sales to his project. Wilkes threatened to sue the city council, because he had offered a slightly higher price than Tom's real estate agency for the houses. Some irate members of the council went to the bishop, who was also very concerned and talked some sense into Wilkes. To get him to drop the threat to sue, he was offered another property at a rock-bottom price. The bishop organized this agreement, working with the city council members. I know this because I had friends on the council at that time. I could tell you more about Wilkes and similar stories about Crenshaw, but there is no need at this point. I'm sorry to tell you all this, but you need to know how evil these guys were."

Mary was shocked and sat there silently for a while. She finally shook her head, grimaced, sighed, and thanked John for the information.

He then said, "Mary, please drop this now. The situation has been resolved with the autopsies, and no one besides you is interested in further investigations. You know how much I care for you and would do anything for you, and this is the best advice I can offer."

Mary responded, "I know that, John, and I really appreciate your friendship, information, and advice. I will miss you so much when you leave us.

"On a more pleasant note, I would like to offer Robert Glover, an internist from the private practice group who works at the medical office building, the position from which you are retiring. I think you know him, and I hope you approve of my decision."

John smiled and said, "Great choice."

Finally, Mary said, "Thank you very much, John. I am very lucky to have a friend and colleague like you."

John smiled and replied as he got up to leave, "And the same back atcha."

After John left, Martha stood at the door to the office and asked how things had gone. Mary shook her head and said, "Martha, I am very conflicted. I am so very fond of Annette and John, but I must be fair to all, even the two horrible men involved. We're all God's creations and must be treated with equity. I need to think about this and discuss it with Dan before I feel I've done my best. I am looking forward to a glass of wine with dinner this evening. It usually relaxes me, so I can think with less anxiety about choices I have to make."

Martha smiled and said, "I think that's a good idea. In fact, why don't you have an extra glass?"

Mary responded, "I just might, except I need to think clearly, and the extra wine might cloud my thinking."

Mary played some of her favorite CDs of classical music in her car on her way home. That usually calmed her and provided some peaceful moments. She deliberately took a long route home and drove slowly so she would have more time to mellow before exposing Mom to what she was going through.

Mom had a special radar screen that picked up Mary's emotions. Mom had always been able to read Mary's and Frank's moods. In a way, that was good because Mom usually knew when to get involved and help, sometimes simply with soothing words. But that was not going to work with this situation.

CHAPTER 22

TIME-OUT FROM PURSUIT

▷ APRIL 26, 2018

On April 26, two days after her meeting with John Bosko, Mary spoke with Dan after Mass. She briefly told him about the meeting and said that after trying to sleep on the matter, she was still concerned about Bosko's possible role in the two hospital deaths. She also continued to have problems with Annette Reynolds's, Ross Stewart's, and the Muslim doctors' and their friend's possible roles in the deaths. She again mentioned that all the physician staff had access to the hospital staff, but she thought the probability of their having had anything to do with the deaths was miniscule.

She was not sure what to do next, and the issue was affecting her sleep and appetite. In an attempt at levity, she smiled and told Dan that when a person of Italian descent had an appetite problem, it spelled real trouble. Then, becoming more serious, she asked Dan for advice.

After silently considering the situation for a few minutes, Dan thought that might be the turning point in getting Mary to stop her pursuit, which he knew would cause a lot of trouble for her and many others. So he told her he thought she should give the issue a rest. "Why don't you forget about this for at least a month? Bosko is not retiring until September, and he will still live here even after retiring. Reynolds and the others are not going anywhere, so there's no need to rush. I think you really know deep down that the Joint Commission will take no notice of the information about the hospital's deaths, because the issue is officially resolved. Therefore, honestly, this is your personal problem to solve.

"Just continue to do what is necessary administratively, and clinically, continue to take good care of patients. Spring has clearly come, with warm weather, trees blossoming, and early flowers starting to bloom. Specifically, I've noticed azalea bushes, crocuses, and tulips are now blossoming. Aren't you the one responsible for the flowers outside your house? Work in your garden, and get your hands soiled, toiling in God's earth."

Mary laughed. "Dan, I knew I could count on you to provide good advice. When I was growing up, in addition to the flowers, my dad, Frank, and I used to plant a large vegetable garden in the back of our house. We loved the fresh vegetables, especially the tomatoes, in the summer. I think a vegetable garden is far more valuable than a medicine cabinet full of vitamin tablets.

"Dad kept it up after Frank and I left home, but after he died, we had the vegetable garden replaced with a grass lawn, which the sons of one of my school friends now care for. I wish I had the time to plant more than tomatoes, but you do the best you can with what you have in time, energy, or whatever.

"Since returning home, I take care of the flowers. But I always put six tomato plants between the flowers in the back garden. As you just advised, there's something very comforting about digging in the soil and something rewarding in seeing the flowers and tomatoes in bloom. It always makes me feel close to God. I think that's exactly what I'll do.

"You know, I love all the seasons, but spring is my favorite. It is wonderful to watch the earth come alive after it has essentially gone to sleep over the winter. It shows the beginnings of life, with buds on the trees and bulbs reaching out to the sun. However, summer is nice because the awakened earth is in full bloom, and the warm sun keeps it awake. Then the fall is also nice, as the earth begins to get drowsy and prepares for the sleep of winter."

Dan told her he agreed but somehow had never been able to describe the seasons so eloquently. He thanked Mary for giving him a new way of looking at the different aspects of the seasons.

That pleased Mary, and she said, "Dan, I still want to continue having our one-on-one lunch meetings. Is that OK with you?"

Dan replied, "Not only OK, but I look forward to our meetings. Next time in your office."

After their meeting, Mary felt so relieved that she smiled all the way back to her office. When she arrived, Martha told her that she looked so happy she wondered if Mary had just met her new Prince Charming. Mary retorted, "Martha, there will only be one Prince Charming in my life, and he was taken from me a long time ago."

Martha inhaled deeply and said, "Dr. D, I am so very sorry. I didn't mean to bring up something sorrowful."

Mary replied, "Please don't apologize. I am so grateful for having had Tom with me even for such a short time. I simply consider it more proof that Dante was correct that God is the Great Comedian, and I'd add that he has a really weird sense of humor."

That made Martha laugh and say, "I think someone else also has a weird sense of humor."

Mary retorted, "Touché. Now, will you please call me Mary at least when it's only the two of us?"

"OK, Mary. But only when we are alone. And will you tell me why you had such a wonderful smile when you came in this morning? That spontaneous smile has been missing for too long."

"You know I have been working on the two hospital deaths that concern me, and this morning, Dan gave me great advice to drop the issue for a month and come back to it if necessary after giving it a rest. That is such a relief that I feel the warmth and light of spring for the first time this year. So look out, Martha; I might come up with something that might cause you more work."

"Bring it on, as long as you remain happy."

Mary went to her desk and spent the rest of the morning on routine administrative issues. After lunch, she spent the rest of the day visiting all the units and floors of the hospital. She was even able to resolve a few problems that were brewing, which reminded her of the importance of continuing the meetings with all the hospital staff.

She left for last the planned meeting with Dr. Robert Glover, the internist who had applied for the position now occupied by John Bosko. The meeting had been set up by Martha for 4:00 p.m. so he could finish caring for his private-practice patients. Mary seldom left the hospital before 5:00 p.m., especially on her administrative days, so a meeting at that time was not unusual.

Robert was a forty-year-old Afro-American doctor, which delighted Mary, who strongly believed in diversification. He had been well educated and trained at Georgetown Medical School, from which Mary had also graduated. He also had done his residency in internal medicine there, plus a year in geriatrics.

Right after he'd finished his training, he'd joined the private-practice group, and he was well regarded. His wife was a high school teacher, and they had two teenagers, a boy and a girl, who attended the school where their mother taught.

Mary met with him in his office in the medical office building attached to the hospital. Much to his delight, Mary told him she would like him to join the full-time hospital medical staff. Although she had made it clear during the interview for the position, she reiterated that the position would not start until September and that while the salary included a good pension plan, it was probably lower than what he was making in private practice.

He responded, "My wife and I have already set up an educational account for our kids, to which we'll continue to contribute, and our pension plan is also secure. I want to spend more time with my family. While officially, I only have been on call one week every two months, because my patients are all older and have many chronic problems, I often receive calls from them or their families when I am not on call. I guess that's my fault, but that's the kind of doctor I am and want to be.

"St. Joseph's hospitalists' call schedule and coverage are much more conducive to the lifestyle my wife and I would like to have. I really want to be free on my days off. My kids are growing up so fast, and I don't want to miss their special events, games, practices, and simply time together as a family."

Mary said, "I completely understand and am really happy you will join us. Although she's had no special training in geriatrics, Jane Chen has had a special interest in caring for the elderly. I hope you will work with her, because so many of our patients are elderly. I also hope you and John Bosko, who as you know will be retiring, will meet so he can fill you in on issues I might have missed."

"I know Jane Chen, and I will be sure to call her tomorrow. It will be wonderful to work with her, I'm sure. She has a great reputation. As for John, he has already called me, and we agreed to meet next week if you appointed me to the medical staff."

Mary nodded, smiled, and said, "That's so typical of John. Also, please know that you can call or visit me anytime, day or night, if necessary. I'll leave you with my card, which has all my contact information on it. Also, all the doctors use our first names with one another. I hope that suits you."

Smiling, he said, "It surely does, Mary."

She handed him her card, took and squeezed both his hands in hers, smiled broadly, and left his office. When she returned to her office, she was still smiling.

What a relief to have that position filled with such a great doctor, and that he has already been welcomed by John is an extra plus, she thought. She knew the other doctors and the nurses and other staff would follow suit and welcome him.

Her drive home that evening was different from those of the past few days. Her appetite had already returned, and she was ready for one of Mom's dinners.

CHAPTER 23

BACK TO NORMAL

On Friday morning, April 27, after the discussion with Dan and her decision to give the investigation of the hospital deaths of Crenshaw and Wilkes a one-month rest, Mary awoke after the best night's sleep she'd had in a long time. When she went to the kitchen before leaving for the hospital, as usual, her mother handed her hot cappuccino in a travel mug and a paper napkin. To her mother's delight, Mary loved to slurp the foam off the cappuccino and needed to wipe her mouth as she drove to the hospital. Mary knew not to put on lipstick until she was in her office. Also, as usual, she kissed Mom on the cheek and thanked her for the coffee before she slurped. Mom always smiled and shook her head at the antics with the cappuccino.

Mary had convinced Mom long ago that she didn't want her to make breakfast, because she preferred to eat something at the hospital cafeteria. Her mother agreed as long as breakfast included fruit. Breakfast was usually oatmeal, to which she added raisins, and a lemon poppy seed or blueberry muffin. After all raisins, lemons, and blueberries were fruits, so she could honestly keep Mom happy.

Mary told Mom she ate her breakfast after Mass, and Mom thought that was nice because she fasted before taking communion, which was an old Catholic custom to which Mom still adhered. It was easier to let her believe whatever she wanted than to try to convince her that was no longer necessary. There was no harm involved, and the belief made Mom feel better.

That morning, Mom stared at her and said, "Mary, what's going on?"

"What do you mean, Mom?"

"You have that wonderful look and smile I haven't seen in a long time."

Clearly, Mom was so tuned in to Mary's moods she picked up on the relief and energy Mary felt with the responsibility for the investigation lifted, even if only for a month. The break would give her time to pursue a normal routine, which hopefully would result in the resolution of the feeling she had to pursue the blasted hospital deaths any further. That was an especially satisfying thought because she didn't know what else she might do or who else she might have to get involved in any further investigation.

"Mom, your antenna is too acute. Let me assure you that I am feeling great because something about which I was worried will very likely no longer be an issue. It is work-related, and you know I don't discuss anything like that with you. You wouldn't understand and would worry too much about things you could not help to get resolved. OK?"

"If you say so. I'm just so happy to see the old Mary back. Now, go to work, and take care of those sick people."

Mary gave her mom a big hug, went out the door, got in her car, and hummed between sips of cappuccino all the way to the hospital.

When she got to St. Joseph's, she picked up her mail and

messages, greeting everyone along the way, which she always did, but this morning, her smile was broader. She no longer had to stop to get her white coat and scrubs that she always wore in the hospital, because wonderful Martha had arranged for five sets of scrubs to be delivered to her office early on Monday mornings. In addition, four laundered and pressed white coats were delivered every month, also on Monday mornings, when the soiled scrubs and white coats were picked up for laundering.

As she entered the reception area to her office, Martha looked at her and said, "Well, obviously you are still happy with your wise decision. Good for you. Have a great day taking care of patients, which I know is what you love most about your responsibilities. No surprise there, because you are a doctor, after all."

Mary smiled at that and went to the chapel. After Mass, Dan smiled and said, "Mary, you look radiant this morning. I'm so happy you decided to take my advice. Even Elana noticed how happy you look this morning and mentioned it to me."

"Dan, I promise to do exactly what you advised. The fact that I feel so good now proves to me that it is the right decision. Let's see what happens over the next month. Incidentally, have you heard from Pedro? I miss him especially at Mass and hope he is happy."

"Not yet, but I expect he'll get in touch with us as soon as he's settled. I'll certainly let you know."

Mary went back to her office with her usual muffin and coffee from the cafeteria. She quickly changed from her street clothes of slacks and a blouse into her scrubs and white coat, and while eating, she went through the mail and messages from some of the private doctors who had patients to be discharged that day. They wanted Mary to write the orders and prescriptions because they would be busy in their offices and didn't want the patients to wait for them to get to the hospital. There were no planned admissions, which was normal for a Friday. That relative quiet would allow her later to catch up on completing the never-ending, infernal insurance forms and some reading of medical journals.

Mary then began her rounds for the day. She was not assigned to the pediatric unit that day, because Emily Marino also was on duty and usually covered the pediatric unit. She began with the patients to be discharged, so they could get home as quickly as possible. She thought no one should have to stay in a hospital any time it was not necessary, except for the doctors and nurses, who sometimes seemed to delay leaving to be certain the care of their patients was assured.

That morning, it was simple and not very time-consuming to discharge the patients. They all wanted to get home quickly, and the orders left by their private doctors were easy and required little explanation.

Mary then went back to the two twenty-bed units to which she had been assigned. She started with the unit where only eleven patients remained. The nurses there reported that none of them needed anything special. Nonetheless, she spent some time with each patient, making sure there was nothing she needed to address. She knew patients appreciated that attention, and they had every right to expect it.

When she finished with that unit, she went to the second unit, where fourteen patients remained. Most were recovering from surgery performed the previous day or early that morning. A few were older patients with serious infections that were under control but not yet resolved.

The one patient about whom the nurses were concerned was a nineteen-year-old woman, Melinda Ramey, who was recovering from a motorcycle accident two days ago that had resulted in a shattered ankle. A well-respected, excellent orthopedic surgeon who also worked and taught residents at the city hospital had done the surgery. He had spent six hours trying to put her ankle back together. He told Mary, the patient, and her parents that the ankle joint would heal nicely but would not function exactly as it had before the accident. He said Melinda would probably be left with a slight limp that could be masked with special shoes. Clearly, her planned college basketball career was over before it really had begun.

That problem might not have been so anxiety-provoking, except the young woman had been an all-star basketball point guard and premed student at a university where she had a full athletic scholarship. She had been home for a long weekend, during which she and her two older brothers, also home from college, had gone on a short motorcycle trip. She had been riding on the back of one of the cycles, when a car had pulled out of a side street onto a country road and hit the front of the cycle, throwing her onto the road, where another car, unable to evade her completely, had run over her ankle.

Her brothers had not been seriously injured, and the driver who had hit the cycle and the one who had run over her ankle had been extremely concerned and called an ambulance and the police immediately. The first driver had been found to be legally inebriated and driving under the influence. He'd been arrested, but that did not help the medical situation.

The second driver, who had run over her ankle, had been so worried about her that he'd followed the ambulance to the hospital and visited her every day. He had not been found negligent, but he had a daughter two years younger than Melinda and was clearly shaken by the experience.

Melinda's parents and her two brothers were devastated, and Melinda was distraught. She was inconsolable, had trouble sleeping, and was eating almost nothing. She was almost six feet tall and lanky and had always been a hearty eater, which was necessary to keep her weight at a normal level. Everyone was concerned that she was losing weight in addition to all the other problems.

Mary thought this encounter was going to take some time, so she left her visit for last. When she entered Melinda's room late that afternoon, Melinda was in traction on an orthopedic bed, staring out the window, while her father sat by her bedside, holding her hand. Her mother had spent the night with her, and the family took turns during the day, so she was never alone. Her father came to the hospital right after work and usually stayed until his son took over, and the son stayed until the mother arrived in the night to stay over.

Mary introduced herself to the father and to Melinda, who turned to look at her. She asked Melinda if she had pain, which she denied, and then Melinda turned away and went back to staring out the window. Her father explained that she had a high pain threshold, and the prescribed pain medications seemed to be working well.

Mary said to Melinda, "I'm sure that as an athlete, you learned to tolerate a lot of physical pain. However, I was also asking about emotional pain."

When Mary said that, Melinda turned her head toward her and angrily said, "What do you know or care about emotional pain?"

Her father said, "Melinda, please. The doctor is trying to help."

Mary smiled and said, "Mr. Ramey, I have experienced and do understand severe emotional pain, and Melinda's reaction is perfectly understandable."

Melinda said, "When did you experience severe emotional pain?"

"I'll be happy to share some of that with you when I get to know you better if I think it will help you."

Melinda looked at her with doubt on her face and said, "Would you really?"

"I always keep my word, but now I have to check your bandages and listen to your lungs, so your dad will have to step out for a few minutes."

Mr. Ramsey said, "Doctor, I was about to leave. My son will be here in a short while and will stay until my wife comes in to stay the night. I know Melinda is in good hands, so I will leave you. Thank you for your kind understanding."

When he left, Mary went to Melinda's side, and Melinda did not resist her checking the bandages and cooperated so Mary could make sure her lungs were clear. Melinda kept staring at her throughout the examination but said nothing.

Mary asked, "Are you using the respiratory device to take deep breaths? That's important until you can get out of bed. You don't want to get pneumonia."

Melinda said she was using the device, and in addition, she was taking deep breaths without the device. She also was getting as much exercise as possible by lifting weights with her arms and uninjured leg and squeezing the muscles in her injured leg.

Mary said, "I understand that you are not eating, and that's very bad. Your body can't heal unless it is properly nourished. The food here is really quite good."

"I know, but I'm just not hungry. My whole life is ruined, and I don't care about anything anymore."

Mary looked directly into Melinda's eyes and said, "I can't imagine anyone your age believing your whole life is ruined. You are nineteen years old and barely getting started with life."

Melinda pressed her lips together and said, "I wanted to be a doctor and had a basketball scholarship for college. I love basketball and was a pretty good player. Now I won't ever be able to play basketball again, and I can never be a doctor."

Mary sighed and said, "Well, you probably won't be able to play well enough to make the basketball team or perhaps not even play at all. But that is no reason to think you can't be a doctor. One of my medical school classmates was a paraplegic, and he became a great doctor."

Amanda gaped at her, wide-eyed, with her mouth open in disbelief. "Is that true?"

"I would never lie to you. In fact, I wouldn't lie to anyone. If you want to discuss a medical career, I'll be happy to visit with you every day I'm here, so we can talk. Would you like that?"

"You would do that?"

"Absolutely." Then Mary pursed her lips, squinted, and sternly said, "However, you must promise me you will eat and stop feeling sorry for yourself, young lady."

Melinda smiled and said, "That's the way my mother talked to me before the accident. Now she only tries to make me feel good by saying goofy things."

"Mothers do that, Melinda, because they love us. Give her a break. So do we have a deal?"

"Yes, we have a deal."

"OK, I'll see you tomorrow."

"How about not tomorrow but Monday? I need the weekend to think about this."

"All right. I will see you Monday afternoon when I've finished my rounds. We can have a nice talk then. But remember to eat, or the deal will be terminated."

With that, Mary took her hand and squeezed it, smiled, and left the room. She was happy that her gut feeling had been correct in that it was best not to be gentle but firm with the young woman. She knew good coaches did not treat athletes gently. She also knew this was going to be a challenge, but she loved challenges, didn't she?

By that time, it was after five o'clock, so she finished her chart work, went to her office, changed into street clothes, collected her things, and went home for the weekend. It had been a good day in that Mary thought she had been able to help some people. Maybe she would be able to find the true meaning of her life after all.

As she drove home, Mary thought about all the wonderful things she was going to do that weekend. In addition to shopping with Mom, she could take a long walk in the woods near the house. She loved the trees and other foliage; the sounds of the birds; the wind in the trees; and the fragrance, even in the winter, from the pine trees. When she walked there alone, she cherished the quiet that allowed her to hear and feel the vibrant silence of the woods that made her feel close to God, who had created such beauty.

On Saturday afternoon, she was going to work on the small herb garden and place the six tomato plants in the flower bed in the back of the house. After all, tomatoes began as flowers, didn't they? She grinned at that thought.

CHAPTER 24

A GOOD-NEWS LETTER

Two weeks after Mary asked Dan if he had heard from Pedro, Dan told her he had with him a letter he'd received the day before from Pedro. The conversation occurred as they were preparing for Mass in the hospital's chapel one morning.

Dan said he would read the letter to Mary after Mass, so Elana, who would be at the service, could also hear it. When she first had been hired many years before, Elana had arranged to work from 8:00 a.m. to 4:00 p.m. instead of the normal 7:00 a.m. to 3:00 p.m. housekeeping shift so she could attend Mass daily, and now she filled in as a eucharistic minister whenever needed, which she enjoyed.

Dan knew that the few minutes Elana would be late in reporting for work that day would be excused because he had explained the situation to her supervisor, Nancy Darcy, who was responsible for housekeeping. Nancy also was happy that Dan had received a letter from Pedro, probably showing that he was healthy and happy in his native country, Mexico. She knew Elana would fill her in on the letter's contents later that day.

After Mass, Dan, Mary, and Elana sat in the front pew, and Dan read the letter to them.

May 1, 2018

Dear Father Dan,

Hello from sunny Mexico. I miss you and my wonderful friends from St. Joseph's Hospital, especially Dr. Defazio, Elana, and Marcos. Please give them my best wishes, and I hope you will share this letter with them and anyone else you'd like to.

I am now settled into my new home. With the money I had saved, I was able to buy a small but comfortable house, where my sister, Rosa, and I live. I also bought a motor bike so I could travel to places too far to walk, including Mexico City, which is the closest city to our village.

I am a eucharistic minister at our local church, and the padre is very happy to have my help. Thank God I also had saved enough money to buy the material necessary to repair the church and a small building next to the church, which we now use as a community center.

The men and women in our village have made the repairs, because many of them are carpenters, some have plumbing skills, and one is even an electrician. Because it is very hard to finish twelve years of public school and few of them did, their construction training was passed on from their fathers or uncles. Now some of the men are passing those skills to their sons and daughters. I know that Dr. Defazio especially will be happy to hear that about the daughters. Before I could provide the financial means, no one had the money to buy the materials, so no repairs could have been made.

The padre has lived on the very small amount of money he receives from the diocese and the tiny amount the villagers are able to put in the collection basket at Mass. Of course, he uses much of the collections to buy altar needs, like candles and altar cloths. Now, with my monthly pension, I can contribute enough to the collections so he has more money to buy whatever he needs.

There are many gardens in the area, so vegetables and fruit have always been available. A few families raise chickens, so eggs and chickens are also available. The nearby streams provide fish, but there is little meat.

The padre is an avid fisherman, and the villagers provide him with whatever fruits and vegetables they can spare. Twice a month, a farmer who raises chickens mostly for sale gives the padre eggs and a chicken, which his wife bakes. The padre even uses the bones and small bits of the chicken to make soup; thereby, he has several meals from the one chicken. I tell you this so you will know how frugal all the villagers are.

Also, with some of the money from my monthly pension check, we buy rice and beans in hundred-pound sacks, and that saves a lot of money, rather than buying the more expensive, much smaller amounts, which was all families could afford.

About once a month, we try to buy enough meat to make sure every family gets some. We use the community center to distribute the rice, the beans, and whatever meat we have every Friday to whoever needs it. Also, every Thursday evening, I teach a class of English as a second language to mostly the children but to anyone who wants to attend. There are now twenty students, so I might have to start another class, because more than twenty is too many to give individual attention.

The American dollar goes a long way here. I am trying to add a little from my pension every month to the small savings I have left in case an emergency happens.

I want you to know how happy I am and how grateful I am to you and all my friends there. For many years, you were my family and took good care of me. Now I am with my Mexican family, and this is where I want to spend the rest of my life. I am trying to live my life as you, my American friends, especially Father Dan and Dr. Defazio, taught me by example. I am passing on the love you gave me to the people who are now part of my life.

God bless and keep you.

Pedro

When Dan finished reading the letter, tears were in all their eyes. All three were taken by the sincerity of their friend and were happy for him. Dan folded the letter and put it in his jacket.

Mary asked for Pedro's address so she might send him a letter. Dan told her that Pedro had provided only a post office box in Texas and had requested that mail be kept to a minimum and, if possible, sent along with Dan's letters. The mail system in Mexico was not as reliable as the one in the United States. His post office box, which was in a Texas city near the village where he'd lived, used the name P. Gonzales, a common name, so he could remain undetected. A friend of his who worked in Texas one day every two weeks would pick up the mail from Pedro's mailbox.

Dan also told her the letter he'd received was postmarked from Texas and obviously had been mailed by Pedro's friend who traveled there. The friend probably lived in Mexico City. However, it was a long trip to Mexico City on a motor bike, and Pedro wanted to keep those trips to a minimum.

Mary wanted to send some money to Pedro for the church's and community center's needs, but Dan told her that was probably a bad idea because of what Pedro had said about the mail system. Pedro's pension was sent directly to a bank near his village, but Dan didn't know the name of the bank; therefore, money could not be deposited there for Pedro. Dan said he would ask Pedro for the best way to send him money for the church and community center and would let Mary know.

When Mary returned to her office, she told Martha about the letter because she knew Martha was also fond of Pedro. He had given her a hand-carved wooden statue of Our Lady of Guadalupe from Mexico when he'd left St. Joseph's. Martha was pleased to know how well Pedro was doing.

Pedro had friends all over the hospital because he was such a kind man. Mary planned to tell anyone who asked how well Pedro was doing. *Once you become a friend of the St. Joseph's staff, you always remain a friend*, she thought.

CHAPTER 25

MYSTERY PATIENT

Over the next few weeks, Mary was happy in being able to care for patients and see to administrative issues without concern for the hospital deaths of Crenshaw and Wilkes.

As promised, she visited Melinda Ramsey, the young athlete who had shattered her ankle, on the Monday after she'd seen her for the first time. She was not sure how Melinda would greet her this time and was surprised that the greeting was cordial.

Melinda looked at her when she entered her room and said, "Hi."

Mary smiled and responded, "Hi back atcha," and that made Melinda smile. "Are you ready to discuss your becoming a doctor?"

Melinda said, "I guess so, if you really think that can happen."

Mary said, "If I didn't think so, I wouldn't be here. I have already signed out for the day, so we can have all the time we need to discuss this. But first, I need to understand a few things about you so I might help. OK?"

Melinda responded, "OK. What do you need to know?"

Mary said, "Let's start with how you are doing in college grade-wise."

Melinda frowned and said, "I had a good but not great first semester because there were a lot of basketball practices and games." Then she smiled and said, "But I'm doing much better this semester."

Mary asked, "Is your scholarship only based on athletics, or is any of it based on academics?"

Melinda closed her eyes and sighed before she said, "I had a decent academic scholarship, but the athletic one was better, so that's the one I have."

Mary said, "Well, the first thing is to find out if you can still get the academic scholarship, because you can't play basketball. Your parents can find that out very quickly. By the way, where is your family?"

"My dad is checking that question about the scholarship situation. He's also working with a lawyer, so we might get some money from the insurance company of the drunk driver involved in my accident. That would make it much easier to pay for my education. My mom will be here later this morning, and my brothers have returned to college."

"OK. The next thing you must do is ace your final exams for this semester no matter what. Can you do that?"

"If I study, sure. I have two liberal arts classes, one science, one language, and one math course, and none are all that difficult. And I have plenty of time to study, not having basketball practice."

"See, Melinda? There's often a positive side to a bad situation if you look for it. Now, get your books and computer, and get going. I will come back to discuss more every weekday until you are discharged, as long as you keep studying."

They agreed to that plan, and they continued their visits, but Melinda became so enthusiastic about school that after five days, most of the visits were short and happy. Melinda's mother met Mary on the third day and wanted to know what

Mary had done to bring about such a wonderful change in her daughter's attitude. Mary knew it was a rhetorical question, so she only smiled in response.

When Melinda was discharged from the hospital, she promised to keep her grades high because she had been provided with an academic scholarship. The insurance company had also agreed to pay a substantial amount of money, which would be used for her education. She also wanted to keep in touch with Mary, and they exchanged email addresses. Mary would provide whatever guidance she could regarding applying to medical schools when the time came.

Melinda's parents were grateful to Mary and made that clear to her and to all the nurses and anyone else who would listen.

Melinda was one of many patients whom Mary helped with issues beyond their medical problems. But the patient care she especially found rewarding was when she contributed to the diagnosis or treatment of an illness. After all, she was a well-trained doctor.

One such patient was a twenty-one-year-old man, Robert Helms, who was admitted in mid-May for the second time in two months. He was admitted again because of nausea, vomiting, watery diarrhea, tingling of his fingers and toes, and a "weird" feeling. He had been evaluated at St. Joseph's a few weeks before for the same symptoms, and an extensive evaluation had found nothing abnormal.

However, his symptoms had disappeared just before his previous discharge from the hospital, and his private doctor was going to monitor him. Mary had not seen the patient during his first visit, so as was her custom, when she was assigned to the unit where he had just been admitted, she carefully read his medical record. His private physician had not yet seen him and asked Mary if she would please do the history and physical exam, because he wanted her opinion about possible diagnoses and knew that a complete evaluation by another doctor, especially one as bright as Mary, might result in more information, leading to a diagnosis.

When Mary spoke with Robert, she found he and his family were farmers who had dairy cows and a large apple orchard. He had two older sisters, who were married and lived in the city. The farm was in a rural area about eight miles from the hospital. They were a strong Catholic family and favored St. Joseph's over the city hospital, where his private doctor also had admitting privileges.

Mary thought about the diagnosis, this time as more of a recurring or potentially chronic disease rather than as an acute problem. However, when she considered a chronic illness, among the possible diagnoses, everything that immediately came to mind had already been ruled out during his first admission.

A careful physical exam was normal, except for her discovery of two small horizontal white lines on each of his fingernails and toenails. She knew they were Mees' lines, which designated arsenic poisoning. That confused her. Arsenic could be in the soil, but why was he the only family member with those symptoms? Did the others also have Mees' lines?

She showed Robert the lines and asked if he had noticed them before. He replied that he had, but he'd ignored them because he thought they were due to scratches from farmwork, even though his father and mother didn't have similar lines. He knew they didn't because he had checked their nails.

She then asked about his diet. Did he eat pretty much the same food as his parents? He said he ate more fast food than his parents and laughed when he said so. Mary shared his laugh and asked if, besides eating more fast food, there was anything unusual he ate.

He thought about it and said he loved apple seeds, so his parents gave him the seeds from the apples they ate or cooked. He would save them until he had a cupful and then chew on them like nuts while drinking beer. When Mary asked him to recall when he had last eaten the seeds, he remembered having eaten the seeds a few days before being admitted to the hospital this time and the previous time.

Mary thought, *Bingo*. She called Robert's private doctor, told him she thought Robert had mild arsenic poisoning, and explained why she thought so. She always remembered a great lesson she had learned from one of her favorite professors during her residency: ordering a diagnostic test was like picking your nose in public. You should first consider what you were going to do if you found something. It was a gross statement, but she knew it would be remembered by any doctor who heard it. She followed that rule to prevent ordering unwarranted or too many tests, but in this case, she knew testing for arsenic was indicated, and she knew what needed to be done if the test was positive.

Robert's private doctor laughed at the warning regarding ordering diagnostic tests but agreed to her testing Robert's urine and hair for arsenic. He said if she was right, he'd owe her a bottle of a fine Italian wine.

It turned out she was correct, and when she and Robert's doctor told Robert and his parents about the diagnosis and the cause, they could hardly believe it. They were concerned because they believed arsenic poisoning was deadly.

They were appeased when they were told that a mild case like Robert's was not lethal but that he and all others should not eat apple seeds from their trees, because the soil where they grew likely contained arsenic. The apples were fine, but the seeds were not.

After Robert was discharged, his doctor asked Mary to

please come to his office in the building adjacent to the hospital. She wasn't sure why he wanted her, but she walked over to his office. When she got there, he presented her with a bottle of fine Italian wine in the presence of many of the doctors and nurses in the office building. They all clapped, and she blushed with embarrassment. However, she was happy she had made the diagnosis and saved Robert from further potentially serious problems.

Some days, getting out of bed was well worth it. She thought to herself, *This surely was one.*

CHAPTER 26

CRENSHAW'S RESTAURANT

Every month or so, Dan and his friends, some of the priests from St. Ann's rectory and the cathedral, would go to dinner at one of the restaurants in the nearby city to discuss the latest happenings in the diocese or anything else that came up. On occasion, they ate in one of the diners in the community, but that was rare and only if they met for breakfast. They had never eaten in the only real restaurant in the community, El Toro, a Spanish restaurant, because it had been owned by Matthew Crenshaw, and it had been his rule that priests never paid for their meals. Like many other priests, Dan and his friends had wanted no part in accepting anything from Crenshaw, because they had known about his dishonest business dealings and how he treated women. However, they also had not wanted to insist on paying, because that might not have sat well with the bishop, who had been a friend of Matthew Crenshaw's and wanted to stay on his good side because of his needed donations of time and money to the hospital and church. The best way to solve the dilemma had been to skip that restaurant and all the others owned by Crenshaw in the city.

But now that Crenshaw had been dead for about a year,

his estate owned all restaurants, though none of his relatives wanted any part of owning a business, so they were pursuing buyers for all the restaurants. More importantly, there was no longer a rule regarding priests' eating for free. So Dan and his friends decided to try the restaurant, which had retained the chef, who had a good reputation, and the staff, who were noted for providing excellent service. The chef's specialty was paella, and that was what all four of the priests planned to order.

When they were seated, they ordered a platter of tapas for starters and a pitcher of sangria. The wine came immediately, and after a toast to a night free of any obligations, one of them asked Dan if he knew what had happened to Crenshaw, because Crenshaw had died in St. Joseph's Hospital. Dan said he knew what he thought everyone knew: Crenshaw probably had had a major heart attack in his sleep sometime in the early morning hours.

One of the priests said, "God forgive me, but that was just too easy a death for someone like him. I know that being a priest, I should never think unchristian thoughts like that, but among my brothers, I feel I can express my feelings."

The two others agreed with him wholeheartedly.

Dan said, "I didn't know him, because I only blessed him and gave him the Eucharist when he was admitted to St. Joseph's, but why do you all feel that way about him?"

The first priest said, "Dan, I didn't really know him either, but he had a reputation for being a dishonest businessman who mistreated women. It wasn't just a few people who said this; there were many. Further, I believe many of us priests were involved in counseling women whom he had sexually mistreated.

"After he died, I was one of several priests who served at his funeral mass conducted by the bishop. At rehearsal, when plans were being made for his lavish funeral, which took place at the cathedral in the city, the funeral director told us he always had felt sad when preparing bodies for wakes and funerals, but that feeling never had come when he was preparing Crenshaw. His feelings were quite the opposite for that man. In fact, he admitted to feeling relief because the world would be a better place without him. He apologized to us and asked us to forgive him for saying such negative things about the man, but it was obviously how he felt."

At that point, the waiter brought the platter of tapas, and the priests stopped the conversation. The waiter said he hoped they would enjoy the tapas as he poured more wine from another pitcher of sangria he had brought for them.

After the waiter left, between bites of food, another priest said, "You know, the only time I heard worse things about anyone was after Calvin Wilkes died. I was asked to serve at his funeral mass in the cathedral, also conducted by his friend the bishop. A different funeral director was involved and said almost the same thing about Wilkes as the other funeral director said about Crenshaw. He was adamant that Wilkes was evil. That was the word he used, and he apologized for talking about the dead like that."

Dan said, "Good heavens, they sound like terrible people, but both had served on St. Joseph's board of trustees. I had assumed the bishop put up with a lot of their behavior because they donated a lot of money to the diocese and provided their money, time, and energy to the hospital. Their financial donations allowed the bishop to support many of the good things the church and hospital did. I certainly don't envy him for having to put up with them to ensure those donations."

Once again, they were interrupted, this time by two waiters who brought the paella to the table and served each one from a giant platter. The priests ate the delicious paella, which lived up to the reputation, and after eating flan for dessert, they paid the bill, leaving a generous tip, which they always did.

They went to their respective cars in the parking lot and said goodbye until the next time. Dan—and, he believed, the others—knew they would probably not ever have a better paella but certainly would have a more pleasant topic next time.

As he drove home, he thought about how much grief and sadness Crenshaw and Wilkes had wrought. Unfortunately, the turmoil had not ended with their deaths, considering what Mary was going through because of the problems stimulated by their deaths. Dan hoped that after she had a month to reconsider what she would do next, she would forget about any further investigation. However, knowing Mary, he worried that was not going to happen.

As it turned out, he knew Mary well.

CHAPTER 27

SISTER THERESA

▷ MAY 21, 2018

It had been three weeks since Mary agreed to forget about the Crenshaw and Wilkes affair for a month. She had spent the past weekend working in the garden and taking long walks in the woods near her home. Mom had even accompanied her on her Saturday morning walk, and they'd had a great time remembering the picnics the family had had there when Mary and her brother, Frank, were growing up.

Completely refreshed, on Monday morning, Mary arrived at the hospital in time to check her mail and messages, change into scrubs, and get the report on patients from the doctor who had been on the units she would cover that month.

As the CMO, she made up the schedule for assignment of doctors to the various patient units. She knew most of the doctors had favorite units because they especially enjoyed knowing and continuing to interact over time with the same nurses who worked on those units, so whenever possible, she assigned them accordingly, at least for the 7:00 a.m. to 3:00 p.m. shifts. For the other shifts, they all covered many units. For whatever reason, none of her colleagues preferred the fourth-floor unit where priests, nuns, VIPs, and children older than twelve were admitted, usually to the special room. Therefore, she assigned that unit to herself most of the time.

After Mass, she went first to the special fourth floor to care for the patients on that unit. There had been only one patient admitted on Saturday morning, who had suffered a badly infected laceration on his leg after falling on a piece of glass while running. The wound was healing nicely after administration of IV antibiotics. He would be discharged on oral antibiotics after being seen by his private doctor later that day.

She went to the nurses' station and chatted with the nurses for a few minutes. They expressed no concern for the fourteen patients on the unit, three more of whom were to be discharged later that day by their private doctors. There were four patients to be admitted later that morning. In the meantime, she would look in on the patients still on the unit.

The other unit for which she was responsible only had patients who were to remain in the hospital. All of them had already been seen or were soon to be seen by their private doctors. The nurses on that unit also had no patient problems they needed her to resolve.

At that point, Mary's cell phone buzzed with a text from Dr. Jim Allen, asking her to please call him on his cell phone as soon as possible. She wondered what had stimulated the unusual request, and she immediately called him, expecting to leave a voice message. To her surprise, he answered the phone after the first ring.

He said, "Mary, I am so happy you are covering the special unit, because I have added one admission: Sister Theresa, whom I think you know from your days at the convent. Mother Superior knew that I take care of all the nuns from that convent and specifically asked if you might also see Sister Theresa. I know Sister Theresa will be there later this morning, but she and Mother Superior know I can't see her until later this afternoon. Would you please see her for me and let me know what you think?"

Mary responded, "Of course, Jim. What seems to be the problem?"

"The only thing I could get from Mother Superior early this morning when she called me is that Sister Theresa awoke crying out in pain. She is so stoic it panicked Mother Superior. Apparently, she has had some abdominal pain for the past two or three weeks, but she refused to have Mother Superior call me, because she didn't want to bother me. However, this pain has become much worse and is now accompanied by loss of appetite, occasional confusion, and headaches."

Mary frowned with concern and said, "I will see her as soon as she arrives and will let you know what I find, OK?"

"That's perfect. Thank you, Mary. I really appreciate your doing this."

"Jim, I know Sister Theresa quite well. She was at the convent during the time I was there as a nun and was very kind to me. I also see her when I visit the convent several times a year, usually on holidays. The last time was a month or so ago, at Easter time."

Mary did not like what she had heard from Jim and was concerned that Sister Theresa might have a serious medical problem. She then busied herself seeing to the care of the patients on the fourth-floor unit, especially the one patient who had already been admitted that morning. None of them required much from her out of the ordinary, and by eleven o'clock, all the discharged patients had left with the prescriptions and follow-up orders she had written.

At 11:25 a.m., while Mary was tending to the second admitted patient of the day, she was notified by a nurse that Sister Theresa had arrived and was getting settled in the special VIP room. As soon as she finished with the patient, Mary went to see a frail-looking Sister Theresa. She was sitting on the side of the bed in a hospital gown and her own robe. A young nun, whom Mary also recognized from passing her in the halls during one of her visits to the convent, was sitting in a chair next to the bed.

Mary immediately went to Sister Theresa, hugged her and kissed her on the cheek, and then did the same to the young nun. She had long ago learned to mask any feelings in front of patients or their families, but she was horrified upon seeing how Sister Theresa looked. The sister obviously had lost a lot of weight, and her eyes were slightly jaundiced. She also had winced when Mary carefully hugged her. None of those signs boded well for a seventy-five-year-old woman of God.

Sister Theresa said to the young nun, "Sister Jean, this is Dr. Defazio, also known one time as Sister Mary Elizabeth when she was one of us. She didn't stay very long with us, but look at her now. We all are so proud of her."

Mary smiled broadly and thanked Sister Theresa for her kind words. She asked her if she'd prefer for Mary to ask questions and examine her when young Sister Jean was not in the room. Sister Theresa said she'd prefer to have Sister Jean remain in the room.

Mary proceeded to ask pertinent questions, revealing that Sister Theresa had first noticed a pain in her lower left abdomen about three or four weeks ago, and it had grown worse with time. She had not been all that concerned, because the pain was mostly on her left side, and she knew her appendix was on the right. Also, the pain had been controllable with acetaminophen and ibuprofen. But eventually, the pain could not be controlled with over-the-counter medications; she could not eat without becoming nauseated and vomiting; and she now had headaches.

When Mary examined Sister Theresa, she found severe abdominal pain even with mild palpation, an enlarged liver, an enlarged spleen, and evidence of fluid in the abdominal cavity. The exam and the rest of her history were consistent with what Mary feared was most likely an advanced malignancy.

Mary finished, smiled, and told Sister that she had to see two more patients who had just been admitted, and she would return as soon as she finished with them and other required chores. She also said she would order a pain medication because it was obvious Sister was in pain. That was met with a big thank-you from both nuns. Mary forced a big smile and said, "Now, don't go away, OK?" which made both sisters laugh.

Mary went to the bathroom in the hallway and washed her face with cold water to get control of her emotions before she called Dr. Allen. She never wore makeup except for lipstick, so she only had to wipe her face with a paper towel. Fortunately, when she called Dr. Allen, this time she had to leave a voice message for him, which allowed her to have some time to think about what she would say. She spent the next three hours caring for the last two patients admitted that day and rechecking a few others who needed her care. Thankfully, no one required much beyond routine care.

She went back to Sister Theresa's room and found her asleep in bed. Sister Jean said she had fallen asleep about a half hour after the nurse gave her the pain medicine about two hours earlier. Mary thought Sister Theresa had probably not slept much last night, so this was good. She told Sister Jean she would return later after she had spoken with Dr. Allen, who she knew would be in to see Sister Theresa after he finished with his office patients.

Since it was after three o'clock, she signed out to the doctor who would be covering that and other units for the next shift. After that, she decided to walk over to Jim Allen's office to speak to him in person. On the short walk over, she reminded herself that self-control was essential now.

When she arrived at Jim's office, he had just finished with his last patient and was happy to see Mary. They went into his office, and Mary told him what she had found. She was relieved she was able to tell him everything without becoming emotional.

Jim said, "Mary, I can only imagine how you are feeling, so please don't think you have to put on a doctor's face with me."

Mary responded, "Thank you, Jim. You know, one of my professors in medical school told us that a good doctor doesn't get personally involved in the care of his or her patients. I never believed that. I think the best doctors are very involved in the care of their patients, but they always must maintain a professional demeanor with a patient and his or her family." She spoke with tears in her eyes.

Jim handed her a tissue and agreed. They then discussed how to proceed by ordering specific tests for now and immediately getting a gynecological oncologist involved. Fortunately, there was a doctor with those credentials who saw patients in the office building twice a week and had admitting privileges at St. Joseph's and the city hospital. Jim would call him as soon as he saw Sister Theresa, which he would do immediately. He asked Mary if she would please accompany him, and she readily agreed.

The visit was difficult for everyone, even though no specific diagnosis was discussed; various tests would be ordered, and then they might call a specialist, depending on the results of the tests.

Mary said she would visit Sister Theresa every day and closely follow her care. Of course, that pleased Sister, who said she was lucky to have two great doctors caring for and about her.

Mary went to her office, changed into her street cloths, and gathered her things so she could leave. She also realized that her stomach was growling; she was feeling a bit light-headed and was very hungry. It was no wonder she was hungry and feeling a bit woozy, because she had eaten nothing that day, having lost her appetite. Her blood sugar needed a boost before she drove home, so she grabbed a protein bar from her desk drawer and ate it on the way to her car.

It was now after six o'clock, and she called Mom before she drove off. When she was going to be late in getting home, she would call Mom so her mother would not wait to eat dinner after the usual dinner time of 6:00 p.m. Obviously, Mary was late in making the call, but Mom understood and told her not to worry but to drive carefully.

That happened a lot on Mondays, and fortunately, dinner on that day was usually leftovers from Sunday dinner. Mary had thought the menu of leftovers would cease when she began taking Martha her Monday lunch from Mom's Sunday dinner. However, Mom only had added more food to Sunday's dinners, so nothing changed.

As she drove home, Mary thought about how difficult that week was going to be, because she knew what was coming for Sister Theresa. Despite being hungry, she didn't feel like eating much when she got home. Mom took one look at her when she came into the kitchen and said, "This must have been a very difficult day for you."

Mary nodded and told her briefly about Sister Theresa, whom Mom knew from Mary's days in the convent.

Mom said, "I'll say extra prayers for her and all her doctors, including you. But you must eat to keep up your strength so you can take good care of Sister and the other patients. Now, eat." It was a typical Mom response.

Mary didn't sleep well that night, and the next morning, she prayed for guidance and strength while driving to work. When she went to the unit to see Sister Theresa, among other things, the covering doctor reported that Sister Theresa had slept all night because the nurses had made sure she had enough pain medications. Another nun had spent the night with her and slept in the chair next to Sister's hospital bed.

After Mass, Mary told Dan about Sister Theresa and asked if she could take the Eucharist to both sisters, and Dan readily agreed. Mary went to the room and found Sister Theresa sitting up in bed and another young nun, Sister Yvonne, sitting in the chair next to the bed. Sister Theresa looked rested, if still frail. Mary gave them both the blessed communion wafers and prayed with them. She told them she would return after she had taken care of her administrative duties for that day.

Because of some administrative issues that needed attention, it was well after two o'clock that afternoon when Mary returned to Sister Theresa's room. Many of the diagnostic tests Jim had ordered the day before had been reported, and all pointed to an advanced ovarian cancer with metastases involving most of the abdominal organs.

Sister had an MRI and bone scan scheduled to be performed at the city hospital at 5:00 p.m. Because Sister had refused to be admitted to the city hospital, arrangements had been made to transport her there for the tests and then back to St. Joseph's. That agreement between hospitals was one of many displays of caring for a patient's needs and not primarily for convenience of the clinicians' protocols.

By Friday morning, when the results from all the tests were in, it was clear Sister Theresa had advanced-stage ovarian cancer with multiple metastases. The only possible treatment was to try a brutal chemotherapy regimen that had a slight chance of buying some months of life.

Jim Allen asked Mary if she would join him when he met with Sister Theresa at 5:00 p.m. that day. Mother Superior also wanted to be there so she would know firsthand what was going on, so she could plan accordingly. At 5:00 p.m., all four of them were in Sister Theresa's room with the door closed and a Do Not Disturb sign placed outside the door. The unit nurses were aware of the importance of privacy in that and other similar cases.

Jim told both nuns the diagnosis, explained the possible treatment, and answered questions from Sister Theresa regarding prognosis with and without treatment. Mary greatly admired that he responded honestly while trying to give some hope and did so while only occasionally getting a bit choked up and coughing. When he was finished, they all sat quietly for a while, and then Jim asked Sister Theresa if she needed more time to decide what she wanted.

Sister, sitting on the side of her bed, responded. "Dr. Allen, this is really no surprise to me. I may be a schoolteacher, but I know how to use a computer. I am seventy-five years old and have had a wonderful life, and if God wants me, I will go to him, having served him all my adult life. I want to live what's left of my life free of the side effects of chemotherapy, which only might give me a few more months of life on earth. I'd like to go home to the convent if Mother Superior will have me."

Mother Superior responded, "Sister, you are family, and you will always have a home at the convent, where you've lived most of your life. With the doctors' help to get us a proper bed and other equipment and medicine necessary, we will care for you."

Jim said he would make all arrangements for what they would need. Mary said she would visit the convent as often as she could, would be on call for them whenever they wanted, and would back up Dr. Allen when needed.

Jim asked if there was anything he could do now and was told no, not at that point. Sister Theresa and Mother Superior thanked him and asked Mary to stay. He left the three women and went to the nurses' station to arrange the discharge of Sister, including a prescription for pain medications and arrangements for a hospital bed and other necessary equipment to be delivered to the convent.

When he was gone, Sister Theresa smiled and said, "I can speak much freer with Dr. Allen gone, and I want to tell you what I've been thinking. It's so ironic that as a nun, my cancer involves the one organ I have never used." They all laughed.

Mary said, "Mother Superior, please forgive me for saying this, but I have always thought and often said that our wonderful God is the Great Comedian and has a very weird sense of humor."

To Mary's surprise, Mother Superior said, "Mary, I think you are correct. I have often wondered about the many ironic things that happen in this world. But who am I to question God?"

Mary agreed with her and then hugged them both and left the room. She knew she would see them often in the next few weeks and perhaps even months. Indeed, who was she to question God?

Mary visited the convent to see Sister Theresa at least four times a week on her way home from the hospital. She also called every day until Sister Theresa died peacefully in her sleep five weeks later. Throughout her illness, she always was surrounded by the other nuns, who took turns sitting at her bedside day and night. Mary was not sure it was a happy ending, but that was not for her to decide.

She had a sad drive home the day she was told Sister Theresa had died, and she did not look forward to telling Mom. But such life events required faith that God would provide one with the courage to do the right thing.

Sister Theresa's funeral mass was celebrated by the bishop, and so many of her friends and former students were in attendance that the cathedral was filled to standing room only. It was truly a celebration of a life well lived.

CHAPTER 28

MARY AND DAN'S THIRD SPECIAL MEETING

▷ MAY 22, 2018

On a Tuesday about three and a half weeks after Mary had resumed her normal routine, during which she took no action involving the Crenshaw and Wilkes incidents, she again met with Dan. This time, the meeting was in her office, where Martha had arranged for their lunch, which was the usual feast prepared by the hospital chef, who refused to prepare anything less for, as he told Martha, two of the most wonderful people he knew. Not to waste food, Mary and Dan gave Martha the extra food, which they knew she shared with Nancy Darcy's administrative assistant. Kindness was contagious.

When they were seated at the table in Mary's office, she smiled at Dan and said, "No tissues needed for this meeting—I promise. I have been so happy these past three weeks or so just being a doctor with some administrative responsibilities. And thus far, nothing unusual has happened. We've had no unusual hospital deaths in the past five months. That gives me confidence that there is no serial killer about whom we need to be concerned." They both laughed at that last statement.

Dan said, "As you well know, I have no problem when tissues are needed, even though I still don't know enough to have an opinion about whether or not angels cry. However, I'm very happy to see you back to your old self. I still think you are overly concerned that another unusual death will occur or that anything else should be done about the other two deaths, which have caused you so much angst."

Of course, Dan did not tell her about the recent conversation about Crenshaw and Wilkes he'd had with his priest friends in the restaurant. He saw no need to pass on more negative information about the dead.

Dan continued. "But now I have a question for you. I've been told that you graduated from medical school at the top of your class and were offered the position of chief resident when you completed your residency. That position essentially ensured you a fellowship and, eventually, an academic position at some medical school. Why did you turn down something that many doctors only dream about?"

Mary nodded, was silent for a while, took a sip of her water, and then said, "Dan, I actually thought about an academic career but only for about two minutes. You see, in academia, everything is geared toward promotion until you reach full professorship with tenure. Supposedly, that is based on teaching, research, and clinical acumen. However, promotion is mostly decided by your publications, mostly concerning your research, primarily in high-impact medical journals. These publications lead to a national and then international reputation in your field.

"While I like teaching, there is usually little or no credit toward promotion for teaching. Ironically, everyone wants to be a professor, but no one wants to profess. But really, who can blame anyone for not wanting to do something that has essentially little or no academic reward? If you're not promoted in time, you will probably have to find a position at another place, which could be very difficult.

"I also love researching medical questions, but I did not want to spend the rest of my life writing grants and papers instead of caring for patients. I love to read but hate to write, and working in a lab or office away from patients is unthinkable for me."

Dan said, "But don't all doctors have to write about patients in medical charts?"

Mary responded, "That's not really writing in the same way. We mostly fill out forms, complete a list of standard questions in medical charts, and write notes filled with medical jargon and alphabet soup. In fact, most doctors are not good writers. One of the reasons I've been so happy the past three weeks, and even before, is that I have had the time to help patients, not being rushed or dealing only with the physical aspects of their illnesses, although that is the aspect I most enjoy. I have cared for many patients whose emotional concerns were far worse than their physical illnesses or whose emotional angst made their serious physical illnesses worse. I've actually been able to provide some advice and guidance to them that resolved at least some of the emotional strain."

Dan looked at her and said, "And how about your emotional health? Are you still having what you called an existential crisis and I call an existential struggle? Because if you are, you need to reconsider your definition of *worth* or do a much better self-evaluation. You told me you were struggling with finding the meaning of your life, but you just described it perfectly. And it sounds to me like a beautiful meaning of life."

"Dan, I was referring to the spiritual aspects of my life."

"Mary, what you are doing, how you respond to people, and how they respond to you is spiritual."

Mary responded, "But is what I've planned and done so far following God's plan for me?"

Dan shook his head and said, "Remember when I told you about Rabbi Sol, who helped me so much when I was just starting out? Well, one of his lessons was that humans plan, and God laughs. So you might think your life is your plan, but God is laughing. Despite what you think, as you've described it, your life is God's plan. Plain and simple. You can always choose not to follow it, but that's not what you've done. And from what I've observed, it's a wonderful plan. So just relax, and carry on. You are doing God's work."

Mary responded, "Do you really think so? But what about my recurring doubt? I want so badly to believe completely, but despite my prayers, it just doesn't come. I know it's ridiculous to pray to a God to help me believe in him." She shook her head, wrinkled her brow, and shrugged. "Why would I pray to him if I doubt his existence?"

Dan sighed and said, "Mary, that is called faith. You need faith if you don't know, and if you know for sure, you really don't need faith. And as you've told me, it made you feel better when you learned that Mother Theresa doubted sometimes. There aren't many who've led a more godlike life than she did, and in her belief, faith was very much a driving force.

"I often think of doubting Thomas, who needed physical proof that Jesus was truly resurrected, yet he remained in Jesus's favor. So I also struggle with doubt sometimes, but in the end, I have faith and strongly believe, which is enough for me to continue with my spiritual life.

"At Mass, when I consume the eucharistic wafer and drink from the chalice of wine, I want very much to feel the presence of God in me. Sometimes I spiritually feel that deeply, and other times, that feeling is less or even missing. But I consider all of that to be a test of my faith. I'll bet you have similar feelings, especially as a eucharistic minister. But you probably focus on the times when you don't feel his presence rather than the times when you do. I suggest you accentuate the times of deep spirituality to carry you through the lesser times and times of doubt."

Mary sighed loudly and said, "Dan, you are a dear friend and spiritual adviser, and I appreciate both very much. Times like this remind me of how I felt spiritually with Tom. Thank you."

At that point, Martha knocked on the door and loudly said, "Father Dan and Dr. D, I hate to interrupt, but lunchtime is over. The kitchen crew is here to pick up the trays, and your next appointments are here."

Mary and Dan laughed and said simultaneously, "Coming, Mother." They had both told Martha jokingly the first time she alerted them to get on with their schedules that she was like a nudging mother. That reminded Martha of her niece, whom she had mothered and who now was grown and had her own children, who called Martha Nana.

Martha laughed at Mary and Dan's response and said, "Thank you." She knew they appreciated her keeping them on schedule, so she just shook her head and laughed after thanking them.

CHAPTER 29

SUSPICIOUS PATIENT

On Friday, May 25, after Mass, Mary went to the fourth-floor unit where she was primarily assigned and reviewed the patient roster for that unit and the other to which she was assigned for that day. When she received the report from her colleague that morning, he reported nothing special with any of the patients.

There were to be six discharges on the primary unit and seven on the other unit and no admissions on either unit, which was typical for a Friday. That meant there would be only fourteen patients on the primary unit and thirteen on the other unit, unless there was an unscheduled admission. All the patients to be discharged had been seen by their private doctors the previous evening and required only that she first make sure there was no reason to delay any of the discharges and then write prescriptions and the final notes in the charts.

Because none of the patients remaining in the hospital needed immediate attention, Mary saw the patients to be discharged first. When that was completed, she began seeing the other patients. Earlier, she had noted, a little to her surprise, that one of the patients on the fourth-floor unit was Ross

Stewart, the patient who had been in the same unit during the times of both Crenshaw's and Wilkes's deaths. He had been admitted late in the afternoon on the day prior to Wilkes's death.

She decided to leave him for last, and by the time she got to see him, it was about two o'clock, but she was in no hurry to leave. If necessary, she could break at 3:00 p.m. to sign off with her colleague who was scheduled for the 3:00 p.m. to 11:00 p.m. shift and then return to complete the interview with Stewart.

Mary first read the notes she had made on Stewart's first and second admissions, which she had retained in her office's locked file drawer. She read them over a brief lunch of salad and iced tea in her office. He had a well-regarded, small family-owned contracting service business, for which he and his two sons did essentially all the on-site work. He occasionally employed other workers he had previously tested for craftsmanship and honesty and used them for big jobs. His daughter, an astute accountant, ran the business office, overseeing all administrative issues. His wife, Melanie, was an excellent former nurse who had worked at St. Joseph's Hospital for many years and retired only recently.

His first admission to St. Joseph's the previous May had been for a large laceration he sustained on his leg while working. It had required many stitches and IV antibiotics for two days. The second admission had been for repair of bilateral inguinal hernias, probably the result of heavy lifting on the job over many years.

It was peculiar that he had requested a late-afternoon scheduled procedure to repair the hernias. That procedure was routinely performed in the morning in the surgical center in the medical office building adjacent to the hospital. Unlike the usual morning hernia operation, which allowed the patient to go home from the recovery room after several hours, his requested late-afternoon procedure had required an admission to the hospital that might not have been covered by his insurance. The possible extra didn't seem to matter to him, but Mary wondered what his accountant daughter thought about that decision. He had excellent health insurance, but that admission might not have been covered, because the procedure usually did not require hospitalization. Thus, it might have cost him the full amount of the hospital bill, though not the cost of the surgical procedure, which would have been billed by the medical office group.

Mary then read his current chart and found that like the first admission, this one was for another accidental injury. This time, he had fallen off a ladder and sustained several broken ribs and a large laceration on the leg opposite his previous injury. This wound also required significant cleansing, many stitches, and IV antibiotics. Obviously, construction work often was performed where a lot of dirt was involved.

When she went to his room, Stewart was sitting in a chair by the window, reading a murder mystery novel. She thought how ironic that was. He looked up and, smiling, said, "Hi, Dr. Defazio. It's really nice to see you, although I would have preferred it to be in other circumstances. My wife sends her best regards to you. Unfortunately, she can't be here until this evening."

Mary responded, "It's also nice to see you, Mr. Stewart, although I agree with you regarding the circumstances. Please give my best regards to Melanie if I am not here when she arrives. Tell her she is really missed. She is a terrific nurse, as I'm sure you know."

He said, "I sure do, and because she is such a good nurse, I can go home tomorrow, and she can give me the IV antibiotics over the weekend. And please do me the honor of calling me Ross."

Mary said, "OK, Ross, and you can call me Mary. But before I examine you, do you need anything for pain?"

"No to both. First, out of respect, I could never call you anything but Dr. Defazio. Also, no to my needing something for pain now. I tolerate pain well, and the medicine I've been getting helps a lot. So please go ahead and examine me."

Mary first listened to his chest and was happy that he was able to take deep breaths and that she could hear good air sounds and nothing abnormal in his lungs. As expected, because of his rib fractures, he winced with the deep breaths. Mary thought that was a sign that his macho sense prevented him from telling her he was in pain. She would remember to tell the evening nurses to make sure he had some pain medication so he would get a good night's sleep.

She then redressed his wound, which was nasty but would heal well with the help of antibiotics because he was a healthy man. She knew his wife would inject the antibiotics, put clean bandages on his wound, and make sure it was healing well. He had already received a tetanus shot during his first admission about a year previously, so he wouldn't need another.

At that point, Mary said, "Ross, I'd like to ask you some questions that have nothing to do with this hospital admission. Please know that you can simply refuse to answer any or all, but I'd like to ask because your responses might help me to make some important decisions."

His reaction was a surprised look. But he said, "Of course. You can ask me anything, and I'll try to help you in any way I can."

Mary said, "Thank you. First, I found that you were on this unit on two previous occasions when a patient on the unit died. I'd like to know if those experiences in any way interfered with your healing. I read your chart for both times, and nothing was recorded regarding your having expressed any concern related to the deaths. But that might not have been recorded, or you were too considerate to complain. Now I can ask you directly, and I want you to be perfectly honest with me."

Ross responded, "You are referring to the deaths of those two bastards Crenshaw and Wilkes." Then he caught himself and apologized profusely, saying, "Oh my, Dr. Defazio, I am so sorry for using that language with you. I apologize; please forgive me."

Mary smiled and said, "Ross, I have heard much worse words, so I take no offense at yours."

Ross replied, "It's just that those two"—he hesitated—"guys were so disgusting that many of us were happy they died. I should be ashamed to admit it, but I was actually ecstatic, especially that I was here to witness the process related to their deaths."

Mary asked why he felt so strongly, to which he responded, "My company had worked for both men, and they were crooks. I refused to cut the corners they wanted for their jobs, which might have caused injuries to others and just wasn't the quality for which we are proud and work hard to maintain. Because they disagreed with me, both refused to pay anything for the extensive and expensive jobs we had already done. I tried to sue them but got nowhere with either case because they had well-connected, dishonest lawyers. My lawyer told me to just forget it because both Crenshaw and Wilkes had been sued many times, but no one had ever won. Both had political connections that guaranteed their success with suits. They donated well to certain politicians' coffers to ensure their success with the law."

He sighed, shook his head, and said, "Dr. Defazio, they were very evil men, and the world is a better place without them."

Mary nodded and said, "I understand. Thank you. I appreciate your honesty. Now I have a question strictly related to my curiosity. On your second admission, when you came here for the hernia repairs, you requested a late-afternoon procedure, which required a hospital admission. That is quite unusual. Why did you do that?"

Ross said, "Well, we were on a job requiring my experienced expertise, and I wanted to get in at least a half day's work before being laid up for a few days. That way, I could show my sons how to handle the situation and complete the job, not requiring them to lose the days I could not work with them."

Mary smiled and said, "It seems your reputation for excellent workmanship is well deserved, which is no surprise to me." She then thanked Ross for his candid responses and left him after shaking his hand.

Later, on the way home, she thought about Ross's responses. Clearly, he had great animosity toward both Crenshaw and Wilkes, but he'd made no effort to mask those feelings. On the other hand, he also had had the opportunity to have easy access to both Crenshaw and Wilkes. She thought, *As a murder mystery reader, he probably knows how to eliminate someone and escape being identified by an autopsy. So now I should add another person to the suspect list who previously I only considered to be on the periphery. Dear God, how am I ever going to get this resolved?*

She went to sign out to her replacement, which she accomplished by 3:20 p.m. That allowed her a few hours to work on some administrative issues, so her weekend could be completely free of responsibilities. She looked forward to a weekend during which she could have time to relax and think more clearly.

CHAPTER 30

FRANK

Mary knew that her one month of taking a break from the Crenshaw and Wilkes investigation was about to come to an end. She soon needed to decide whether she should drop the investigation or pursue the issue further and even more intensely. After speaking with Ross Stewart the previous Friday, Mary wanted to discuss the Crenshaw and Wilkes situation with her brother, Frank, who was a judge at the city courthouse. Surely, because he knew her so well, he could provide some well-founded guidance to her.

After Mom told her it would be fine with her, Mary called Frank and asked if she might spend an hour or so discussing something important with him before he and his wife, Megan, had the usual Sunday dinner with Mom and Mary at the Davino home. He readily agreed after discussing it with Megan, who thought it would be a great time for her and Mom to prepare dinner together. She always enjoyed time alone with Mom, when they discussed all sorts of things, and Mom told her funny stories about Frank and Mary's childhood.

So on Sunday, May 27, Mary and Frank decided to walk in the woods near the house so they could have privacy. There was a bench about a hundred yards down the wooded path, where they could sit together and enjoy the peaceful surroundings.

As soon as they started the walk, Frank looked at Mary and, with a serious expression, asked her what was going on. He said, "Mary, you seemed to be extremely troubled a month or so back, and then whatever was bothering you appeared to have gone away, but now it looks like it's back. What is the problem, and how might I help?"

Mary said, "Frank, I have always looked up to you, and you have helped me more times than I could count. Now I need your expertise as a lawyer and judge, but I'd like this conversation to be kept between us, at least until it is resolved in my mind. Would that be OK with you?"

Frank smiled and said, "Of course. But what is so serious that you need a judge's opinion?"

Mary responded, "Well, when I assumed the position of chief medical officer, I wanted to become familiar with various aspects of St. Joseph's administrative issues. I also wanted to prepare for a Joint Commission on Hospitals inspection that will occur in a year or so. Therefore, I investigated all sorts of general data, such as total admissions, types of diagnoses, any untoward events, and hospital-based deaths. In all those investigations, the only disturbing thing I found was the occurrence of two unusual deaths about six months apart that were so similar it was uncanny.

"Both incidents involved wealthy, very influential men who had been St. Joseph's Hospital board members and friends of the bishop. Both generally were in good health but had been complaining of some nonspecific chest discomfort. They were admitted so their doctor could be assured that a heart procedure involving the placement of stents in the coronary arteries, which perfuse the heart, performed for both a few years previously was still functioning.

"They both died on the eleven o'clock to seven o'clock shift. The first one was discovered about seven o'clock on the morning after admission when an orderly came to deliver him to the radiology suite for a cardiac catheterization. The patient had been fine when a laboratory technician put in an IV around four thirty that morning. He apparently died between that time and probably between five and six, because he was not warm to the touch when the doctor arrived.

"The same private doctor who cared for both men ordered the second patient to be hooked up to a monitor with an alarm system in case a problem occurred with his heart, as had happened with the first patient. About a half hour after the laboratory technician set up the IV for this patient, again at about four thirty, the alarm went off. The doctor and nurses on duty in the hospital ran to his room immediately, but despite all attempts to resuscitate him, the patient died.

"Because there was no obvious reason for these deaths, the same medical examiner performed full autopsies on both patients. Incredibly, he could find no reason for either death, so the official recorded cause of death for both men is nonspecific cardiac arrest. I have never seen that diagnosis on a death certificate before. The medical examiner commented that in his many years of experience, he had never seen anything like two patients dying in such similar ways in the same hospital and so close together in time.

"This issue has been bothering me ever since I discovered it. I can't let it go, because something simply does not seem right. My colleagues disagree with me and advise me to let it go. However, it makes no medical sense to me, but I'm not sure what to do next. So, my dear big brother, what do you think, and what would you do?"

When Mary was finished, Frank said, "Mary, you are so honest and sensitive, always wanting to do the right thing, no matter the consequences. Before I respond to your questions, I need to tell you something important that is pertinent to the way you are responding to this situation. I've never told you, but you once taught me something very important for which I will be forever grateful."

Mary said, "What are you talking about? I don't think I've ever taught you anything. Quite the opposite is true."

At that point, they had reached the bench, and they sat down before Frank continued.

"OK, here's the story. Remember the day when you broke Mom's treasured vase given to her by her grandmother, who'd brought it from Italy when she came to America via Ellis Island?"

Mary laughed. "Are you kidding? How could I ever forget that day? I was mortified, and it's embarrassing to think about it even now."

Frank said, "Well, you had just turned nine years old and were dancing in the living room while listening to your new small portable radio, which you'd received as a gift for your recent birthday. It was raining outside, and all games had been canceled, so we stayed at home. Mom had gone to a widowed neighbor's house to deliver some of what she'd prepared for dinner. I warned you that she would be angry if she found us frolicking in the living room. We were always supposed to walk carefully in there because of the treasures she had on the credenza.

"You were being a brat, wouldn't listen to me, and kept dancing. Then, suddenly, you twirled to the music and knocked her treasured Italian vase off the credenza, and it broke in half. Fortunately, it landed on the thick rug, so it broke neatly in half. You looked terrified, and I told you we should leave it on the floor and go outside on the back porch to play chess before Mom returned. Maybe she'd think it had fallen somehow on its own.

"About five minutes after Mom returned, we heard a loud 'Oh my God!' and we knew she had found the vase. Then we heard, 'Frankie and Mary Elizabeth Davino, get in here—now.' Knowing it was not going to be pleasant, we trooped into the living room, where she was standing with her hands on her hips—always a bad sign. She angrily asked, 'Who broke this vase?'

"Instead of saying nothing, like I did, you confessed and told her you had done it. She said, 'What? How did you do that?' and you admitted that you had been dancing in the room.

"Mom just glared at you and said, 'Didn't I tell you never to play in here? You have the large recreation room downstairs, a big garden, and the whole neighborhood to play in.' Then, as we all knew was coming, she took you by the arm, sat on a chair, put you over her lap, and spanked you. Afterward, she said, 'I should also ground you for a month, but I won't because you told the truth. But go to your room right now, and don't dare come down until I call you.'

"Mom was the disciplinarian but rarely spanked us. It was always a memorable experience. Usually, it took only a look to get us to behave. Unfortunately, the warning look had not been possible in that situation.

"About ten minutes after you ran up the stairs, Dad came home and found Mom sitting with the broken vase at the kitchen table, sobbing. I didn't know what to do because I had never seen her cry except during a sad movie on TV. Dad hugged her and asked why she was so upset. She told him what had happened with the vase and said she had spanked you. She seemed to be upset about both.

"He looked at the vase, smiled, and told her he could fix it. He also said you had certainly deserved the spanking. That seemed to mollify her, and she stopped crying.

"Dad was a quiet, peaceful man who looked for the best

in people and seemed to always find a way to see something positive in even bad situations. He told me to get some tissues for Mom and to stay with her until he returned. He then went downstairs to his workshop. Mom smiled, told me she didn't need tissues, and went into the bathroom on the first floor to wash her face. When she came out, she asked me to help her set the table for dinner. Dad came back a short time later, smiling, and told her the vase was all fixed and would look as good as new in the morning, as soon as the special glue solidified. That made Mom very happy, and she hugged and kissed him.

"Then he asked for dinner because he was hungry. We quickly finished setting the table, and Mom told me to go upstairs to get you while she was finishing what she had cooked for dinner. When I entered your room despite your telling me to go away, you were sitting on the bed, still sniffling. I told you that Dad had fixed the vase and that Mom wanted you to come to dinner, so I said to blow your nose, wash your face, and come downstairs. Which, thankfully, you did.

"When you came downstairs, I saw Dad narrow his eyes and shake his head at you, but then he smiled and winked. And that made you smile a little. You hugged Mom and told her you were very sorry, and she hugged you back. We ate dinner and never mentioned this again.

"Before we went to bed that night, I went to your room and asked you why you had admitted to breaking the vase. You knew I would never have squealed. You told me that if you hadn't responded to her question and admitted to doing something wrong, it would have been a lie. It also might have allowed someone else, probably me, to be blamed. You told me that lies are stealing the truth, which is very bad. And if someone else were blamed, it would be the same as bearing false witness. So not admitting guilt would have been breaking the

Seventh and Eighth Commandments: 'Thou shalt not steal' and 'Thou shalt not bear false witness.'

"At the early age of nine, the nuns had certainly done a good job with you. Even though you only lasted a short time as one of them, you've obviously never forgotten what you were taught.

"I learned two valuable lessons that day that I've tried to live up to all my life. First, Dad taught me how to gently comfort a distressed woman and a little girl, and second, you taught me never to lie."

Mary responded to Frank's story by nodding and smiling. She felt happy that Frank thought she had done the right thing so much so that he wanted to emulate it, and she told him so.

Frank continued. "Now I will respond to your request for advice, because I think you have found yourself in a situation very similar to that day long ago. For some reason, you think it is your duty, considering the deaths of two patients, to make sure everything that should be investigated is indeed investigated. You want to be sure the truth is not hidden, so justice can be done. Am I correct?"

Mary said, "Absolutely. And at this point, I'm not sure the situation has been fully vetted."

Frank said, "OK, now I need to ask some questions. First, have you any evidence that something adverse or someone might have contributed to these deaths?"

Mary responded, "Well, the same doctor signed both death certificates. He was on duty during the night when the first death occurred, but no one alerted him or anyone else during the night that the patient was in distress. There was nothing that could be done when the alarm came from the orderly. That patient was pronounced dead after the seven o'clock day shift started, but the doctor in question had not yet signed out, so he was officially still on duty, and therefore, he completed the paperwork.

"For the second death, during the night, the alarm went off on a monitor to which the patient was attached as a precaution. According to the same doctor and nurse who had been on duty for the first patient, everything possible was done to attempt to resuscitate the second patient, but to no avail.

"There also was another doctor in the hospital both nights. She was called in to the ER and discharged the patients from there on both nights with plenty of time to either go home or sleep in the hospital until she reported for duty on the seven o'clock to three o'clock shift, which is normally what happens. However, she and her husband are avid campers and have equipped their van so that they can sleep in it overnight no matter the weather. And that's what she supposedly did, but no one checked to be sure she really did sleep there and did not enter the hospital units.

"Both of these doctors are wonderful people, but they expressed great animosity toward the patients who died. They both told me the world is much better off without them.

"There also was an incident involving both patients' attempted molestation of a Muslim nurse who works at St. Joseph's. Her fiancé, her brother, and the brother's closest friend are doctors who see patients and sometimes admit patients to St. Joseph's. They might have done great harm to these terrible men were it not for the intervention of the bishop. They agreed to keep the incident a secret for the sake of the nurse and her family's reputation but warned that if these men attempted anything like that with any Muslim woman, they would be seriously injured.

"There also was a patient who, for very good reasons, had great animosity toward the two men. He was admitted to the same unit as the patients when they died.

"Thus far, I have done nothing with this information except discuss it with Dan."

Frank said, "OK. Now, what makes you question the medical examiner's record?"

Mary said, "I don't question it at all. I just find it so unusual that the diagnosis for both cases was unspecified cardiac arrest, a very unusual diagnosis on a death certificate. The medical examiner also commented that he'd never seen anything like that before."

Frank said, "Mary, you have told me that being a doctor is like being a medical detective or judge. You are presented with a case that is a patient with a medical issue, rather than a legal problem. You then gather information and make a diagnosis, rather than a legal decision regarding guilt. It seems to me you've done all possible investigation for this situation. So what else might you do now to reassure yourself that all t's have been crossed and all i's have been dotted?"

Mary said, "I want to be sure I haven't missed something, so I guess I'd have to report my concerns to the bishop or, more appropriately, to the police so they can legally investigate."

Frank sat back, shook his head, sighed deeply, and said, "Mary, if you told the bishop, you know he would tell you that you are overreacting, and he might think less of you.

"As for calling in the law, the consequences are much graver. First for all the involved doctors, for the suspect patient, and for the Muslim nurse and her family and the brother's friend. It would damage their reputations, no matter what is found. Second, the hospital's reputation also would be damaged no matter the final finding. Third, the consequences for you in this case would not be a spanking like when you were nine years old but ruined friendships with the doctors, the suspect patient, and the Muslim nurse involved and probably also with your other doctor and nurse colleagues.

"Knowing you, if I thought there was anything amiss, I would certainly advise you to pursue further legal investigation, no matter the consequences. But that is simply not the case. Nothing further should or could be done.

"Finally, I must admit that I know you are referring to the deaths of Matthew Crenshaw and Calvin Wilkes, two well-known, notoriously evil people."

Mary sat up straight and, in exasperation, said, "Frank, why does it matter that they were terrible men? They were God's creations and therefore worthy of equity—that is, being treated the same as anyone else. Remember that Jesus said, 'Render to Caesar that which is Caesar's and to God that which is God's.' Caesar, in this case, is the United States, and our laws should be rendered equally to all. I know that is not always the case, but that doesn't make it right."

Frank sighed and said, "Mary, you are a truly wonderful woman, but I think you are being unreasonable in this case, especially with yourself. There is nothing further to investigate legally or otherwise. You've done all the investigation possible. You'll just have to live with the uncertainty of the situation. Surely you have encountered other situations of uncertainty like this in medicine."

Mary responded, "I guess you are right. But I know that sometimes the law gets in the way of truth and justice. I was concerned that might or might not be the case with this situation. But you have made me feel more confident that I have done as much as I possibly could.

"Frank, I am so grateful that you are my brother and that I can always count on you for very good advice. I guess I'll just have to live with my uncertainty. Now, let's get back before Mom and Megan come looking for us."

On the walk back, they both were silent and in deep thought. When they reached the street, Mary took Frank's hand as they crossed, as she had when they were growing up. She looked at him and said, "Big brother, I love you."

Frank smiled and responded, "I love you too, little sister."

CHAPTER 31

MARY AND DAN'S FOURTH SPECIAL MEETING

▷ MAY 29, 2018

Because their previous meeting had occurred only three and not the promised four weeks into the time Mary was to forget about the Crenshaw and Wilkes issue, Martha had set up another meeting with Dan for Tuesday, May 29.

Dan had told Mary he was looking forward to discussing the Crenshaw and Wilkes situation again after she'd had time, as he'd put it, to rest her soul. Since her conversation with Frank the previous Sunday, Mary had spent a great deal of time thinking about what she would say to Dan that day.

This time, they met in Dan's office with the same incredible lunch waiting for them. Sensing it was to be an important meeting, Martha had wisely scheduled them to meet for an hour and a half instead of the usual hour. Of course, she had advised Dan and Mary of the extended meeting only that morning, which had made both laugh loudly. It was a typical Martha maneuver.

As they settled in and began munching, Dan looked at Mary and said, "Well?"

Mary told him she had discussed the Crenshaw and Wilkes situation with Frank. Dan wanted to know about that discussion in as much detail as Mary felt comfortable relating. He said that would help him understand whatever decision she made.

Mary said, "Dan, I am comfortable telling you everything. So here goes. I first described the situation to Frank, omitting the names of the doctors, nurses, and patients involved. Of course, Frank told me later into the discussion that he was aware that Crenshaw and Wilkes were the patients whose deaths were involved, because of the general knowledge in the community about what happened with them. He understood that I was concerned that truth and justice must be served no matter who the victims or the culprits were or the consequences that might well ensue. He reminded me of a situation that happened when I had just turned nine years old that he believes was almost the same as where I now find myself."

Dan said, "Now you've really made me curious. Nine years old? What happened?"

Mary blushed and replied, "Well, this is embarrassing to admit, but because I've told you that I am comfortable telling you everything, here goes. I was being a real brat, dancing to music on my new radio in our living room despite our having been told that we must never play there, because of the treasures in that room. Frank warned me to stop, but I wouldn't listen and, consequently, accidentally broke the vase Mom treasured. It had been given to her by her grandmother, who had brought it with her from Italy when she came to Ellis Island. You might remember seeing it when you visit our house."

Dan said, "I know that vase. I saw it intact, sitting on the credenza in your living room. It is very beautiful, and I admire it every time I come for dinner. However, I did notice that the first time I saw it, a certain look passed between you and your mom, and you blushed. But I decided not to pursue it back then."

Mary responded, "Dad fixed the vase so nicely you cannot tell that it was once broken in half."

Dan nodded and said, "I'm sorry to have interrupted. Please continue."

Mary continued. "Well, Mom knew either Frank or I had broken it, and when she angrily asked us who had done it, I admitted that it had been me. As we all knew would happen, as expected, she spanked me—which, thankfully, was a rare event—and sent me to my room. However, she also said she wasn't also going to ground me for a month, because I had told the truth.

"Later, Frank asked me why I had admitted to breaking the vase instead of keeping quiet, as he had, especially because I knew he would never squeal on me. I told him that keeping quiet was lying, and lying is stealing the truth. In addition, because I knew that he or someone else probably would have been blamed, my not admitting the truth would have been the same as bearing false witness.

"Therefore, I could have broken two commandments, the seventh and eighth: 'Thou shall not steal' and 'Thou shall not bear false witness.' Admitting my guilt was the truth, and justice was the spanking. I guess the situation now is somewhat similar."

Dan shook his head and said, "Mary, that was incredible thinking coming from a nine-year-old. In fact, it's pretty sophisticated coming from an adult. I don't see it quite that way, but if that's what you believed, you did the right thing. But how does that relate to the Crenshaw and Wilkes situation?"

Mary said, "Well, Frank understands that I am seeking truth and justice for these men. I must be sure that a thorough investigation reveals the truth so justice can be done. As a judge, he asked me questions about the situation and what I had done to find the truth.

"He asked me what I thought I would do next if I am not satisfied that everything possible was done to find the truth. I told him I would probably report the situation to the bishop or, better, to the police. He pointed out the dire consequences of either of those options to the nurses, patients, and doctors possibly involved; to St. Joseph's Hospital; and to me personally. However, if the investigation for the truth was not thorough, he could see my going ahead with those options, because he knew I would not rest otherwise.

"But as a judge, he concluded that everything possible to find the truth had been done, and nothing further was needed or even possible. He said I'd just have to live with the uncertainty, as I probably had to with some medical situations."

At first, Dan had been anxious about what Mary was about to tell him. However, now feeling that things were probably falling into the proper place, he sat back and was silent in thought for a while and then said, "So where are you now?"

Mary thought for a minute or so and took a sip of her iced tea. She then said, "I guess I must live with the uncertainty. However, Dan, it still doesn't feel right. As a doctor, I know that something is amiss, but I'm just not smart enough figure it out. But at this point, what else can I do?"

Dan felt greatly relieved at that news. He reached out and, taking her hand in both of his, said, "Mary, you are very smart and have done everything you could to find the truth. The situation is just one of those unsolvable mysteries that are part of life."

Mary laughed and said, "Well, if this is another example of the Great Comedian playing with me, I hope he is having a good time."

Taking his hands back from her, Dan said, "So now you

are responding to God as if he were right here. That's a very good sign that maybe your doubts are dissipating. What do you think?"

Mary narrowed her eyes, shook her head, and said, "I guess if I had no doubts, I'd not argue with him."

Dan laughed. "So why not argue with him? Or better, why not have an authentic dialogue with him? Talk and listen so you might engage in the deep levels of your thoughts. That's what is called prayer. See where that might take you and your doubts."

Mary sighed and said, "Even if I am frustrated and miffed at him?"

Dan responded, "Especially so. God already knows how you feel. I think he's just waiting for you to admit it."

Mary shook her head but said, "OK. I'll try that."

At that point, Martha knocked on the door and said, "OK, you two, time's up. Now, get back to work."

And that was what they did.

On the way home that afternoon, Mary remembered the lesson from her favorite mantra from Psalm 46:10: "Be still, and know that I am God."

CHAPTER 32

DR. CLARISSA WILKES DUNNING

Mary spent the rest of that week and the weekend trying to work effectively while not projecting her inner turmoil, which persisted despite her conversations with Dan and Frank. She succeeded at the hospital by keeping busy, and Mom said nothing of concern at home, so she was relieved at her apparent success in hiding her inner feelings.

The only person with whom she routinely shared her feelings about the situation was Dan, who was her anchor. At night and other times when she was alone, following Dan's advice, she spoke with God in a manner she had never dared before. Her dialogue consisted of first asking and then pleading with him to help her understand why he had burdened her with this problem. Why couldn't she simply forget about the Crenshaw and Wilkes situation and get on with her life, trying to help people? That was what people she trusted and even one of God's chosen priests had advised her to do. Some nights, she became teary-eyed with frustration. She was once again sleeping badly. She would fall asleep while having the dialogue with God and would awaken frequently, taking up the dialogue where she had left off.

On weekdays, as was their custom when Mary returned from work, she and Mom ate dinner, cleaned up, said the rosary, and watched the news while Mary worked out on the exercise equipment in front of the TV, and then both retired to their rooms to read. Both were avid readers, and Dad had built bookshelves that covered a full wall in Mary's room, in front of which was the desk where she worked on her computer.

The books they read were quite different. Mom preferred crime novels, murder mysteries, and biographies of famous people, especially women. Mary could not share her computer because it contained confidential hospital and patient information, so she wanted to buy Mom her own computer. Mom refused, but she accepted and liked her iPad and iPhone, each of which she used to communicate with her family and friends.

Despite their having Wi-Fi access, Mary doubted Mom used the internet often, if at all, and she knew Mom never read Kindle books online. She and Mom both preferred the feel and fragrance of printed books. There was nothing as pleasant as curling up in bed with a book, especially in the winter. She couldn't imagine doing that with a computer or iPad.

Mary preferred books on philosophy and religion and biographies of famous philosophers, saints, and the like. She kept only a few medical books in her room. When she wanted to know more about a specific medical problem or illness while at home, she read what she needed online, having access to the same internet as was in the hospital.

At work in the hospital, she mostly used her office computer for email and to read journal articles and other medical information via the hospital's internet access. The doctors' on-call room had two computers and a few dozen medical textbooks. They nicely met the needs of all the medical staff.

Because of the anxiety she was feeling, Mary had taken down from her bookshelf Thomas Mann's *Magic Mountain*, Kierkegaard's *Fear and Trembling*, Paul Tillich's *The Courage to Be*, and the complete short stories of Flannery O'Connor and put them by her bedside, near her Bible. She wanted to read parts of them again, hoping to find answers or at least some solace in them.

She remembered that years ago, she'd found meaning in a few lines she had read by Tillich. He had written that having an awareness of the ambiguity of your highest achievements as well as your deepest failures was a definite symptom of maturity. She smiled wryly, thinking that at least she could feel mature. *Such irony!*

She spent the weekend with Mom, as usual, going to Mass, going to the hairdresser, doing grocery and other shopping, and just spending time talking to her on Saturday. On Sunday, she attended morning Mass with Mom, Frank, and Megan and dinner with all of them after she had helped Mom cook. Then they all helped with cleaning up after they finished eating. She was grateful because spending time with her family was always uplifting.

By Monday morning, June 4, she was beginning to feel some relief and even had slept well the previous night. Perhaps God was responding in his own way. At the hospital, after she signed in, she served at Mass with Dan and told him about the past few days. He was delighted that she finally was finding some peace with God.

After Mass, she collected her messages and mail, went to the cafeteria for her and Martha's coffee and muffins, and returned to her office before visiting the units where she was assigned for that week. Martha thanked her for the goodies, including the food from Mom's Sunday dinner, as she always did on Monday mornings.

None of the patients who were to be admitted had yet arrived, and the patients to be discharged had been taken care of by their private doctors. The remaining few patients could easily wait.

She had received a few letters, which she read in her office while eating the muffin and drinking coffee. The only letter of any consequence was, according to the return address, from a doctor in upstate New York. Her curiosity was piqued, so she opened it to read the message.

> May 31, 2018
>
> Dear Dr. Defazio,
>
> Please excuse my impertinence, but I need some information, and you are the only person I have found who might be able to help me. I am Clarissa Wilkes Dunning, a family doctor, and I practice in a small town in upstate New York. I have lived here essentially all my life, except when I was in medical school and residency.
>
> My birth father was Calvin Wilkes—

Mary's gut wrenched at this information, but after taking a deep breath, she kept reading.

> My mother divorced him after twenty-seven months of marriage; I was only thirteen months old at the time. Therefore, I have no memory of him, nor do I want any.
>
> My mother immediately moved to where we now reside. She has told me very little

about my birth father, but I know he must have been a terrible person, because my mother, a strong Roman Catholic, was able to get a dispensation for the divorce from our bishop because of the circumstances leading to the divorce. She supposedly could have easily received an annulment but declined because of me.

Hence, I carry his name but not for much longer. My wonderful real father, who officially adopted me, is Alfred Dunning. After I marry, I will keep his name and drop the Wilkes, because I have more than enough names already.

I will be married in a few weeks to another doctor, whom I met during residency training. And that gets me to the reason I need your help. We plan to have a family and would like to know any genetic issues that might need to be addressed for our children. My fiancé knows about his family history, and I know my mother's family history, but we don't know about my birth father's history. I couldn't find the name of his primary care doctor and know only that he died in St. Joseph's Hospital, where you are the chief medical officer. Might it be possible for you to provide that information? If you can and would, I would be very grateful to you.

Sincerely yours,
Clarissa Wilkes Dunning, MD

Mary was stunned by what she had just read. She wanted to help her colleague, but she first needed to check with Jim Allen, who had been Wilkes's doctor; the bishop; and the hospital's lawyer, because patient information normally was given only to those the patient allowed or, in the case of death, the patient's legal agent, the one with power of attorney. Obviously, Dr. Dunning did not have that power of attorney.

As soon as she completed her patient responsibilities, Mary planned to call Jim Allen to alert him and then turn the letter over to him for response. If, as she suspected, he did not want to respond to the letter himself but wanted her to respond, she needed to know if there were any pertinent genetic issues Dr. Dunning needed to know about. As soon as Mary heard from him, she would then call the bishop and the hospital's lawyer to alert them.

After she took care of her patients' needs up to that point, instead of eating lunch, Mary called Jim Allen, and she was happy he came to the phone immediately. After she read the letter to him, she asked if he wanted to respond. He immediately said, "No way. I want to remain anonymous, if you'd be so kind to allow me that favor and handle it. Of course, I will get involved if needed. As far as any genetic issues, there are none.

"I cared for Wilkes for more than thirty years, including his mild myocardial infarction and stent placement almost three years ago. That condition was the result of his horrible diet, essentially no exercise, and heavy smoking. To his credit, after the stent placement, he stopped smoking, changed his diet, and joined a health club, which he attended twice a week. As a result, he lost twenty-five pounds, and I believe that's why his coronary arteries and the stent were patent at autopsy."

Mary thanked him and agreed to respond to the letter as

soon as she received guidance from the bishop and the hospital lawyer. She would keep Jim posted. He thanked her profusely.

She then called the bishop and the hospital lawyer and explained the situation to them, including her conversation with Wilkes's doctor. Both asked her to fax them a copy of the letter from Wilkes's daughter and said they would get back to her. She asked Martha to send the faxes, allowing her to read the letter, knowing she would keep it confidential.

Mary returned to the patients on her assigned units and waited for the responses from the bishop and lawyer to guide her on what to do. Those responses didn't come until the next day, so that night, she didn't sleep well. She considered that the letter might have been more than it seemed on the surface.

When she thought the letter might have been a prelude to a legal suit or worse, she worried that she was becoming paranoid. Thankfully, the legal aspect was now in the hands of others. However, the letter was a reminder that the Crenshaw and Wilkes issue was somehow still in play. Exasperated, she said out loud, "God, why are you not releasing me from this never-ending saga?"

The next morning, after another sleep-deprived night, she told Dan about the letter and promised to let him know what the bishop and lawyer advised. Later that morning, when she was in her office, working on some administrative paperwork, with her door open as usual, Martha came into her office and told her the bishop had called and asked if he and the lawyer might meet with her in the bishop's hospital office in an hour. She readily agreed to the meeting, hoping it would provide the guidance she needed in responding to the letter.

An hour later, she went to the office next door and met with the two gentlemen. They greeted her with big smiles and handshakes, which immediately relaxed her. After the bishop introduced her to the lawyer, all three sat at the small table in the office corner, where Martha had placed coffee and tea that she had ordered.

The bishop, a tea drinker, began with a laugh and said, "Mary, I'll bet you never thought you'd have issues like this when you agreed to be the CMO."

Mary smiled and responded, "Well, I must admit I've found the medical part to be a breeze compared to the administrative issues. But so far so good."

The bishop said, "No, not 'So far so good,' but 'So far so great.' I am very happy you have taken on this responsibility. I can't imagine anyone better to handle these tricky situations."

Mary thought to herself that he might not have thought so if he had known what she was going through with the Crenshaw and Wilkes situation. But she smiled and responded, "Thank you very much, Your Excellency. You are very kind."

The bishop then said, "Well, after discussing this issue at length, because I am only too aware of the situation between Mr. Wilkes and his former wife, who is a wonderful woman, we see no harm in responding to Dr. Dunning's request. However, it must include only that there are no genetic issues of which we are aware, and you can tell her that he died of cardiac arrest, providing a summary of why he had a bad heart. We need to read the letter before you send it, to protect you and the hospital. We want no harm to come to anyone in this situation."

Mary was relieved and said she would draft the letter, fax it to them, and make any suggested changes they had before she sent it. They said they did not need to be copied on the letter, but they would send her a note confirming they were involved in the letter. Again, this would protect her. Clearly, she was working with men who cared about people in general and her specifically, and that made her feel secure.

Before she went home that evening, she drafted a handwritten response. She printed the letter because her handwriting was so terrible, and she found it easier to think while writing and not typing. Further, there would be no paper trail on her computer of the exchange. She then faxed the letter to the two men from the machine in her office. For confidential purposes, she did not want to use the hospital email system. She hoped the bishop and lawyer would get back to her soon so she could finish with it on her next administrative day at the latest.

That night, she once again felt conflicted and greatly agitated. For several hours, she continued reading the books she'd put by her bedside and continued her dialogue with God, having been stimulated by the contents of the letter from Wilkes's daughter. *My God, why do you continue to tease and agitate me with this issue? What do you expect of me?* She didn't sleep well for the second night in a row.

The next morning, she went to the nurses' station in the primary unit where she was assigned and signed in with her colleague. Fortunately, there were no pressing problems with patients or anything needing her immediate attention. She then went to Mass, after which she updated Dan and then went back to the units to take care of the patients' needs.

At lunchtime, she returned to her office, where Martha handed her a typed letter that had been hand delivered to the office earlier that morning. She was pleased to note there was only an added comma to the letter she had written.

An attached note advised her to call the bishop's office with her approval, and subsequently, the letter would be typed formally on St. Joseph's Hospital stationery and delivered back for her signature. The letter would be mailed from the legal office, and a copy would be kept on file there.

The letter to be mailed read,

June 6, 2018

Dear Dr. Wilkes Dunning,

I am writing in response to your recent letter requesting medical information about your birth father, Mr. Calvin Wilkes, which might affect your children. I can happily report that based on information we have about him over the thirty years he was followed here, there is no need to worry about any specific genetic problem Mr. Wilkes might have passed on to your children. He died of cardiac arrest, and his heart problems most likely resulted from a history of poor diet, lack of exercise, and heavy smoking.

I hope this information relieves you of any worries you might have had in this regard. I wish you and your family long, healthy lives.

Yours sincerely,
Mary Davino Defazio, MD
Chief Medical Officer
St. Joseph's Hospital

With that task out of the way, Mary returned to her routine clinical work scheduled for that day, including informing Dan and Wilkes's doctor, Jim Allen, of the resolution. Dr. Allen was greatly relieved and thanked her again, and Dan thought the letter was a good way to resolve the issue.

When she returned home late that afternoon, she once again felt the dread of verbally battling with God. The weekend's relief had disappeared. How was she ever to get this problem resolved?

CHAPTER 33

MOM MEETS WITH DAN

▷ JUNE 6, 2018

At ten o'clock on Wednesday morning, Mary was on the fourth-floor unit, caring for patients. During that time, the phone rang in the office on Martha's line, and when Martha answered, she heard, "Martha, this is Beth, Mary's mom. I hope she is not there, because I need to speak with Father Dan, but I don't want her to know."

Martha responded, "Beth, are you OK? Is everything all right?"

Beth said, "I'm fine, Martha, but I really need to speak with Father Dan about Mary. I am very concerned about the way she's been acting lately. But please don't tell her I called. That would really get her upset."

Martha said, "Of course I won't tell her. You have called Father Dan, not her, so there's no need for me to inform her of your call. Father is now with the family of a patient who is very sick. He's been gone for some time, so I expect he'll be back soon. I will have him call you as soon as he returns to the office. Or do you want me to call him now?"

Beth immediately said, "Oh no. It's no emergency. Any time today would be fine."

Martha thought about what Beth had said and considered telling her that she also had noticed Mary's preoccupation with something. However, she decided against saying anything, because she didn't want to add to Beth's worry. So she said only, "I'm sure Father will call you as soon as he gets here. Please know that if there's anything I can do to help, all you have to do is ask. You know how fond I am of Mary."

Beth responded, "I know that, Martha, and I appreciate it very much. It might only be my overreacting to something that's not very serious."

They chatted a bit more about general things but nothing important and then said goodbye and hung up.

About a half hour later, Father Dan returned to the office, and Martha gave him the message immediately, saying only that Beth wanted to speak with him, had provided no reason, and didn't want Dr. D to know. Martha asked if she should call Beth for Dan. He seemed concerned and told her that was a good idea. He then went into his office and closed the door.

As soon as Beth answered the phone, Martha told her she was going to connect her to Father Dan. She did so and hung up so they could speak in private. As much as she would have liked to listen to that conversation, she would never have done so. That would have been a severe breach of confidentiality and morally wrong. She would wait to see if Father Dan informed her of his discussion with Beth.

When Dan picked up his phone, he said, "Beth, what is the matter? Is everything OK? Are you ill?"

Beth responded, "Father Dan, I am fine, but I am very concerned about Mary. I've been worried about her for a while, but she seemed happy over the past month or so. She seemed to have resolved whatever was bothering her. Then this past Monday, it started all over again. I wanted to discuss it with you, but I couldn't when you were here, because she was also present. I know you are very busy, but do you have time for us to discuss my concern on the phone?"

Dan knew she was at home and, having nothing pending at the hospital, asked if he could come there now so they could discuss her concern in person.

Beth said, "Oh, Father Dan, that would be wonderful."

He said he would be there in twenty minutes or so and immediately went to his car.

When he arrived, Beth was at the door, waiting for him. They went to the back porch and sat in the chairs at the table, which had been set with lemonade and homemade cookies. Taking a cookie, Dan smiled and said, "Beth, you know the way to every man's heart is through his stomach. Now, tell me what you are concerned about."

Beth responded, "Well, for a week or so in April, I was concerned about Mary because she seemed preoccupied about something, but then she seemed to be fine for about a month. Then, for the past week or so, it started all over again but only worse. I know she is not physically ill—after all, she is a doctor—but I am her mother and know something is wrong. A mother always knows when her child, no matter how old, is ill either physically or emotionally.

"She is not sleeping, and well, she's just not the same. Father Dan, Mary is the kindest and most resilient person I know. When her Tom died, I thought she'd never get over her grief, but she pulled herself together, and look at what she's accomplished. After Tom died, she moved in with her dad and me while she was working and going to school to get the courses she needed to apply to medical school. It was wonderful to see her fight through her grief and become happy again. When she went to medical school, we were so proud of her, and she called us several times a week to keep in touch. She was so happy then and during her residency.

"During her last few months of residency, she informed us that she had secured a position at St. Joseph's Hospital, to the delight of all of us. At our request, she planned to move back into this house with us.

"Then my husband, Frank, was killed in a freak accident. He had just finished repairing a leak in the roof of the convent, where he worked for the nuns. He stepped onto the ladder, which slipped, and he fell and hit his head on the stone walkway. He died instantly. He was only sixty-five years old, and I was sixty.

"We had been married forty-one wonderful years. We both grew up in the city and met at a cathedral's dance for young people. We married six months after our first date and lived in a city apartment until we could afford a house. We were able to buy this house because it needed a lot of work and was available at a low price. You see what my Frank did to make it a beautiful home.

"He was so handy he even built a small greenhouse for the nuns at their convent. He planted four rosebushes, and the nuns planted other flowers to ensure they would have fresh flowers of some variety year-round for their chapel.

"After he died, I was very depressed. However, despite her grief at losing her father, whom she loved very much, Mary became my solace. I'm not sure I could have made it back to happiness if not for her.

"Of course, Frankie and Megan were also wonderful, but they had two children to care for, and they were relieved Mary would be here to take care of me. Now she insists I take care of her more than she takes care of me, but she's wrong.

"She refuses to allow me to pay for anything, despite my having nice savings and checking accounts and my Frank's pension and Social Security. He also had a substantial life insurance policy, which Frankie invested for me. The nuns, who were so sad at Frank's death, did not have insurance. They wanted to pay us something for the accident, but of course, we would never allow that.

"After my Frank's death, when I wanted to sell our car because I didn't need it anymore, Mary insisted on buying it from me. She refused to just take it.

"Now she is so concerned for me that she wants to buy me a car in case of an emergency, but I refuse. At her request, I never gave up my driver's license, and she insists I drive her car every week or so to keep in practice. And my name is also on her car insurance. I have always driven a manual-shift car, so driving Mary's automatic car is like sitting in a living room chair. No big deal, but it makes her happy, so I drive her car when she wants me to.

"I don't need a car. My friend Sarah picks me up every day that we go to the soup kitchen together. Our house is on her way. She refuses to take gas money, so instead, I give her whatever dessert I make on Sunday. She loves desserts.

"But I have digressed. I'm so sorry, Father Dan. But it is so easy to talk to you, and I wanted you to know us a little better."

Dan smiled and said, "Beth, I am very happy you have told me all this. I often wondered about your husband, Frank, but didn't want to ask, for fear of getting into something better left alone. Thank you for allowing me to know all this."

Beth replied, "Let me get back to the reason I asked you for help. Mary has gone through some interesting ways to hide her anxiety from me. She is a great joke teller and continues to tell me a joke or show me a funny cartoon on her computer almost every day. But it's just not the same. Her heart is not in it.

"She also has snapped at me several times for no apparent reason and then apologized. That is simply not like her. Oh, we've always argued about things, but that's normal. These current arguments are different because they come out of nowhere.

I've even heard her swearing when she thought I couldn't hear. She even muttered the f-word one day. Ordinarily, I would never let her get away with that, but I pretended not to have heard it. I knew she realized how terrible it was to say it in my presence when she quickly looked at me. She was obviously relieved that I apparently hadn't heard it. There'd been no need for my admonishment. However, I never remember her swearing before, no matter how provoked. I know something is wrong.

"Please don't misunderstand me. Mary's recent mood in no way changed her basic principles. She has always sought the truth and would never lie. Even as a child, she wouldn't lie, no matter the consequences to her. She won't tolerate treating anyone unfairly or differently because of who or what they are. She says we all are God's creations and deserve to be treated the same.

"But now she is struggling, probably because of her beliefs and kindness. I don't want to watch her struggle, but it's something I don't understand. Is there anything I can do to help her?"

Dan sat quietly for a while, nodding, and then said, "Beth, you have her pegged perfectly, which is no surprise because you are her mother. Mary is working on an issue that has come up at the hospital. She and I have been discussing it, and I know she has also discussed it with her brother.

"Everyone thinks the issue has been resolved, but Mary feels it is her responsibility to be absolutely certain that everything necessary has been done to be fair to all involved. Because of her integrity and intense sense of fairness, she still is not certain the issue is completed. This is something only she can resolve for herself. We can only help her to deal with the struggle she is enduring.

"I will continue to work with her on this from my vantage

point. So please continue to bear with her for a while longer. As you said, she is very resilient and is in no danger either physically or emotionally. The issue will be resolved in due time. In the meantime, just continue to be her mother as only you know how. You are her rock at home, and that's very important."

As Dan left, Beth hugged him and thanked him profusely, handing him a bag of her cookies, which made him laugh and say, "Does anyone escape a visit to your home without leaving with a bag of goodies?"

Beth laughed, feeling proud at the accolade.

On the drive back to the hospital, Dan thought about what his next steps should be to get the matter resolved. His planned next step was sure to force Mary into a situation that would take a great deal of fortitude on her part to reach a conclusion.

He silently prayed he would be able to help her get through the grievous situation.

PART 3
RESOLUTION

CHAPTER 34

MARY AND DAN'S FIFTH
SPECIAL MEETING

▷ JUNE 22, 2018

After speaking with Mary's mother on June 6, Dan made the decision to act and finally get the terrible situation resolved once and for all. To achieve that result, he needed to set up a meeting with Mary. So after Mass on Wednesday, June 20, he asked Mary if they could meet in his office at 4:00 p.m. on Friday.

Mary readily agreed to meet then. She said she would be grateful for the meeting because she still hadn't found the peaceful resolution she had been seeking for so long. She knew it was affecting her interactions with people she loved in her family and with her colleagues, for whom she cared a great deal. That bothered her because she did not want to cause anyone to feel that she didn't care for his or her feelings, and although she'd had no negative feedback from anyone regarding her patient care, she was worried she might have been less effective with patients. She also told Dan she'd been upset with herself lately and hoped that feeling was not shared by those around her.

Dan was relieved Mary had agreed to the meeting, because the timing would allow him a day to think about how he would approach her and what he might do to help her. Importantly, she would be finished with her work for that day and would have the weekend to contemplate what he told her. He could only imagine what that was going to be like for her.

When Mary arrived at work that Friday morning, she felt the real meaning of ambivalence. On the one hand, she needed and wanted the meeting with Dan, but on the other hand, she dreaded what might result from the meeting. In any case, they spoke little about the meeting after Mass that morning, except to exchange a "See you at four" before they left to complete their responsibilities for the day.

While Mary was busy caring for the patients on her units, Dan called her mother. As usual, Beth answered the call immediately with a "Hello, Father Dan." She still refused to call him Dan without the added *Father*. "Is everything OK?"

He responded, "Well, yes and no."

She was alarmed and loudly said, "What do you mean?"

Realizing her distress, Dan immediately said, "I mean yes, everything is fine now, and Mary is certainly OK. However, we are going to meet at four o'clock, and our discussion might cause her great anxiety. I will provide her with the information she has been seeking, the lack of which has caused her to be so preoccupied and act in a way that has caused you, me, and others concern. My hope is that the troubling issue ultimately will be resolved with the information I give her, but I can't be certain. In any case, as she works through it, she will need a lot of support and space from you, Frank, and Megan this weekend."

Beth responded, "Well, Frank and Megan will not be here. They are going to spend the weekend visiting their daughter at her college. So Mary and I will have the weekend to ourselves.

I can certainly arrange for her to have as much time alone as necessary while being here for support if she needs me."

Dan said, "Beth, that is wonderful. Please know that I will also be available to her, or both of you, if anything is needed from me. I will stay at the hospital or close by just in case my support is needed. You only have to call me, and I will respond immediately."

Beth said, "Father Dan, you have been such a wonderful support and friend to Mary and to all of us. I trust you completely. No matter what happens, I know you will have done your best to help her. I will pray that what I provide will also help her get through this troubling mess."

Dan replied, "Beth, you are the very best mother anyone could ever want. Just be yourself, and together we will help get her through this matter."

With that, they hung up, and Dan prayed the outcome would be as they wished.

As soon as they hung up, Beth called her friend Sarah. She then called Mary and left a voice mail for her, asking her to call when she had a chance. As usual, Mary returned her call as soon as she had a break from needed patient care. In this case, it was less than a half hour later.

"Mom, is everything OK?"

Beth answered, "Everything is great, Mary. I hope you won't mind, but I just spoke with Sarah, and she and I are going to the movies and dinner tonight. She is going to pick me up at six o'clock so we can have dinner at El Toro, the Crenshaw restaurant in the community, and make the seven forty-five movie show. So please don't wait up for me. There is some cold roasted chicken in the refrigerator and all sorts of stuff for a salad and other things you like."

Mary laughed and said, "Mom, there's enough food in the house to feed a small army. Please don't worry about me. Have a great time, and I'll see you in the morning."

Beth said, "OK, honey, see you then."

Mary then returned to her patients and soon became so busy discharging some and caring for those who would remain that when she looked at her watch, it was 2:30 p.m. She went to the cafeteria for a quick, light lunch. At 3:00 p.m., she went back to the units and signed out the remaining patients to her colleague. Then it was time for her meeting with Dan.

When she arrived in the office suite she shared with Dan and the bishop, who, as usual, was not there, Dan was waiting for her with a forced smile. Martha had left for the weekend. Friday was the only day when she left by 4:00 p.m.

Dan said, "Well, Mary, I guess it's time we had this meeting. Would you mind sitting in my office, so we can talk without being disturbed? I will close the door."

Mary looked at him with a worried expression and said, "Of course, Dan, but you look so serious. I hope nothing is wrong with you."

Dan responded, "Nothing is wrong with me, but as you've admitted, something has definitely not been right with you lately. When you told me after Mass one day that you were upset with yourself and didn't like yourself very much, I knew I had to do something to help you work out that ridiculous thought. I believe all your angst and self-deprecation revolve around your trying to be sure you've done everything to solve the darn Crenshaw and Wilkes deaths. So I have something to give you that will solve this great mystery."

Mary said, "I don't understand. What do you have?"

Dan answered, "I have a letter for you. However, I want you to promise to only read the first paragraph and then stop, so I can say something. Then you can read the rest."

Mary was perplexed but said, "Of course. I'll do as you ask and only read the first paragraph and stop before reading further. Now, where is this letter?"

CHAPTER 35

LETTER TO MARY

Dan handed Mary an envelope dated June 12, 2018, which had her name on the outside. She looked at him with narrowed eyes, opened it, and read the following:

June 12, 2018

Dear Dr. Defazio,

Father Dan has told me that you have been very troubled about the hospital deaths of Matthew Crenshaw and Calvin Wilkes. He said you want to be sure their deaths were treated fairly, because you find the explanations about their deaths given so far to be unsatisfactory. Therefore, please know that I am responsible for both of their deaths.

At that point, Mary turned ashen and cried out, "This simply cannot be! Not Pedro! Oh, Dan, how horrible." She began sobbing.

Dan went over to her; handed her a box of tissues; and, kneeling, put his arms around her, saying, "Mary, I tried to protect you and Pedro from this revelation, but your God-given intelligence and integrity just wouldn't allow you to let it go. Now I want you to read the rest of the letter while I go to the cafeteria to get us some coffee. I'll return, and we can discuss the next steps after you've read the entire letter. OK?"

With tears in her eyes, Mary looked pleadingly at Dan and responded, "Of course. But please do come back soon. I already desperately need your help and advice."

Dan left the office, closing the door. Mary dried her eyes, took a deep breath, silently pleaded for God's help, and continued reading the letter.

> I told what I did to Father Dan in the confessional before I left the United States, and he granted me God's absolution. Because of the sanctity of the confessional, he could not tell you or anyone else what I confessed.
>
> But recently, he wrote and told me about your worrying and being very upset, so I am confessing this to you. I would never want to cause you any worries or to harm you in any way.
>
> Now I hope you will read the rest of this letter so I can explain why and how I ensured this world was rid of those two horrible men. Yes, I know they were God's creations, just like me, but I have never felt that what I did was sinful or wrong. I never believed, nor do I now believe, that I was doing anything against God's will. I only revealed it in the confessional because Father Dan convinced me that my getting rid of those two evil men was sinful. I did not want to ever do anything

sinful, so I confessed it so God would forgive me.

Now I will explain my actions. In early
January 2017, my sister, Rosa, who had been a
housekeeper for Calvin Wilkes, and I traveled
to Mexico for our mother's funeral. After the
funeral, my sister told me she had decided
not to return to the United States. This was
a great surprise to me because I'd thought
Rosa was happy and had a nice, well-paid job
working for a good man.

Rosa had been an illegal alien in the
United States for more than twenty years,
working for Calvin Wilkes, who, as you
know, was an influential, rich businessman
who owned a lot of real estate in town and
was a special friend of the bishop. Wilkes
had a reputation for being a successful businessman and supposedly was considered by
many to be a pillar of the community. From
the beginning, he had convinced Rosa that
he would take care of her and that she did
not need to apply for a green card or citizen-
ship. By the time she knew better, it was too
late, because she already had been working
here illegally for several months and feared
deportation.

However, Rosa told me that during all
the years she worked for him, Wilkes and his
colleague Matthew Crenshaw, another friend
of the bishop and an influential man who
owned three restaurants within fifty miles of
town, had abused and repeatedly raped her

and threatened to report her to the immigration officials if she told anyone.

As it turned out, Crenshaw also had an illegal alien Mexican woman working for him, and both men treated her the same as Rosa, including the same threats. Rosa and the other woman had been friends in Mexico, and Rosa had recommended her to Crenshaw, so she felt responsible for her.

When Rosa told me why she was not going to return to the United States, I wanted to seriously hurt those men or at least report them to the police. My sister begged me to promise her that I would not do anything that might put me or the other Mexican woman at risk for retribution, even though I was a documented citizen.

I promised her I would not report them, but I still wanted to harm those terrible men, because although I couldn't prove it, in addition to what Wilkes had done to my sister, after she left, he hired another undocumented Mexican woman, and I thought it was very likely the disgusting treatment of the two Mexican women continued.

I vowed to punish those men for being so cruel and began to plan how I might do that. I considered what I was planning to be God's will, so I didn't want their deaths to look man-made.

I knew that both men attended St. Ann's parish, across the street from the hospital, and were admitted to St. Joseph's Hospital for all their medical needs. I was well regarded by all the staff in the hospital and was trusted not to reveal what I heard. When I was on duty, no one ever stopped me from overhearing many discussions about patients. Therefore, I knew that both men had heart conditions and had been admitted to St. Joseph's several times for evaluation or treatment, including the placement of coronary artery stents.

I knew they were provided the best treatment, with both being admitted to the special, large private room on the fourth floor of the hospital reserved for clergy, nuns, and so-called VIPs or special patients. I also knew that patients admitted to that room had special food prepared for any overnight stay, so all tests and treatments could be completed in a relaxed, comfortable environment. And I knew that room was located across the hall from the doctors' locker room.

I had access to the list of all scheduled admissions, so I would know when the men were to be admitted. Because I knew in my heart they would be admitted sometime in the future, I bided my time. In that time, I had to find a way to get rid of them without being caught, making each look like a natural death.

I knew I couldn't use drugs or any poisons that could be discovered on autopsy, which I was sure would be necessary. I also knew from reading medical textbooks that injecting air into their blood supply would require forcing air preferably into an artery, which would be quicker, and not a vein; however, there would be no reason for either of them to have an arterial line in place while they were in their room. Also, whether using an arterial or venous line, I'd probably be caught forcing the air into them if they cried out for help before they died.

I have always been an avid reader of mystery novels, and in my reading, I discovered that someone could die if a large intravenous injection of potassium was delivered, without the method of death being discovered if an autopsy was performed.

As you know, I worked the night shift from 11:00 p.m. to 7:00 a.m., and one of my jobs was to empty the wastebaskets in the hospital pharmacy. I began collecting the small amounts of potassium chloride liquid left in discarded vials. I knew that relatively small amounts of this solution were added to intravenous solutions frequently, and the vials containing the remaining solution were discarded. It didn't take very long for me to accumulate many full vials of the solution, and I could easily accumulate more if needed. I also had easy access to syringes and needles of all sizes.

My first opportunity to accomplish what I considered God's will came in May 2017, when Matthew Crenshaw was admitted electively because his cardiologist wanted to make sure the two stents in his coronary arteries were still open. He had had the stents placed two years previously. On this occasion, he was admitted in the late afternoon for an examination, and a cardiac catheterization was to follow the next day.

I knew the cardiac catheterization required the placement of an IV line so a test dye could be administered later in the radiology suite. I had watched this routine carefully over the years and knew the IVs were routinely placed between four and five o'clock in the morning, depending on how many patients needed them. The laboratory technician usually placed the special-room patient's IV last, so he or she could have the longest undisturbed sleep.

Being very cautious not to be discovered, I called in sick with a supposed problem involving vomiting and diarrhea the day I knew Crenshaw was to be admitted. I claimed to have probable food poisoning, and my supervisor, Ms. Nancy Darcy, knew that probably meant I'd be away for two days. Because she knew I rarely took a day off, she kindly told me to take it easy and not to return until I felt well and to call her if I needed a doctor or anything else.

The day Crenshaw was admitted, after eating a large early dinner, I entered the medical office building annexed to the hospital in the late afternoon and was pretty much unnoticed because of the number of staff, visitors, and venders in the hallways. I then hid in a seldom-used utility closet until the building was locked at 9:00 p.m. I then carefully walked through the office building halls and the empty connecting tunnel to the hospital.

Making sure no one was in the halls and stairwell, I silently went up the stairs from the second to the fourth floor, where I hid in the doctors' locker room across from Crenshaw's room. I knew that during the week, the doctor on the night shift never slept in the call room, because there were so many patients in the hospital who needed their care. They all stayed awake, even if no patient needed them at that moment, because they wanted to be immediately available, knowing they almost always could go home the next morning to sleep. If there happened to be a doctor in the room, I planned to leave after emptying the wastebasket and hide elsewhere, but that turned out not to be necessary.

That night, I stayed in the call room, dozing but never actually sleeping. I was anxious and couldn't sleep. So when the technician entered Crenshaw's room, I was fully awake and ready to act.

After the technician left the room, I put on a white coat borrowed from the doctors' locker room and entered Crenshaw's darkened room. I smiled at the dozing Crenshaw and injected a full fifty-cc syringe of the potassium solution into the IV well and tubing and left the room. I went across the hall, removed the white coat, quickly but silently went down the hall to the back stairs and to the second-floor connecting tunnel, and waited in the utility closet in the office building until I knew the building's outside door was open at 7:00 a.m. I left the building, again unnoticed because I made sure the flow of physicians, patients, family members, and delivery service people had started.

Meanwhile, I knew that in the hospital, at 7:00 a.m., when an orderly came to Crenshaw's room to wheel him to the cardiac catheterization room in the radiology suite, he would be found unresponsive, and the orderly immediately would call the doctors and nurses. All attempts at resuscitation would fail. This would cause a great deal of anxiety among the doctors and nursing staff, but by then, I was on my way home. I stayed at home for the full two days.

The second opportunity for me to finally accomplish what I believed to be the will of God happened six months later, in November 2017, when Calvin Wilkes was admitted late one afternoon. He also was admitted electively for evaluation of two stents that had been placed two years previously. Wilkes's evaluation also required a cardiac catheterization to be performed the next morning. This time, I reported for my usual night duty and worked fast to finish my routine work. At four o'clock in the morning, I hid in the physicians' locker room across the hall from the special patient room, where Wilkes had been admitted.

Now, there were two differences from what had happened with Crenshaw. The first was that I already was on duty in the hospital and didn't need to hide in the medical office building. I only had to hide in the doctors' locker room. The second difference was that Wilkes was hooked up to a vital-signs and electrocardiogram monitor. His private physician, who had also cared for Crenshaw, had ordered the monitor as a precaution.

This time, after the technician left the darkened room, Wilkes was almost asleep when I entered his room. This allowed me a short time to watch and very softly whisper, "This is for Rosa," as I injected the potassium solution into the IV well and tubing. I then said, again in a soft whisper, "Goodbye, you bastard." Please forgive my language, Dr. Defazio, but that's what I said, and I want you to know it. I then rapidly left the room and went into the doctors' locker room across the hall because I knew the alarm would soon sound.

After I removed the white coat, while still hidden in the nearby doctors' locker room, I silently watched the emergency team's initial efforts to resuscitate Wilkes. Soon after the team was fully engaged in Wilkes's room, I quickly and silently sneaked down the hall and halfway down the back stairs. From there, I could secretly watch the rush of more nurses to Wilkes's room, caused by the monitor alarm sounding.

After I was sure the resuscitation attempts would fail, I went back to my normal work. This time, I personally witnessed the distress of the hospital staff, which made me very sad because I really like and respect them all. I didn't want to cause them to feel bad, but I believed what I'd done was necessary for me to accomplish God's will.

After Crenshaw died, I paid for his housekeeper to return to Mexico, and I have been supporting her and my sister since then. You know what else I have been doing since my return to Mexico, and I hope you approve of my efforts here.

You see, Dr. Defazio, I didn't consider my actions to be sins or wrong, but rather, I thought I was doing what God wanted. The world is now a better place without them doing very bad things to people, especially women. However, if you think differently, I will understand and hope you will forgive me.

As you might know from Father Dan, no one knows where I live in Mexico. I have only a post office box in a Texas town under my name, which is very common in Mexico. My friend picks up my mail every week or so and gives it to me when we meet in a place near the border. It would be very hard for anyone to find me, but if it's God's will that they do, so be it. We all must do what we believe is right.

You have always been a great supporter and friend to me, and I will always be grateful

for your kindness. No matter what you do
with this information, I will understand and
still feel nothing but fondness and love toward you.

Yours in Christ,
Pedro

When Dan returned with the coffee, Mary was sitting
in the chair in shock and had tears running down her cheeks.
She wiped her face with a tissue and told Dan she could hardly
believe what she had just read, and it was going to take some
deep thought to get it straight in her head.

Dan responded, "You see, Mary? This shows why you need
to be careful what you ask for. I know this is a decision you'd
have preferred not to deal with. We all want decisions like
this to be easy and fall into neat categories, but that is not how
much of life is. Pedro thought he was being an angel, but others
might think he was acting as the devil's advocate. I believe that
decision is not so black and white; it's gray.

"This is not unlike your decision regarding Julia, the
woman who aborted her fetus and died in your arms. You are
certainly pro-life, but in that case, you considered both the
life of the baby and the life of the mother. Although abortion
might only be understandable in rare cases, it is not all black;
it is gray.

"In this situation, you wanted the truth so justice could be
done. Well, now you have the truth, and therefore, you must
decide what you will do with this information. You'll have to
decide if Pedro was acting as an angel or the devil's advocate
or something in between. Then you must consider what justice
you believe would be appropriate in his case.

"I know you will spend the weekend thinking about this,

and I will be here if you need to discuss anything or just need a shoulder. I must admit I am glad you know what happened, and I also know I must be part of the resolution. No matter what you decide, I will support you."

Mary answered, "Thank you, Dan. That means a lot to me. I think I need time this weekend to decide about Pedro and what I will do. I hope I will get back to liking myself, because I know my decision will have a significant effect on how I feel about myself.

"I'm going home now to figure out what I must do. Thankfully, Mom will be out with her friend, and I have the rest of today and night to myself. And Frank and Megan are away visiting with their daughter, so there will be no Sunday dinner with them. So that day also will be relatively free for me. Funny how all that happened."

Dan smiled, nodded, and said, "Yep. Funny how things like that happen. It looks like the Great Comedian has a good sense of how to use his humor in directing people's actions. I'll see you Monday, if not sooner."

Mary knew it was going to be, in her own words, one hell of a weekend.

CHAPTER 36

LETTERS

Before Dan set up the June 22 meeting with Mary, he needed
a letter from Pedro. It had become clear that because of
Mary's constant pursuit of truth, fairness, and justice, she was
not going to rest until she could honestly believe she had done
everything possible to resolve the peculiar circumstances involved in the deaths of Crenshaw and Wilkes to the full extent
of her duty and capability.

He prayed for guidance and finally knew that he also had
a duty to help her reach a fair and peaceful decision. Therefore,
he decided it was time to ask Pedro for a letter to Mary, de-
scribing what he had confessed to Dan before his departure.
So he sent a letter to Pedro's post office address, hoping Pedro
would soon respond.

June 6, 2018

Dear Pedro,

It was wonderful to hear from you recently
and find that you are doing so well and

helping so many people in your village. Your padre sounds like a very good pastor, and your working as his eucharistic minister seems to please both of you very much. I pray for you every day, knowing you are doing God's work.

Now I write to ask a special favor that I hope you will be able to grant. I need for you to write a letter to Dr. Defazio, explaining what you confessed to me on March 23, the day before you left the United States.

As you know, she was appointed as the chief medical officer at St. Joseph's in February. As part of her new position, she wanted to learn whatever she could about the hospital, including looking at all deaths for the past five years. She discovered that Matthew Crenshaw and Calvin Wilkes died similar deaths that required examination by the county medical examiner and that the examiner could find no medical reason for the deaths and, thus, diagnosed both deaths as nonspecific cardiac arrest, which Dr. Defazio found to be very unusual and peculiar for two cases within six months or so.

Of course, no one else has a problem with this result, and the matter should be considered closed. However, as you know, Dr. Defazio is a very smart and conscientious woman. Her investigations and personal knowledge revealed that both men were not very nice and were detested by everyone with whom she spoke. Because no one, including her, liked either man, she wonders if their deaths may not have been given a fair investigation.

She looked at everyone who was present for both deaths and found that one of the doctors signed both death certificates. She discussed the situation with him and other staff who also were present for both deaths. But she still has doubts about his role because he expressed a grave dislike for both men.

Also, at the times of both deaths, she found another doctor also had been in the hospital or at least in the emergency room, having been called in to care for patients. That doctor was scheduled to be on duty in the hospital for the 7:00 a.m. to 3:00 p.m. shift the next day. When that happens, the doctor involved almost always sleeps in the doctors' call room when he or she has finished in the ER. However, this doctor supposedly slept in her specially equipped van parked in the ER parking area reserved for the on-call doctor and not in the doctors' call room, which Dr. Defazio found to be very unusual. Moreover, in the past, this doctor had described the men to Dr. Defazio as despicable.

Dr. Defazio even discussed the Crenshaw and Wilkes situation with a patient who was present on the same unit when both deaths occurred. He admitted to detesting both men because of previous business dealings with them, so she also considered him to be a suspect.

In addition, there was an unfortunate incident with Crenshaw and Wilkes involving a St. Joseph's Hospital Muslim nurse. Her husband, her brother, and the brother's best friend are doctors who sometimes see patients in the annexed medical office building and occasionally admit patients to St. Joseph's. They were livid with Crenshaw and Wilkes and threatened to harm them if they tried to treat any woman as horribly as they had the Muslim nurse.

While Dr. Defazio doesn't want to accuse anyone falsely, she also wants to be sure everyone, including the two men who died, is treated fairly. It's important to know that after her initial discussions with various people, she has not revealed her continued concern to anyone but me.

She wants very much to be rid of this issue, which continues to torment her. But it seems that every time she has been willing to drop the issue, something comes up to bring her attention back to the matter.

She now has told me she wonders if God is nudging her to continue the investigation by reporting it to the bishop or the police. Both these options would be very harmful to her, to all the people suspected, and to St. Joseph's. I want to stop her from making such a harmful report, but she is tormented and very sad, so it's time to get this issue resolved.

Therefore, knowing I cannot reveal anything, I hope you will be willing to send her the letter I am requesting. If you will, please write the letter to her, and put it in an envelope with her name on it. Then send the letter in another envelope to me. I will give it to her only because I believe it is necessary, and there is no other way to resolve this issue for her. I pray that you agree.

Because you have no geographic or email address and no phone number and only have a post office box in a Texas town close to Mexico under the common name of P. Gonzales, I doubt anyone could find you. I thank God for your businessman friend, who is surely special to carry your mail to and from the post office in Texas.

Pedro, I am so very sorry to make this request, but I am forced to ask now. I promise to take special care of your letter so no one will have access to it but Dr. Defazio and me. We know she also will be very careful with it.

I will await your response.

God bless you and keep you safe, my brother.

Yours in Christ,
Father Dan

To Dan's relief, he received a large envelope from Pedro on June 20. In it were a short letter to Dan and an unsealed envelope addressed to Dr. Defazio. The letter to Dan read,

June 12, 2018

Dear Father Dan,

I have no problem sending Dr. Defazio a letter admitting that I am responsible for the deaths of Matthew Crenshaw and Calvin Wilkes and explaining why and how I did it. I have great respect and admiration for her. If she decides to alert the police or anyone else, I will understand and have no ill feelings toward her. She is very much a woman of God and must do what she feels is the right thing.

I have not sealed the enclosed envelope and ask only that you read what I have written in the letter to her, to be sure I have explained it correctly. I also would appreciate your letting me know her reaction and what she will do.

As you will read in that letter, I don't think it will be easy for anyone to find me, but if it's God's will that they do, I accept it.

Thank you for all you have done and continue to do for me. Please also be there to help Dr. Defazio. God bless both of you.

Your brother,
Pedro

Dan silently read Pedro's letter addressed to Mary and had a lump in his throat while reading it. It was a beautiful letter clearly displaying his respect for Mary and the truth. Neither Pedro nor Dan had any idea how Mary would react to it or what she might do with the information.

In his heart, he believed her kindness and generosity of spirit would bring peace to all of them, but he had no guarantee. *After all, how well do we really know another person?* he thought. *God, please let my belief in Mary be accurate.*

CHAPTER 37

MARY AND GOD

▷ JUNE 23-24, 2018

After Dan left his office on June 22, Mary changed into street clothes in her office. As she drove home, she was still in a state of disbelief. All the way home, she mumbled to God in a disjointed array of words that barely made sense to her, but she hoped they would be understood by God. She was clearly at a loss to understand what just had been revealed to her. Further, how was she going to resolve her requirement to ensure that her decision was fair to everyone involved? *Dear God, what do you expect of me?*

When she got home to an empty house, she locked the front door; went upstairs; and took a long, hot shower. She then donned cool summer lounging pajamas and went down to the kitchen to make something to eat. Although she was not very hungry, she had not eaten much that day—just a bowl of vegetable soup in the hospital cafeteria. She had finished the soup only in order not to insult the chef, who was so kind to her. Also, she didn't want to lose any more than the few pounds she'd lost over the past few weeks while struggling with the Crenshaw and Wilkes issue.

She made a chicken salad sandwich with light mayo on

multigrain bread, put it on a plate with some olives, and poured a glass of pinot grigio. She took the food and drink out to the table and chairs on the back porch, along with the letter and her cell phone. It was a warm June evening, and there was a cool breeze in the backyard. As she munched on the sandwich and sipped the wine, she again read the letter, this time slowly.

When she finished, she went up to her bedroom, feeling physically and mentally exhausted. She brushed her teeth and crawled into bed, even though it was only a few minutes after nine o'clock. She wanted to read something by Kierkegaard she had read several nights before that remained in her thoughts.

Essentially, he'd written that the experience of alienation of the ego was a necessary prelude to awareness of the Self. *Self meaning God?* And that alienation was never attained except through despair. *Is that why I hate myself and feel so horribly?* Clearly, she needed to sleep on this and consider it in resolving her dilemma.

At ten o'clock, she shut off the light, closed her eyes, and immediately fell asleep.

She did not wake up until six o'clock the following morning. After she showered and dressed in jeans and a polo shirt, she went downstairs, where Mom was sitting at the table, drinking cappuccino and eating one of her homemade muffins.

Mary did not want to reveal her feelings to her mother, so she smiled and said, "Good morning, Mom. Did you have a good time last night?"

Mom answered with a smile, "Good morning. We did. As it turns out, the El Toro restaurant is now the Carmen and Carlos Restaurant. Two young siblings whose grandparents migrated from Mexico bought it a month ago when the Crenshaw estate sold all three of its restaurants. The chef from El Toro and a local businessman bought one of the other Crenshaw restaurants in the city, so you can still get great

Spanish food there. It's a good thing Sarah made reservations at Carmen and Carlos, because the place was packed, with a long waiting line.

"I wasn't sure I was going to like Mexican food, because I'm not especially fond of tacos or burritos, but I was in for a pleasant surprise. The menu was full of traditional Mexican food patterned after the recipes in the book *Like Water for Chocolate*. I loved the book, and now I know I also love the food. It was delicious.

"And the romantic comedy movie was very enjoyable. I know you don't like that kind of movie, but Sarah and I really enjoy them. I came home well after ten o'clock, and when I checked, you were fast asleep and looked so peaceful I didn't disturb you."

Mary responded, "That's wonderful. We'll have to go to that restaurant sometime. But I can't believe I slept so long. I guess I was very tired."

Mom said, "Well, as you've often told me, your body will tell you what it needs."

Mary smiled. "How about if we shop early this morning? Because I must do some important things this weekend."

Mom replied, "Great idea because I want to make some cookies and visit one of the neighbors who just lost her husband."

When they returned from shopping, Mom went to the kitchen and then the neighbor's house, and Mary went for a long walk in the woods near their house. This time, she chose the full circular five-mile path in the woods, which began about a hundred yards from the house.

She slowly walked and then stopped to really see the trees and flowers, listen to the birds and the light wind, and deeply breathe in the fragrance of the lilac bushes. She often wondered where the wind came from, and where did it go? *Is it the same as the human spirit?*

When she resumed the walk, she argued with herself and, in a way, with God. She considered all the things she had experienced over the past few months, including what she'd read while wrestling with her existential struggling; the weeks of battling the Crenshaw and Wilkes issue; and, finally, Pedro's letter. At the end of the walk, she still was confused but decided to keep pondering how she should react to it all.

When she returned home about four hours later, Mom had dinner ready, so they ate and watched an old 1950s musical movie on TV. Mom loved those oldies, and Mary was grateful because she could quietly sit with Mom while not paying much attention to the movie. Her mind was still in a whirlwind of thoughts she needed to sort out.

After the movie, Mary told Mom she wanted to get some work done in her room. That was fine with Mom because she was well into one of her murder mystery novels, which Mary thought was ironic, given the current situation.

The next morning, after Mass and a late brunch, Mary changed into jeans and a polo shirt and told Mom she again wanted to walk in the woods, but this time, it would not take more than a few hours. Mom said that was fine because she wanted to make eggplant parmigiana and cherry pies for dinner.

Mom said, "It's going to rain, so you should take an umbrella."

Mary answered that she would be home before it rained, so an umbrella was unnecessary. She didn't want to be burdened with carrying anything. She just wanted to walk and think.

After leaving the house, Mary took the same path in the woods she'd taken yesterday, but this time, she had sorted out her thoughts. She was grateful there was no one else on the path, probably because of the gloomy weather.

As she slowly walked, she thought, *OK, God, this is where*

I am. I know you have a plan for all of us, and you have given us the free will to follow it or not. I have tried to follow what I thought was your plan and lead the kind of life where your grace would allow your loving spirit to flow through me toward others. But recently, I have been confused about the true meaning of my life and whether my life is such that you would want your loving spirit to flow through me.

I hated what I had become. For a long time, I begged for your guidance to help me with my struggle with this existential anxiety. You guided me to read a lot and to discuss many things with Dan, whose friendship and counseling you blessed me with. He has gone through so much, knowing all along that Pedro was responsible for the deaths of the two men who have driven me to distraction but not being able to, and probably not wanting to, tell me. Finally, you guided me to read Kierkegaard Friday night. I now know that I had to reach despair and essentially destroy my ego to truly find you.

Also, recently, I asked for your guidance to resolve the truth-and-justice issue with the Crenshaw and Wilkes deaths, which you seemed to keep nudging me to resolve. I think you have answered my prayers by combining my two struggles.

To resolve my existential struggle, I needed to understand how to receive your grace, which I now believe is the state of being one with you. I also know that we don't earn or merit grace; rather, it is freely given, if only we know how to recognize it. Thankfully, I have a much better idea of how to recognize it.

As for the truth-and-justice issue, I know that like all humans, I have on occasion deviated from your plan, and at times, I have sinned, but you've always forgiven me. While my worst sins, thankfully, have not included deliberately taking another person's life, I believe you would forgive me if I had, if I was truly sorry I had done so.

There is so much violence in the world, including wars, the Crusades, and even the taking of human lives in the Bible, especially in the Old Testament. You even asked Abraham to sacrifice his son, Isaac, by taking his life to show his obedience to you.

Abraham was completely devoted to you, and he was prepared to take Isaac's life. However, was Kierkegaard correct when he said that Abraham believed he could take Isaac's life but still have him, and that was why he was willing to sacrifice him? In any case, you did ask a father to take his son's life as a test of his faith. While you didn't take Isaac's life after all, can the taking of another human's life ever be justified?

When I sought truth and justice with the Crenshaw and Wilkes issue, you provided me with the truth through Pedro. But was he justified in taking their lives? As I thought about Crenshaw and Wilkes, I remembered their funerals, even though I did not attend either of them. I heard about them from a few of my friends, each of whom did attend at least one of them.

There were many so-called mourners, but I didn't hear about any displayed grief. Perhaps that's because grief is a private emotion, but even Wilkes's wife and daughter didn't express grief or mourn him. I was worried that because there was so much animosity toward these men, their deaths might not have received a fair investigation and justice.

You have guided me to a true understanding of judgment and justice, or righteousness. One of my favorite psalms, 143:2, says, "Do not bring your servant into judgement, for no one living is righteous before you." At this point, I understand what that really means. Pedro committed a mortal sin, or a heinous crime in legal terms. But how could justice for his or other similar sins ever be done, or put another way, why do you forgive him, me, or anyone who commits mortal sins? Where is the justice in your forgiving? For truly the first time, I comprehend that through Jesus, you compensated for all human sins.

You sent your only begotten Son, Jesus, to become the Son of man so he would receive the most horrible, ignominious death by crucifixion. The crucifixion of Jesus is the justice that covers even the most horrific sin of any human being. He lovingly offered his sinless life and horrendous death as a willing reparation and penance for the sins of all of us. That is the true and ultimate justice.

I assume that is why some people believe that through the sacrament of the confessional, a priest—a man acting as an agent of God—can offer God's forgiveness. For others, they communicate and confess directly to you and ask for forgiveness.

I have thought about the one other experience I've had with a person taking a human life. That was Julia, the young woman who aborted her baby, whom I cared for when I was a nun working as a nurse. She was so afraid that you would condemn her, but after listening to her story, I had no doubt that you would forgive her, and I managed to convince her that was true.

Just before she died peacefully in my arms, I had this wonderful feeling of being at one with you, and I believe she also felt it. In the past, I wondered if that feeling was grace. Now I know it was, and that is what I've been seeking with my existential struggle. I really want to receive your grace and be at one with you.

The experience with Julia caused me to leave the convent because I could not be a hypocrite and support a rule of the church that I felt was wrong in some possible rare cases.

So if I had no problem putting kindness of spirit over justice with Julia, why would it be different with Pedro? Clearly, it wouldn't. If I truly want grace, I must put kindness first. You have asked us to love one another as you have loved us. I believe that kindness is a manifestation of love. We must always allow kindness to meet truth and peace to meet justice.

Mary arrived at the end of the circular five-mile route and sat on the bench located there. After a few minutes of deep thought, she felt the same peaceful warmth she had felt with Julia that day long ago and often had felt with her beloved Tom. She was completely absorbed in her feeling of the presence of God. At that moment, she knew grace was hers.

A while later, she came alert and realized she had been weeping—in fact, sobbing—with relief. What a glorious walk with God it had been.

But she was worried because her face was wet with tears, and her nose was running. She didn't want Mom to see her like that, but she had no tissues. She thought about using her polo shirt as a tissue, which she hoped she could wash out before Mom saw it.

However, as she walked the last hundred yards or so to her house, the sky darkened, and a drenching rain poured down. She thought that solved her problem; she looked up at the sky and let the rain wash her face and clear her nose. She kept walking at a slow pace, feeling the rain soak her. She laughed and thought, *I guess this is God's way of washing away my anxiety.*

When she arrived home, Mom was waiting at the open front door with two large bath towels. She pursed her lips, shook her head, and said, "I told you to take an umbrella. You are soaked."

Mary was feeling so happy she decided to get playful with Mom, as she frequently had in the past. She responded, "I know, Mom, and I don't want to mess up the carpet, so I have an idea. I will simply strip naked right here and leave all my wet clothes on the porch."

Mom looked at her as if she were crazy and loudly exclaimed, "Mary Elizabeth!"

Mary laughed and said, "Mom, I was joking. You know I would never do that."

Mom replied, "I would hope not. Now, take off your shoes and socks, and leave them on the porch. Then step inside on the towel I've put down, and take off your clothes after I've shut the door."

After Mary had shed her wet clothes, Mom said, "Look

at you—you're covered with goose bumps. Now, dry off, wrap yourself in this towel, and go upstairs to get warm before you catch pneumonia."

Mary said, "This kind of chill is not how you get pneumonia."

Mom replied, "What do you know?"

Mary shook her head and, rolling her eyes, just laughed and said, "Well, so much for my medical education, training, and experience."

She went upstairs wrapped in the towel; took a long, hot shower; and washed her hair with the lavender soap and shampoo she'd bought for Mom and herself. She thought about why hot baths and showers were so comforting and decided they were, in some ways, an emulation of the warmth and comfort offered in the womb. *Why not?*

She also thought about how many gifts God had bestowed upon her and her family. Tom, Father Dan, friends and colleagues, a wonderful profession—the list went on and on, with big things and many small gifts, such as how lucky she was to have hair that needed no special care. She simply would brush it, and after she washed it, she could blow it dry and brush it afterward.

When she came down to the kitchen in dry, warm jeans and a polo shirt, she discovered that Mom had wrung out her wet clothes, which were in the washer along with some other clothes. Mom also had set the table for dinner and was taking the pies out of the oven. *More special gifts!* The aroma of eggplant parmigiana blended with the aroma of cherry pie in the kitchen, and Mary felt hungry for the first time in weeks.

Mom squinted and said, "My dear daughter, whatever has come over you?"

Mary immediately answered, "God."

Mom exclaimed, "What?"

Mary responded, "Mom, I know I've been a real pain in the rear with my preoccupation and moodiness the past few weeks, and I am very sorry for the worry I've caused you. I have been dealing with some issues that I've now resolved. You have the real me back, such as I am. I need for you to know it's very important to me that you please tell me if I ever do anything unkind to you or anyone else."

Mom replied, "Oh, Mary, I am so glad to hear that you have resolved your issues. I have been very concerned about you, and I must admit I even discussed it with Father Dan. But you look so happy now, and that makes me happy too. And as for kindness, I have never seen you be unkind, even when you were a child and being a real brat. However, I will certainly tell you if that ever happens."

Mary smiled broadly and said, "Mom, you are the greatest. Now, how about that dinner? I am famished."

While they ate, Mary asked Mom if she wanted to hear a joke, to which she replied, "I love your jokes and have missed hearing them lately."

Mary then told her the joke, assuring her first that it was not a dirty joke and asking her to bear with her. She never told unclean jokes and was not about to begin now, especially not with Mom.

"A man was driving down a two-lane highway and saw the following advertisement on a billboard: 'Five miles to a convent where you can be screwed by a nun.'"

Mom winced but said nothing, remembering Mary's promise that it was a clean joke.

"He noticed the same ad every mile he traveled, with the number of miles decreasing, until the final one instructed any driver interested in being screwed by a nun to take the next right turn. The man decided that as unlikely as it was, he would follow the sign, and when he made the next right turn, he saw a convent. Being very curious, he went to the front door and rang the bell. The door was soon opened by a nun in full habit, who introduced herself as the mother superior. She said, 'If you are a man who is interested in our advertisement, please follow me.'

"Being a good Catholic trained by nuns, he responded, 'Yes, Sister,' and followed her down a long hall. About half-way, she stopped and asked him if he would like to make a hundred-dollar donation to the convent. He thought that was a fair price, so he handed her a hundred dollars.

"She then led him down the hall to a door, opened it, and told him to pass through, which he did, and he heard the door close and lock behind him. He found himself outside the convent, and looking up, he saw a big sign that read, 'You have just been screwed by a nun. Thank you for the donation to our convent.'"

Mom laughed and said, "That's a good one, but I don't think you should tell it to Mother Superior at the convent when you visit next time."

Mary laughed and said, "Who do you think told me that joke?"

Mom shook her head and said, "Whatever is this world coming to?"

Mary responded, "Nuns are human just like us. Remember, I once was one. The only difference between them and me is that I left, and they stayed."

After devouring a large helping of the eggplant parmigiana, Mary asked for a piece of the cherry pie.

Mom answered, "Coming up the way you like it: with some chocolate ice cream."

Then they both said the rosary, went downstairs to watch the news, and retired to their rooms to read and work. That night, Mary wrote a letter to Pedro, printed two copies, and deleted it from her desktop. She put one copy, along with

Pedro's letter, in a file in her locked desk drawer and the other copy in her briefcase for the hospital. She planned to let Dan read it. Hopefully he would agree to send it to Pedro for her.

That night, she slept soundly, knowing her concerns would no longer interfere with her love of God; her love for herself; or the joy she derived from her family, friends, colleagues, and work at the hospital.

CHAPTER 38

FINAL MEETING

Mary awoke the next morning spontaneously at her usual five o'clock and felt wonderful, having slept soundly again. When she came down to the kitchen, Mom was puttering around humming.

Mary decided to maintain her playfulness and, smiling, said, "Good morning, Mom. See? I didn't get pneumonia."

Mom also smiled and replied, "Don't you get smart with me, Doctor. You know how I took care of you, Frankie, and Dad when you were growing up. And I was not a trained doctor or nurse."

Mary had to admit Mom was right, so she answered, "I'm sorry. Mom. I was trying to be playful, but it came out with my sounding like a smart-mouth. You are right, because you had a home remedy for every common illness, sign, or symptom, such as putting saliva on a mosquito bite, even though you'd never heard of salivary amylase; treating an upper respiratory illness with Vicks VapoRub to the chest and milk laced with honey, garlic, and whiskey; and using olive oil for any rash and, for constipation, steamed spinach or endive with the ever-present garlic and olive oil. God help us with that remedy. Frank and

I had a discussion on that one when we were early teens and decided the treatment was far worse than the problem. The interesting part is that all your remedies worked."

Mom laughed and said, "They still do."

Mary hugged her and kissed her on the cheek. "You look very happy this morning." After a short pause, she said, "You know I do really love you."

Mom smiled and replied, "Look who's talking about looking happy, and I love you too." As she handed Mary her travel cup of cappuccino, a napkin, and a package of food for Martha, she added, "Now, go take care of all those sick people."

Mary hummed all the way to work, feeling better than she had in many weeks. When she got to her office, she put Martha's package of food on her desk and changed into scrubs, and then she went to the fourth-floor unit to sign in. Afterward, she went to Mass, arriving just in time to assist Dan.

After Mass, Dan looked at her questioningly, and she said, "I'm back. Can we meet at four o'clock this afternoon?"

Dan smiled and said, "Absolutely. See you then in the office."

She went back to the office to check in with Martha, who said, "Good morning. Judging by the spring back in your gait and the look on your face, you had a great weekend. What happened?"

Mary responded, "Let's just say I resolved the issue that has been bothering me for the past few weeks."

Martha said, "Thank God for that."

Mary said, "Exactly!" and she went off to the fourth floor and the other units she was covering that day.

By three forty-five, she had signed out to her colleague, finished her work on the units, and returned to her office. Martha was packing her belongings and said, "Dan told me you two are meeting here at four o'clock, and I want to skedaddle so you can meet in peace. Please tell your mom I thank her again for another delicious meal. I can't wait to get home to eat it. And, Mary, I'm so glad the real you is back with us. See you tomorrow." Off she went.

As Martha went through the door, Dan came in with arms outstretched and took both her hands in his. "Mary, please tell me what happened over the weekend. I didn't hear from you, and you look so happy now, so I hope all is well."

As they sat in her office, Mary told Dan what had transpired over the weekend, especially detailing her experience during the walk in the woods on Sunday. He was relieved to hear what had happened and said, "I prayed you'd finally understand grace and deal with Pedro as I knew you would."

Mary responded, "Dan, I have a letter I'd like you to mail to Pedro. It basically says what I believe, and I want you to read it. Then we can discuss how right you were when you explained that I would find my way out of my existential crisis, which you said was really a struggle with my existential anxiety." She handed him the letter to Pedro:

> June 24, 2018
>
> Dear Pedro,
>
> I want you to know how grateful I am to you for having sent your letter to me. You need to know that this whole episode and your letter helped me find out who I really am.
>
> I spent this past weekend thinking about what you wrote. I now understand why you acted as you did. In truth, I probably would not have acted in the same way. I can never know for sure, but it doesn't matter. God has

forgiven you, so who am I not to do the same? He has also forgiven my many transgressions, and for that I am grateful. I am sure you feel the same about yours. As Kierkegaard noted, the opposite of sin is faith. Sin separates us from God, but faith restores our connection to God. You clearly have faith and are therefore connected to God.

I know that you are truly one of God's special people, and I want to always remain your friend. You act with kindness to so many people, and I'd like to help you. I am enclosing a check for $10,000 for you to use for your church and community center. I'm sure you will put it to good use. I also want you to know that if you ever need anything I might provide, all you need to do is contact me. I will always be here for you.

So, my brother, for now, let us keep in touch and both continue to act with kindness and love toward all with whom we come in contact.

God bless you,
Dr. D

When Dan finished reading the letter, he sighed and reached out to hold Mary's hand. After a while, he said, "I am so relieved that I did not make a mistake in trusting that you would understand and act with your ever-present kindness and love. I hope you now know who you are and what grace means for you."

Mary responded, "Dan, I don't really know how I got to

this point, but I do know who I am, and I like that person. And even though I probably will continue to have occasional bouts of struggling with existential anxiety, I will always find grace, because it is everywhere.

"I also know that my experience in seeking truth and justice is not much different from what many people face every day. That includes parents dealing with disobedient children, police officers, lawyers, judges, administrators, military personnel, and leaders of all kinds. The degree of seriousness of the deed, or truth, might be different, but determining appropriate punishment, or justice, is the same. Justice should always be determined and meted out with kindness, mercy and grace."

CPSIA information can be obtained
at www.ICGtesting.com
Printed in the USA
BVHW091029300822
645842BV00001B/80

9 781665 725811